W9-CEK-489

WHO THINKS EVIL

Also by
Michael Kurland

THE PROFESSOR
MORIARTY NOVELS

The Infernal Device
Death by Gaslight
The Great Game
The Empress of India

SHERLOCK HOLMES
ANTHOLOGIES

My Sherlock Holmes
Sherlock Holmes: The Hidden Years
Sherlock Holmes: The American Years

THE ALEXANDER
BRASS NOVELS

Too Soon Dead
The Girls in the High-Heeled Shoes

MICHAEL KURLAND

WHO THINKS EVIL

A PROFESSOR MORIARTY NOVEL

MINOTAUR BOOKS
NEW YORK

This is a work of fiction. All of the characters, organizations, and events portrayed in this novel are either products of the author's imagination or are used fictitiously.

WHO THINKS EVIL. Copyright © 2014 by Michael Kurland. All rights reserved. Printed in the United States of America. For information, address St. Martin's Press, 175 Fifth Avenue, New York, N.Y. 10010.

www.minotaurbooks.com

Design by Jonathan Bennett

Library of Congress Cataloging-in-Publication Data

Kurland, Michael.
    Who thinks evil : Professor Moriarty novels / Michael Kurland.—First Edition.
        p. cm.—(A Professor Moriarty novel ; 5)
    ISBN 978-0-312-36545-5 (hardcover)
    ISBN 978-1-4668-4739-2 (e-book)
    1. Moriarty, Professor (Fictitious character)—Fiction.   2. Abduction—Fiction.   I. Title.
    PS3561.U647W46 2014
    813'.54—dc23

                                                        2013045933

Minotaur books may be purchased for educational, business, or promotional use. For information on bulk purchases, please contact Macmillan Corporate and Premium Sales Department at 1-800-221-7945, extension 5442, or write specialmarkets@macmillan.com.

First Edition: February 2014

10 9 8 7 6 5 4 3 2 1

This book is for Sam and Archie,
boon companions who are sorely missed.

ACKNOWLEDGMENTS

I would like to thank Ms. Linda Robertson for her unerring eye, and for always telling me what I needed to hear.

honi soit qui mal y pense
[shame to him who thinks evil]

—Motto of the Most Noble Order of the Garter

AUTHOR'S NOTE

In some small ways my relating of this history of various events occurring during the later Victorian era may differ from that found in contemporary chronologies, journals, reports, and such. In all such areas of conflict my version is, of course, the correct one. However, all persons appearing in this book shall be regarded as fictional regardless of their resemblance to important historical personages or your Great-Aunt Harriet.

WHO THINKS EVIL

[PROLOGUE]

LONDON PROFESSOR DETAINED IN CONNECTION WITH RECENT WIDDERSIGN OUTRAGE

SPECIAL TO THE STANDARD

Friday 11 July 1890

ACTING on information received, detectives of the Criminal Investigation Division of the Metropolitan Police have detained Professor James Moriarty of 64 Russell Square, Camden. Professor Moriarty is being questioned in regard to the attempted robbery on Saturday last at Widdersign-on-Ribble, the country estate of His Lordship Baron Thornton-Hoxbary, located just outside the town of Wedsbridge in Nottinghamshire.

In what has become known as the Widdersign Outrage, six masked men armed with revolvers forced their way into the manor house at or about midnight, after first assaulting and tying up the gatekeeper, two grooms, and the senior coachman. Once inside, they assembled the occupants of the house in the dining room, where one of the villains guarded them while three smashed their way into the small museum where His Lordship keeps a priceless collection of Greek artifacts acquired at the beginning of the century by His Lordship's grandfather. The other men ransacked bedrooms on the upper floor, gathering up jewelry and other valuables of His Lordship and Lady Hoxbary and their sixteen houseguests.

James Mercer, the chief butler, who had been tied up in the lower pantry along with the cook, an upstairs maid, and a serving girl, as well as a maid and two valets in the service of several of the houseguests, managed to free himself by the expedient of breaking a glass and sawing at his bonds with a sharp shard. Mercer immediately released the two valets, whereupon the three of them repaired to the gun room on the ground floor. Arming himself and the others with three rifles, a shotgun, and a Webley .445 service revolver, Mercer led the way up the servants' staircase to the upper floor, where he and the other two intrepid servants accosted the robbers.

In the ensuing gun battle two of the robbers were killed and one shot in the leg. The others escaped into the forest, and it is believed that at least one of them was wounded. One of the valets, Andrew Lamphier by name, received a bullet in the shoulder and is now recuperating in Queen Anne's Hospital and Infirmary in Nottingham.

The robbers fled without any of the items they had attempted to steal, although a small Mycenaean vase dating from the fourth century B.C. was found shattered in the grass. The Nottinghamshire police believe that the remaining culprits will shortly be apprehended.

Baron Thornton-Hoxbary declined to release the names of his houseguests, stating he did not wish to add notoriety to injury, but it is believed that among the guests were the Duke and Duchess of Pennaugh and Sir Arthur Sullivan, the noted composer. It is not known in what way, if any, this outrage is related to the series of robberies of great homes that have plagued the countryside around the East Midlands for the past year. Readers of *The Standard* will remember our account of the daring robbery at Cramden Pimms, the Nottinghamshire estate of Lord Chaut, in March of this year, when thieves broke in through a window in the middle of the night and made off with several important jewels including the so-called Bain of Thorncroft, a twenty-carat imperial topaz, believed to be the world's largest, owned by the Marchioness of Cleves, who was a houseguest of His Lordship at the time.

Professor Moriarty, quondam holder of the Thales Chair of Mathematics at Midlothian University, is well regarded in mathematical and astronomical circles for his monograph *The Dynamics of an Asteroid*. What information he is expected to supply the police in regard to this unfortunate affair is unknown.

UNIDENTIFIED BODY FOUND IN THAMES

Special to The Standard

Friday 11 July 1890

On Thursday evening at about 8:30 P.M. an unclad and severely mutilated body was found floating in the Thames River below Blackfriars Bridge. Dr. Phipps, the police surgeon, who was called out to examine the body, declared it to be that of a woman of between 18 and 25 years, who had been in the water for at least three days before she was found. Neither the woman's identity nor the cause of her death has yet been established.

CHAPTER ONE

IN THE DOCK

"If the law supposes that,"
said Mr. Bumble . . . ,
"the law is a ass—a idiot."

—CHARLES DICKENS

IT SEEMED STIFLING HOT TO BENJAMIN BARNETT, sitting in the rear of the courtroom, but Mr. Justice Hedge did not seem inclined to have any of the four oversized windows opened. In all the trials he had covered at the Old Bailey, Barnett did not remember ever seeing them opened. Barnett, owner and managing editor of the American News Service, sat in the back pew of the visitors' gallery with his notebook open on his lap and a carefully sharpened Tiffman's No. 2 lead pencil in his hand. Professor James Moriarty had just been brought up from the cells and taken his place in the dock. A tall man with a hawklike face and piercing eyes, the professor stood passively, his shoulders slightly hunched in his black frock coat, giving the impression that he was the only adult in a world—or at least a courtroom—of children. His trial as an accessory in the Widdersign murders had gone on for four days before it was given to the jury, and those good gentlemen had now been out for three. Now, at four thirty in the afternoon of the third day of deliberations, the judge had reconvened the court. The bewigged barristers had returned from wherever barristers go while awaiting a verdict, the judge had donned his red robes and assumed the seat of the Queen's Justice, and the jury was filing in.

Mr. Justice Hedge waited until the last juror had taken his seat and then leaned forward on his elbows and tilted his head, the better to peer over his wire-rim eyeglasses. His gaze focused on the foreman. He frowned. "I received your note," he said. "It's been three days."

The foreman rose. "We know, milord. Three days."

"Are you absolutely sure?"

"We are, milord. Absolutely."

"You can come to no agreement?"

There was a stir in the small audience, which was quelled by a stern glance from the judge. The foreman, a thin, small, nervous greengrocer with a large, red-veined nose that gave character to his otherwise pinched and undistinguished face, nodded vigorously. "Yes, milord. That's so, milord." He clenched his hands into fists and thrust them behind his back to keep from fidgeting. "As you say, we've been at it for three days, milord, and we don't seem to be getting nowheres at all."

"I suppose, then, that giving you a few more hours to consider would be of no help?"

"No, milord."

"Or another"—his lordship grimaced—"day or two?"

"No, milord."

"You understand the charge?"

"Yes, milord."

"You all, singly and collectively, understand and agree," His Lordship began, pushing his glasses farther up on his nose, "that if the defendant, James Moriarty, has, as charged, been responsible for planning the robbery at Lord Hoxbary's country manor house known as Widdersign, he is perforce therefore as guilty as any of the felons who were actually present at the scene of the crime?"

"We does, milord."

"And that, as the robbery resulted in the taking of human life, the defendant would be as guilty of the crime of murder as the one who fired the shot, even though he was not actually present at the time the crime was committed?"

"Yes, milord."

"And even though the victims happened to be two of the criminals?"

"Yes, milord, your lordship has gone over that quite thoroughly. At first some of us had trouble seeing the justice in that, but your argument was quite persuasive. We has no longer any problem with that."

"You're quite sure?"

"Yes, milord."

"Perhaps if I had some of the testimony read back to you?"

The foreman looked horrified and responded quickly, "We don't have no dispute over the testimony, milord, nor any questions pertaining to it."

"I see." Mr. Justice Hedge paused to adjust his wig, which had recently adopted the annoying habit of inching its way forward until his forehead completely disappeared. "Well then," he said, peering down at the foreman as though the poor man were a hedge flower of some unexpected and particularly undesirable color. "What does seem to be the problem?"

"Well, milord, we can't agree as to whether or not he did that he is charged with, based on the evidence as we've heard it, is what it comes down to, milord. He may have done, but there's some as thinks he may not have done."

"By 'he' I assume you mean the prisoner at the bar," the judge specified, glancing down at the court stenographer.

"Yes, milord. The defendant, Professor Moriarty, that's who we mean."

Mr. Justice Hedge pushed his glasses back into place with a forefinger and glared at Moriarty. "It would seem I have no choice but to declare a mistrial. Three days and no verdict. Unheard of."

Barnett scribbled "unheard of" on his pad and underlined it. He would have to arrange to visit Moriarty, who had been a friend and mentor to him in the not-too-distant past, and see if there was any assistance he could offer. Anything, he thought wryly, short of arranging a prison break. That, Barnett was sure, the professor could manage on his own.

The Honorable Eppsworth, QC, appearing for the prosecution, rose and fingered the lapel of his judicial gown. "I would like to move, milord, that a mistrial be declared."

"It would seem I have little choice," said his lordship.

Sir Humphrey Lowenbog, appearing for the defense, rose and bowed gravely, if briefly, toward the judge. "If it please your lordship," he said, "my client Professor Moriarty and I would be quite willing to spare the crown the expense and trouble of a new trial. A directed verdict would suffice, I would say."

"A directed verdict?"

"Yes, milord. Of not guilty, milord."

Mr. Justice Hedge leaned back in his judicial chair and glowered down at the bewigged barrister. "I'm glad to see, Sir Humphrey, that you have not lost your sense of humor during these proceedings,"

Professor Moriarty turned in the dock to look up at the gallery. He took a pair of pince-nez glasses from the breast pocket of his jacket and polished the lenses with a piece of flannel while he studied the faces of those who had been studying his back.

"I would like to suggest," said the Honorable Eppsworth, "that a new trial date be set for as soon as practicable."

"I would think so," said Mr. Justice Hedge. "I doubt whether we could possibly get a second jury so blind to the obvious." He slammed his gavel down on the bench before him. "This case is closed, a mistrial is declared, this jury"—he paused to glare at the jury—"is discharged. Their names will be stricken from the rolls. The clerk will set a new court date."

Moriarty put the pince-nez back in his pocket as his eyes met those of Benjamin Barnett in the gallery. He nodded ever so slightly and turned back to face the judge.

Sir Humphrey took a half step forward. "I would like to renew the matter of bail for my client, milord."

"Humor, Sir Humphrey," said Mr. Justice Hedge severely, "can be taken only so far."

Barnett closed his notebook and rose. So there would be another trial. That brief nod from the professor was surely a sign that Moriarty wished to see him, he reflected. He would visit the prison as soon as possible. If there was any way he could help, he would certainly do so. Barnett's knowledge of Moriarty, gained from two years working with the man and being privy to at least some of his secrets, told him that Moriarty was almost certainly not guilty of this particular crime. However, guilt or innocence was not a part of this equation. There was a question of honor involved. Moriarty had done as much for Barnett once, and from an Ottoman prison at that. Barnett's wife, Cecily, might not see it in quite the same way, he realized—women tended to think of "honor" as a man's excuse for behaving like a child. Barnett exited thoughtfully onto Newgate Street.

[CHAPTER TWO]

MOLLIE'S

Come, give us a taste of your quality.

—SHAKESPEARE

IT HAD BEEN SATURDAY, September 13, 1890, for four hours, but Friday took a long time dying at the gentlemen's establishment known as Mollie's, a three-story white brick building at 33 Gladston Square, London. The last client had been ushered out, except for a marquis and a colonel of the Guards, who were using the establishment as a residence for the night, and five loo players of various ranks and stations in an upstairs room who probably wouldn't be staggering out into the chill, damp fog until sometime Tuesday. The maids were gathering the soiled bed linens to be washed and ironed, the glasses to be scoured, the bottles to be rinsed and returned to the vintners, and the various frilly garments and special costumes to be cleaned, examined, and repaired if necessary. The *filles de joie* were enjoying the luxury of sleeping alone.

Then suddenly there came a tapping as of someone strongly rapping, rapping at the outer door.

"A bit late for visitors," muttered the porter. "Or a bit early, if it comes to that." He slid open the eye slot and peered out. The orange-white glow of the gaslight above the door showed two men in evening clothes standing outside clutching their silk hats in their gloved hands: a thin young man with muttonchop whiskers and the appearance of

8

studied solemnity; and an older, thicker one with a bushy brush mustache and a touch of humor in his ruddy face.

"Closed for the night," the porter called out to them. "Come back tomorrow—or later today, as it happens. Say along about three in the afternoon. Glad to see you gentlemen then, I'm sure."

The young, thin gentleman brought his eye close to the eye slot. "Sorry to bother you, my man," he said. "We're here to retrieve Baron Renfrew. He's late for his next, um, engagement. Has he changed his plans? Is he spending the night? Could we speak with him, if you don't mind?"

"Baron Renfrew, is it then?" the porter asked. "Well then, come into the parlor, gentlemen." He pulled the door open and escorted them to the front room. "You just wait here for a minute, and I'll fetch Miss Mollie."

No more than three minutes later Mollie Cobby, fair, buxom, fast approaching forty, and pleasant to look at from the red silk ribbons in her dark hair to the black satin slippers on her feet, came through the inner door, tying the cord of her silk wrap firmly around her waist. "What's all this?" she cried. "The baron left these premises more than an hour ago, I believe—it might be two hours even. And what might you be wanting with him at this time of the morning, if I may ask?"

"Left, has he?" asked the younger one, pursing his lips and brushing his nose thoughtfully with the tips of his fingers.

"Sorry, miss," said the older one with the thick brush mustache, jumping to his feet and standing as ramrod straight as a sergeant on parade. "I'm Mr. Mortimer, and my associate here's Mr. Pellew. We don't mean to be a bother, indeed we don't. But the baron's coach has been awaiting the baron in the mews, horse, coachman, and all, for these past five hours, and the baron has not appeared in its vicinity. If you could tell us just when he left, or where he was headed, we would be most appreciative. It's our job, you see, to look after the baron, and it's as much as our job is worth to lose track of him. Sadly, he's not always thoughtful enough to enumerate his comings and goings before he comes and goes."

Mollie looked at them thoughtfully. "You're a pair of his watchdogs, then? Why didn't you come inside all this time and wait in comfort, such as it is? Like that Mr., ah, Fetch, who follows him about everywhere."

Mr. Mortimer smiled. "We're his outside watchdogs, miss."

"Speaking of which," said Mr. Pellew, "where is the aforesaid Mr. Fetch?" He peered about the room as though he expected Fetch to spring up from some chest or cabinet like clockwork.

"Why a young, handsome gentleman like the baron needs to be guarded and escorted hither and yon is more than I know," Mollie said. "P'raps you could explain it to me."

"It's just the way of things, ma'am," Mr. Pellew said, spreading his arms wide in explanation.

"It's his mother, you see," added Mr. Mortimer, "and his grandmama. They don't want to know just what he's doing, if you see what I mean, but they don't want him to get into any trouble while doing it."

"Well," Mollie said, shaking her head. "That's as may be, I suppose."

"You say he's gone?" asked Mr. Pellew. "And Mr. Fetch with him? Do you know just when they left?"

"I don't keep a watch on my gentlemen callers," Mollie said severely, dropping primly down onto the couch and waving the two men into seats.

"Not even to receive, ah, recompense?" suggested Mortimer, cautiously settling into an overstuffed chair.

"Come now," Mollie said severely. "Do you think we're a gaggle of streetwalkers in here?"

Mortimer considered the question and decided not to say just what it was he thought.

"So you don't keep track of the comings and goings of your guests?" Pellew asked, cocking his head to one side and peering at her like a sparrow inspecting a beetle.

"Only as it happens in the course of providing for their amusement," Mollie told him. "The porter sees them in, but there's a side door by which they may depart, if they've a mind to. At the end of the evening the girls tell me what, ah, services have been provided, and it's put to the gentleman's account."

"So you can't say for sure that the baron and Mr. Fetch have indeed left, is that so?"

Mollie shifted nervously in her seat. "I didn't see them leave, if that's what you mean, but it was some time past. I was in the upstairs hall, it must be a good hour ago, and Mr. Fetch was no longer in his chair outside the room. And when Mr. Fetch is gone from the hall, it stands to reason that Baron Renfrew is gone from the room."

"Excuse me?" asked Mr. Mortimer.

"Mr. Fetch, like a faithful dog—perhaps that's why he's called Fetch, do you suppose?—always waits outside his master's door. I have no notion of what he fancies he's guarding his master from, but he's quite earnest about it. One of the girls once offered to entertain him in her room while he was waiting, as an act of kindness, you might say, but he would have none of it. Very serious and dedicated, Mr. Fetch. Nancy was quite put out. No one had ever turned her down before; it's usually her what does the turning down. So we give him a comfy chair and a bit of fizz from the gasogene, with just a touch of brandy to take away the nasty taste, as he says, and there he sits until the baron emerges."

Mortimer nodded. "I see," he said.

"So, since Mr. Fetch is gone, the baron likewise must have emerged."

"But you didn't actually see him leave?"

"I can't say I did, no."

"Did anyone?"

Mollie sighed. "It's quite late. Most of the girls are asleep."

Mr. Pellew sat primly on the red plush sofa behind him and began absently playing with one of the tassels that formed a fringe around the sofa's edge. "With which young lady was the baron spending the evening?" he inquired. "Perhaps we could speak with her."

Mollie pushed herself to her feet. "Needs must as wants will, I always say." She sighed once more and shook her head sadly and left the room.

Half a minute later they heard her scream.

Mortimer and Pellew jumped to their feet and rushed upstairs, followed closely by the porter, who brandished a great oak cudgel that had mysteriously appeared in his hand. The screams stopped as they reached the long, dimly lit hallway, but doors were opening and the young ladies of the establishment, their flannel nightgowns held tightly around them against the draft, were peering cautiously out. At the end of the hallway one of the loo players, cards in hand, had emerged from the cardroom and was sniffing the air cautiously. Fire was a constant worry in these old buildings. Seeing nothing of that sort amiss, the man retreated back into the cardroom with one last aggravated sniff and a muttered "Women!" and slammed the door.

Several of the girls had gathered around one of the open doors. Mortimer paused to turn up the gas on a wall sconce near the door, and bright white light from the mantle filled the hallway. The bedroom was a rectangle about fourteen by twenty feet, holding an oversized bed, a nondescript night table, a drop-front bureau in the style of Queen Anne, a rose-colored wardrobe with a frieze of somber angels painted around the top, and a washstand with a porcelain washbasin. A colored etching of a schooner in a windstorm, an oil painting of a cow, and two framed mirrors hung on the walls, which were otherwise covered with a flocked wallpaper in a tulip pattern.

A girl lay stretched out on the bed, and Miss Mollie was bending over her. The light from the hall bouncing off the mirrors onto the walls and ceiling cast weird reflections around the room and kept most of it in deep shadow as the men entered, and for a second it seemed that mysterious half-seen entities were gliding about in the unlit corners.

A shaft of light illuminated the face of the girl, a pretty, freckled-faced young redhead. She lay on her back, naked, with a sheet thrown over her middle for modesty, her hands and feet spread apart and tied with some sort of thick satin cord to the four bedposts. Some trick of the lighting seemed to cast a dark shadow across the sheet.

"I didn't know our master was a devotee of the Marquis de Sade," remarked Mr. Mortimer quietly.

"Let us not dwell on this," said Pellew, turning away and gazing earnestly at another part of the room. "Untie the girl, Miss Mollie, and I'll see that she gets an extra two—no, five—pounds for her, ah, trouble."

"Rose, she called herself," Mollie said without looking up. "Because of her coloring, if you see what I mean; red hair, red cheeks. Rose."

"*Called* herself?"

One of the girls in the hall lit a second gas mantle, which threw more light on the bed. Mortimer stepped closer and peered over Mollie's shoulder. Rose's eyes stared sightlessly at the mirrored ceiling. Her mouth was open, her lips shaped into an oval O—an eternal silent scream of horror. A deep gash splayed open her too-white skin from her throat down between her breasts and disappeared beneath the sheet. What had seemed a dark shadow across the middle of the bed was a pool of slowly congealing blood.

"Well, I'll be . . . ," began Mortimer, taking an involuntary step backward, his hand across his mouth. After a few moments of silent gulping, he managed, "What a horrible thing! Horrible!"

Pellew turned back and stepped closer to the bed to examine the carnage. "Awful, indeed," he said. "Tragic. Such concentrated fury attacking this poor girl. I haven't seen anything like this since—well, for some time." He turned to Mortimer. "You don't think this could be the work of . . . our master . . . do you?" he asked in an undertone. "There were . . . rumors . . . at the time, I remember."

"Bosh," said Mortimer. "Then and now—bosh! Don't believe it for an instant. Something horrible has happened here, but you can't think that . . . the baron . . . had aught to do with it."

"Well, where is he, then?" asked Pellew, peering around the room.

Suddenly Mollie screamed once more and jumped back from the bed. "Something grabbed my leg!" she shrieked.

The gaggle of girls gathered in the hallway outside shrieked in sympathy, then shrieked again as an arm emerged from beneath the bed, its hand reaching . . . reaching . . .

Mortimer and Pellew jumped for the arm and pulled. It was attached to a wizened little man in a white shirt and black breeches who slid out from under the bed and lay prone and motionless on the floor. The girls shrieked once more.

"Why, it's Mr. Fetch," Mollie said, peering down at the man.

Fetch opened his eyes and blinked at the light. "Where am I?" he croaked, rolling over. "What happened?"

"Never mind that," Mr. Mortimer said severely. "Where's the baron?"

Fetch tried to sit up but lay back down with a weak groan. "I was bumped," he said. "Banged. Bopped aside the head. Something grabbed me from behind, and—oww!" He had tried to touch the spot above his left ear where the damage had been done, but the pain was too great.

"What sort of something hit you?" Mollie asked.

One of the girls outside the door put her hand to her mouth. "Ghosts and ghoulies," she whispered in a loud and earnest whisper. "There's strange things walks these corridors at night."

"Mighty strange," one of the other girls agreed. "I have felt their presence as a cold, clammy hand on my back in the dark!"

"None stranger than yourself, Gladys Plum," Mollie said severely. "Go back to your rooms now, all of you, and stop frightening each other, or you'll be feeling my cold hand where it'll do some good."

The cluster of young women looked at her wide-eyed and made no attempt to move.

"Where is your master?" Mortimer repeated, bending over the prostrate Fetch. "Where is the baron?"

"Don't know," Fetch mumbled. "Where am I?"

Mollie squatted on the balls of her feet next to Fetch. "You're in Rose's room," she told him. "Until moments ago you were under Rose's bed."

Moving his head gingerly, Fetch looked around the room. "I was?" he asked, wonderingly. "What was I doing there? Where's the baron got to, then?"

"Wait!" Mortimer said. "What's that sound?"

"Sound?" Pellew straightened up and looked searchingly around the room.

"Be quiet and listen," Mortimer instructed, holding his forefinger to his lips.

They listened silently for a few moments. A couple of the girls in the hall giggled nervously, but Mollie looked sternly at them and all giggles subsided.

"What sort of sound?" Mollie whispered.

"It's a sort of soft scratching, thumping, sobbing sort of sound," Mortimer said. "Coming from . . ." He looked around him, trying to locate the sound. "There it is again, but I cannot tell where it's coming from."

Mollie lifted her eyes to the ceiling and held her breath. "I do hear it," she said. She waved a finger around the room like a compass needle gone wild and then steadied it to point to the wardrobe. "There," she said. "It comes from there."

Pellew tiptoed over to the wardrobe with exaggerated caution and paused in front of the door to look back at Mortimer. Mortimer nodded and, standing behind him, the porter raised high his cudgel.

Pellew stood to the side of the wardrobe and yanked at the door handle—with no effect. He yanked again and again it did not budge, but this time a loud squeal emerged from inside the wardrobe.

Pellew frowned and, moving in front of the door, took the ornate round knob firmly in both hands. Spreading his legs to brace his feet against the sides of the wardrobe, he yanked again with all his might. There was a creaking and a snapping and the door flew open, throwing Pellew onto his back in an undignified sprawl.

In the wardrobe were hanging a few frocks and jackets, a teal blue velvet cloth coat, and a red silk dressing gown with Japanese pretensions. Crouched under the dressing gown in as tight a ball as she could manage was a small girl in a frilly white chemise, her pert round face wet with tears and red with the long effort at suppressing a scream—a series of screams—that now began to tumble forth.

Mollie squinted at the girl and took a step forward. "Here now, here now, Pamela," she said sharply. "Let's have none of that. You must control yourself. Whatever were you doing in the wardrobe? You must take a deep breath and control yourself."

Pamela gulped and stopped sobbing long enough to take a deep breath, then broke out into a fresh paroxysm of sobs.

Mortimer moved up and took the girl in his arms, patting her sympathetically if awkwardly on the back. "There, there," he said. "I have a gel at home just about your age, maybe a peck younger. You mustn't upset yourself so. What were you doing in the wardrobe?"

Pamela sobbed.

"Were you there while . . . it . . . happened?" Pellew asked. "Whatever it was? Take a deep breath, now."

Pamela looked at him, took a deep breath, and sobbed.

"I don't think," Mollie said, "that deep breathing is going to help."

Mortimer took an oversized white handkerchief from his jacket pocket and wiped off Pamela's moist face. "So it would seem," he agreed.

"I'll take her into her room," Mollie said, gathering the girl into her own arms. "We'll talk to her later, after she's had a chance to . . . whatever it is she needs to do."

Mr. Mortimer looked at Mr. Pellew, and Mr. Pellew looked at Mr. Mortimer. "Go for the specials," Mortimer told Pellew. "I'll stay here and do what can be done."

"Put someone at each door," Pellew said.

"Of course," Mortimer agreed, "but I fear the horse is long gone."

"What horse?" Mollie demanded. "What specials?"

"The Special Household Branch of the CID, at Scotland Yard, ma'am," Mortimer told her. "There's nothing for it, I'm afraid. There's been murder done, and His—ah, Baron Renfrew is missing."

"What household?" Mollie squealed, her hands flying up to her face. "I don't want the rozzers in here," she protested, looking around wildly as though she expected them to jump through the window any second.

"Oh, these aren't the regular police," Mortimer assured her. "This is a very discreet group of gentlemen specially trained to handle situations like this. Mr. Pellew will take our coach and fetch them. Will you please see that all outer doors are secured?"

"Situations like what?" Mollie asked. "Just what is this'ere Special Household Branch?"

"Go, Mr. Pellew," Mr. Mortimer said, taking charge with a firm hand. "See to the door, if you please, Miss Mollie. All will be revealed to you in the fullness of time. Which in the present case will probably be within the next half hour, I should say."

Mr. Pellew trotted off down the corridor, the cluster of girls parting before him like the Red Sea before Moses. If, Pellew thought, a religious simile wasn't too inappropriate at a time like this.

"I say!" a voice bellowed from down the hall. "Will you girls please keep it down? We're trying to play cards in here!"

CHAPTER THREE

INDECISION

*Pleasure is nothing else
but the intermission of pain.*

—JOHN SELDEN

MUMMER TOLLIVER, Professor Moriarty's diminutive assistant, perched precariously on the seat of the green damask armchair in the Barnetts' sitting room. His small patent-leather-shod feet swung to and fro viciously, a visual counterpoint to the sharp anger in his voice as he spoke.

"You got in to see the professor, is what," he said.

"Just barely," Benjamin Barnett admitted from the depths of his overstuffed easy chair.

"But they won't let me see him, is what," Mummer continued, "and they wouldn't pass along the bundle of necessaries what I had brought for him. 'Concerned for his safety,' they says. Me, what's been the professor's confidant and midget-of-all-work for the better part of two decades. And it ain't just me what they're so-called protecting him from. Mr. Maws is upset 'cause they won't let him bring no cleaned and starched and pressed clothes to the professor. It ain't right is what he says for the professor to be without his shirts and collars and suchwhats. And if it comes to that, it ain't right is what I says."

"Mr. Maws?" Barnett's wife, Cecily, looked up from her seat at the writing desk between the tall front windows. "Oh yes, the professor's butler."

"Butler and facto-te-tum and bodyguard when such is called for—not that the professor can't take care of 'imself in a scrap."

"The authorities are making it quite difficult to get in to visit the professor," Barnett agreed. "Special forms from the Home Office, special permission from the governor of the prison, neither of which they seem inclined to pass along easily. It took them four days to process my request, and I'm a journalist."

"Yes, well, I'm a midget," said the mummer. "Ain't midgets got no rights in this'ere queendom?"

Cecily raised an eyebrow. "Queendom?"

"Stands to reason, don't it?" said the mummer. "T'ain't nary a kingdom at the present moment, is it?"

"No, t'ain't," Cecily agreed.

"Even when I got to see the professor," Barnett expanded, "they didn't make it easy. They brought me into a tiny stone-walled room with a guard at the door—inside the door, mind you, and sat me across from him at a wooden table that was screwed to the floor. And the chairs—they also were fastened in place. Which place was too far from the table to comfortably write or whatever. A truly large guard stood between us and glowered down at us as we talked. The professor was wearing manacles, which the guards refused to remove. And they searched me twice—at the inner gate and then again at the door to the room. I had to empty my pockets. I was allowed to bring in nothing but my notebook and a pencil. Only one pencil, mind you. I was worried the whole time that the point would break while I took notes."

"I could've been a journalist," the mummer said. "I wrote something once. It concerned a large fish." He stared at the wall glumly, as though the experience were one he didn't want to think about any further.

"I thought persons awaiting trial were permitted visitors," Cecily said.

"Some are and some are not," Barnett told her. "The professor, for some reason, is one of the are-nots."

"A jellyfish," the mummer expanded.

Cecily paused in her note writing, her pen poised to continue. "Why, do you suppose, they're making it so difficult to see him?"

"What I think," the mummer offered, "is they're afraid he'll blow the quad and depart for a spot what offers more room to move about. P'raps they think I'll smuggle him out in my knapsack."

Cecily smiled at the image. "You have a knapsack?" she asked.

"O'course," the mummer said. "I has to have a place to carry about my whatnots and doodads, don't I?"

"Of course," Cecily agreed.

"There are those who would like to get a glimpse of my whatnots," the mummer said darkly, "but I can tell a hawk from a handsaw."

Cecily smiled. "Good for you," she said.

Barnett got up and began pacing the floor. He stared thoughtfully at the ceiling, remembering the bizarre conditions under which he had first met Moriarty. Some six years earlier Sultan Abd-ul Hamid, the second of that name, had been considering purchasing the Garrett-Harris submersible boat for use in his navy. The *New York World* had sent Benjamin Barnett, its ace foreign correspondent, to Constantinople to report on the craft's sea trials. Barnett had first encountered Moriarty running down a street in Stamboul with a gang of street toughs in close pursuit. Barnett and Lieutenant Sefton, a British naval officer, had rescued the professor, who thanked them for their assistance although, he assured them, he could have handled the situation quite well on his own. Shortly thereafter Sefton had been murdered, and the Ottoman authorities had decided in their wisdom that Barnett was guilty. Professor Moriarty had rescued Barnett from an Osmanli dungeon, where he was awaiting trial. Despite his innocence it was probable that when the authorities finally got around to trying him, the wheels of the sultan's justice would have ground him fine.

A year later, while Barnett was working for Moriarty in London, he first met his beloved Cecily. He owed much to Professor Moriarty, a debt he felt he could never adequately repay. "If the professor needs help—" he began.

"Did he say so?" Cecily asked.

"No, as a matter of fact, he didn't, but then it would have been difficult with the Cardiff Giant sitting between us."

"He'll find some way to let us know, to tell us what he wants us to do," Cecily said firmly. "If you try to interfere blindly, you'll probably only make a mess of things."

Barnett paused before the sofa and sighed. Why is it, he wondered, that when a woman marries a man she immediately loses all respect for his intelligence and ability? The thought that perhaps she never had any such respect in the first place crossed his mind, but he thrust it out again. "Mummer's probably right," he said, resuming his pacing. "The prison authorities are taking precautions against the professor's reputed omniscience. They're afraid he's going to escape."

"As well they should be," the mummer observed.

"Sometimes," Cecily reflected, "having a reputation for being clever works against one's best interests." She turned back to her note writing.

"The professor usually don't tootle his own flute," the mummer said, "but there's others what tootle it for him. So he's got a reputation among the villainous classes for knowing everything what there is to know, which is pretty much on the square, and for doing everything what gets done, many of which he wouldn't nohow touch."

"The whole thing is ridiculous, of course," Barnett said. "To think Moriarty could have done such a thing—been so stupid—it's ridiculous."

Cecily put her pen down carefully on the blotter and took a deep breath. "Stop pacing," she said. "You make me nervous."

"Sorry." Barnett flopped down onto the sofa.

"I know you owe him a lot," Cecily said, "but even you must admit that he has at times, let us say, performed acts that are contrary to the laws of Her Majesty's Government. What makes you so sure he wasn't involved in that Widdersign idiocy?"

The mummer left the chair and dropped to his feet before Barnett had a chance to reply. "No way!" the little man asserted. "It ain't his sort of lay at all!"

Cecily turned to him. "Well then, what makes *you* so sure?"

"Well, for one thing, I'd know if the professor were involved, wouldn't I? He and me, we ain't got no secrets from each other. At least none of a pro-as-it-were-fessional nature. Besides, the busies have it that he planned this here Widdersign job, and he don't plan no such sloppy plans. If he had planned the job, those who was supposed to be tied up would right enough have stayed tied up—you can bank on it."

"I think you're right, Mummer," Barnett mused.

Cecily cocked her head to the side like a curious sparrow. "So it's not his honesty or morality but his proficiency that makes you think him innocent?" she asked.

Barnett considered for a second. "That's right," he agreed, "and I'd say it's a much more reliable indicator. What can one really know of another's degree of honesty or morality? Tell me that."

Cecily smiled again. "What indeed?" she agreed. "How did the professor seem when you saw him?"

Barnett thought for a moment. "Gray," he said, "and, I don't know, stolid. As if he wasn't going to let any of this bother him, but it took considerable effort to manage it."

"What did you discuss?" Cecily asked.

"We didn't so much discuss," Barnett said. "The professor spoke, I listened. He told me his side of the case." He stood up and began pacing again. "Well, no, not his side so much as what he thought must have happened. Since he wasn't actually involved, he said, there were a certain number of assumptions in what he told me, but it was the most logical way for it to have happened."

"There, you see?" The mummer hopped to his feet. "What was it he said? And what do he want us to do about it?"

"If there was anything he wanted me to do, he couldn't tell me because the guards were right there in the room and whatever he said would get right back to the prosecution."

"So just what did he say?" Cecily asked.

"And how did he look?" the mummer added. "He looked like he was losing weight when I seen him in court."

"He looked fine," Barnett told the mummer. "He told me that he hadn't done it, in case I had any doubts, and that he couldn't determine why Esterman was lying."

"Esterman?" Cecily asked.

"The surprise witness," Barnett told her.

"Was he one of the robbers?"

"Not likely!" said the mummer. "He ain't steady enough to make an honest robber. I seen him on the stand, twitchin' and blinkin', and then, when he was answering questions, turning to stare steadylike at the jury with every syllable what came out of his mouth."

"I've always thought," said Cecily, "that a steady gaze is the sign of an honest soul."

"That's what they sez," the mummer agreed. "And they sez it often enough so every swindler and liar and two-peg sit-down man in the world has learned to stare you right in the mug when he's busy lying to you. Nothing breeds confi-blinking-dence like when the bloke's staring you right in the mug."

"There were six men in the gang that assaulted Widdersign," Barnett explained to Cecily.

Cecily sighed. "I guess you'd better tell me about it," she said, "as it involves the professor, and I do care about the professor. Also, it looks as though it's going to involve you, and I—you know."

"Yes," Barnett said. He rubbed the side of his nose with his index finger, a gesture he had discovered helped clarify his thoughts, and picked up his notebook. "Two of the robbers were killed in the, ah, fracas," he began, flipping through the notebook to find the right page. "One was wounded and captured, and the other three escaped into the forest with little to show for the escapade except, it is believed, a particularly fine topaz necklace belonging to Lady Hoxbary. On the other hand, Lady Hoxbary may have merely mislaid the necklace; she has been known to do so before."

"And the wounded man?" Cecily asked.

"A few number-eight shotgun pellets in the leg," Barnett told her. "Fully recovered by the start of trial."

"He'll never fly again," the mummer offered. "He walks with a bit of a limp, which he was glad to display and, if you was to ask me, exaggerate for the jury, when he come to give testimony."

"He gave testimony against Professor Moriarty?"

"Well, he had to, didn't he?" asked the mummer.

"He pled guilty," Barnett explained, "and received a lighter sentence for informing on his companions."

"Ten years in quod, it were," expanded Tolliver. "Seeing as how he could have swung, like as what they're trying to do to the professor, I'd say he come off it pretty light. Particularly as how he couldn't do all that much informing on account of which he didn't know who any of them were. Or so he said. My sources," the mummer went on, tapping the side of his nose suggestively, "had it that the prosecutor offered to go even lighter on him if he could somehow produce some of the swag from the earlier robberies, no questions asked, as it were."

"I didn't know you had sources," said Barnett.

"I has my nose to the wheel," Tolliver explained.

"Any 'swag' in particular?" asked Cecily.

"A good question," said the mummer, "and it would seem that the answer is 'indeed so.' The Marchioness of Cleves, whose husband is some biggywig in Her Majesty's Government, is anxious to get her bauble back."

"The, ah, Bain of Thorncroft," Barnett remembered. "A big topaz."

"Twenty carats," said Cecily, who had a fondness for jewelry and an impressive knowledge thereof. "Possibly the world's largest imperial topaz."

"What makes it imperial?" Barnett asked.

"Its color mostly. This one is a sort of pinkish orange."

"So," the mummer went on, "this'ere robber, Manxman Benny by name, he cops a plea, but he don't give the rozzers anything for it they can chew on—except the professor."

"The authorities believed him?"

"It must've gone summat like this," the mummer offered. He raised a hand in supplication and assumed a high, shrill voice, " 'Honest, Inspector, I can't peach on any of me mates, 'cause I never seen them before the job, and I don't know nothing about any other jobs, and I don't know who they are when they're at home. But I happen to know who the big boss is, and I'll swallow my fear of his retri-as-it-were-bution and give you his name. Which is Professor James Moriarty. S'welp me, governor, that's all I knows.' "

"And on that evidence they put the professor on trial?" Cecily asked incredulously.

"There was a bit of detail to add corroboration," Barnett told her, "but basically, that was it."

"Until the Honorable Eppsworth, what appeared for the prosecution, opened his sleeve and Esterman fell out," the mummer expanded.

"Esterman's the local publican," Barnett explained. "Owns the Fox and Hare in Wedsbridge. He claims that Moriarty stayed there for two nights the week before the robbery. Signed the register with the name Bumbury. Moriarty, on the other hand, says he was never anywhere near Wedsbridge. On the nights in question he was at his observatory on the Moor, but the only one there with him was his caretaker, an old ticket-of-leave man named Wilcox, who testified to that effect. When asked by the prosecutor whether he would lie for Moriarty, he replied, 'A'course I would,' which sort of ruined the effect."

"That's what you get for telling the truth in this man's world," the mummer said darkly.

"Maybe not," Cecily suggested. "After all, *something* hung that jury."

"True," Barnett agreed.

"Someone should have hung Esterman for a lying dog, which is what he were," the mummer added with a vicious upward swipe with his left foot.

"What in the world—what's this?" Barnett suddenly demanded. He had closed his notebook and thoughtlessly turned it over as he was laying it down. There were some words crudely written in pencil on the stiff back cover:

look in binding

"Where'd that come from?" Barnett demanded. "What binding? The binding of what?"

Mummer Tolliver picked up the notebook and turned it over and over in his little hands. "It's spirit writing," he announced

The Barnetts, husband and wife, looked at him.

"A ghost sneaked in and wrote that bit on my notebook?" Barnett asked, with the hint of a smile.

"It weren't no ghost. The professor wrote that bit," Mummer explained.

"Ah! So Professor Moriarty snuck in and scribbled on my notebook?"

The mummer looked annoyed. "It's spirit writing," he explained patiently, "what is done onstage or in a séance by the medium to produce a manisfetation . . . manifestation from the spirit world. The medium holds up a slate or pad so the assembled multitude can see that there ain't nothing wrote on it, and then he turns it over and holds it upside down with a member of said multitude holding the other end. Then he whinges for a bit for the spirits to answer their call. Then he turns the slate or likewise the pad over, and writing has miraculously appeared from the spirit world."

"Ah!" Barnett said.

"What has happened unbeknownst to said multitude is that the medium writes the message—*I am watching over you,* or *Have faith!* or *Give the swami fifty quid,* or whatsomever seems appropriate to the occasion—upside down with a bit of chalk or pencil lead held in by his fingernail and a lot of practice to get it right."

"The professor has practiced this art?" Cecily asked.

"He can call the spirits from the vasty deep," the mummer affirmed. "Sometimes they come when he calls them."

"So, upside down, eh?" Barnett took the notebook in his hands and considered. "The professor did hold the notebook once," he recalled. "It fell to the floor, and he picked it up and handed it to me. That was shortly before the end of the interview."

"It just fell to the floor?" Cecily asked.

"Yes, it . . . wait a minute! No. Moriarty knocked it to the floor with a sweep of his arm. Then he picked it up and apologized. He—" Barnett closed his eyes and pictured the event. "He held it toward me for perhaps thirty or forty seconds while he was apologizing and then handed it over. I did think it strange at the time. The professor isn't one to spend time apologizing, but, you see, the stress of confinement, I thought . . . Anyway, that must have been when he did it."

"What does it mean?" Cecily asked. "Look in binding?"

The mummer gave an excited hop. "It must be the binding of the thingummy, doncher see? The notebook."

Barnett examined his trusty reporter's notebook as though he had never seen it before. It was about six inches wide and eight high, slightly under an inch thick, with two stiff covers of some sort of paperboard, surfaced in a glued-on beige fabric that wrapped around to serve as the spine. It had a stitched binding, like a book, as the pages were not designed to be easily torn out. He turned it over and over in his hands. "I don't see—"

"Here!" the mummer said suddenly. He took the notebook and opened it flat and then turned it upside down. "See the way the cloth pops away at the spine when it's opened like this? Take a dekko and see if anything's inside that there space."

Barnett tried to peer inside the space thus revealed. "It's too dark," he said. "Wait a moment." He lifted the notebook, still spread open, up to the light from the window and looked through. "Something," he said. "Some sort of tube." He tried poking at it with his forefinger, but it wouldn't budge.

"Here," the mummer offered, producing a very large pair of tweezers from his jacket pocket. "Try with these."

"What on earth?" Barnett asked. "Why are you carrying these monstrous things around?"

"Very useful for opening doors," the mummer told him, "if the key should happen to be on the other side of the lock."

Cecily looked closely at the oversized device. "Does the need for this come up often?" she asked.

"You'd be surprised how many untrusting people are abroad in this world," the mummer told her.

Barnett inserted the tweezers into the space and gently pried at the cylinder, pulling it from its resting place. "It's a tightly rolled-up piece of—it feels like silk," he told them.

"Fancy that," said the mummer.

"Perhaps you should unroll it," Cecily suggested.

Barnett complied, flattening it out on the table as he did so. The eight-by-eight square of fine silk fabric thus revealed was covered with tiny writing in Professor Moriarty's meticulous hand.

Barnett studied it for a minute.

"Well," he said, "I believe we have our instructions."

CHAPTER FOUR

DURANCE VILE

I know not whether Laws be right,
Or whether Laws be wrong;
All that we know who lie in gaol
Is that the wall is strong;
And that each day is like a year,
A year whose days are long.

—OSCAR WILDE

IT WAS FAST APPROACHING MIDNIGHT AND, the governor of Newgate Prison being a thrifty man, the gaslights in the stone corridors of the Old Block had been turned down to a faint orange glow, the barest hint of which penetrated the slots in the more favorably positioned cell doors. In the silence one could hear the dripping of distant water and the scurrying of small, quick animals.

Professor James Clovis Moriarty, MS, ScD, PhD, FRAS, quondam holder of the Thales Chair of Mathematics at Midlothian University, author of *The Dynamics of an Asteroid*, *Some Thoughts on an Absolute Value for* π, and *A Few Hesitant Steps into the Fourth Dimension*, as well as a score of other well-regarded papers on mathematics and astronomy, paced slowly back and forth the six steps his cell would allow.

Stone walls did not, for the moment, a prison make; Moriarty had turned his mind in another direction. Scarcely aware of the roughness of his gray prison garb, the damp chill of his cell, or the shackles on his hands, he mentally roamed the vast space between the stars, considering what the spectra of certain nebulosities indicated about their composition and structure—a problem that he had been wrestling with for some years. Still it must be admitted that he would have preferred the convenience of his observatory on the Moor, with the new 14-inch refracting telescope, specially crafted for him by Bascombe & Brandt Ltd. and just installed the week he was arrested. Or the comfort of his home on Russell Square, where he could peruse the books and journals in his library at leisure.

The sound of footsteps echoing the length of the narrow corridor outside his door pulled Moriarty from his contemplation of the infinite, and he turned to sit on the edge of his cot and await his visitor.

With little else to listen to for the past weeks, Moriarty had accustomed himself to interpreting the staccato footsteps of any who traversed the corridor, the mutterings of conversations he could overhear, and even the muted breathing of those who passed by. He listened. Two men approached, the one in the lead short and heavy, wearing thick-soled boots that squeaked slightly under his ponderous tread, his breath coming in sharp puffs. That would be the warder, Jacobs, a jowly, pig-eyed, mean-spirited, rapacious great toad of a man. He would not do a favor for any man, but Moriarty had decided that, if the need arose, he could be bought.

The other footsteps Moriarty did not recognize. His ear told him that they were those of a tall, slender, elderly man, with a slight roll to his walk and just the trace of a limp. By the occasional sharp tapping sounds, the man carried a walking stick but, from his casual use of it, was not dependent on its aid.

When they reached the cell door the warder snapped open the latch on the tiny observation window and, pulling it open, peered inside and went through a great show of sliding bolts, turning locks, releasing catches, and pounding on metal before the plate metal door swung open. He then stepped aside with a subservient bow. "This is 'im, your worship. I'll wait outside like what you said, your worship. Be careful of this'ere professor, your worship. 'E's a killer, is what 'e is."

The visitor edged around the chubby warder and entered the cell. "I'll be watchful, Jacobs. Just close the door, there's a fellow, and leave the lantern. I'll call when I want you."

"Yessir, your worship." Jacobs hung the bull's-eye lantern on a peg by the door, touched a knuckle to his forehead, and backed out of the cell, shutting the door with a forceful snap behind him.

Moriarty's visitor was tall and notably thin except for a hint of the rotundity of age around his middle. The cut of his pearl gray sack suit could only have been accomplished in one of the hidden corners of Savile Row, where the tailor would not take your custom unless his grandfather served yours.

Moriarty rose. "Please sit down," he said, indicating the only chair in the room, a spindly, backless wooden stool of great but undistinguished age. "I apologize for greeting you in my shirtsleeves, but these irons on my wrists make it impossible to put my jacket on properly. The warder seems to consider you a person of note, but I welcome the highborn as well as the low to my humble domicile."

His visitor sat down carefully and brushed some perhaps not entirely imaginary dust off his knees. "Amusing, isn't it? The chap hasn't the slightest idea who I am. Governor Makepiece ordered him to escort me to your, ah, accommodation but, at my request, he failed to mention my name."

"Jacobs's assumption is understandable," Moriarty said, resuming his seat on the edge of the cot. "You do have a certain air about you."

His visitor took a silver cigarette case from his jacket and removed two brown-paper-wrapped tubes. "So do you, Professor," he commented, tapping the cigarettes thoughtfully on the case before handing one to Moriarty and lighting the two with a small silver lighter. "Despite the rather dingy gray garment and the manacles, you still achieve, if I may say so, a commanding presence."

Moriarty smiled. "The opportunities for command are limited in these surroundings," he observed.

"That would seem to be so," his guest agreed. "Why the manacles, by the way? They seem rather redundant in here."

"Ah!" said Moriarty. "To quote Reverend Dodgson's dormouse, 'Mine is a long and sad tale.' But truly I doubt whether it's of interest to anyone other than myself."

"Nevertheless, it is curious."

"True."

"Then, if you will, assuage my curiosity."

"Very well. There is a gentleman who calls himself a 'consulting detective,' whatever that may be. A certain Sherlock Holmes."

"I know his brother, Mycroft," the visitor interrupted.

"A gentleman," Moriarty said. "Brother Sherlock is, ah, of a different stamp: lean where Mycroft is stout; quick where Mycroft is stolid; a terrier where his brother is a bulldog. They are both possessed of a high order of intelligence, but where Mycroft is steady and methodical, Sherlock is prone on occasion to bypass his rather considerable powers of deduction and jump to what I may call an escapable conclusion."

"What has this to do with your, ah—" The man gestured at the manacles.

"Mr. Holmes—Mr. Sherlock Holmes—came to the conclusion some years ago, based upon some interaction between us, that I am a blackguard. 'The wickedest man unhung,' I believe is what he has called me. 'The Napoleon of crime.' He would have it that I am responsible for all of the crimes committed to the west of the English Channel. Over the years he has managed to convince some of the gentlemen of Scotland Yard and a few others in authority in one capacity or another. As a result I have been put on trial for a capital offense based on evidence that wouldn't convince a thrush, were I regarded by the authorities as an honorable man, and your friend the governor of the prison has been told that I am some sort of miracle man, capable of escaping from ordinary confines. So he has put me here, in an underground dungeon in the oldest part of this ancient structure, with thick stone walls, and kept these on"—Moriarty raised his hands and shook the iron cuffs back and forth—"for added emphasis."

His visitor nodded thoughtfully. "Could you?" he asked. "Escape, that is."

"Possibly," Moriarty admitted. "Given sufficient incentive."

His visitor pursed his lips. "The present circumstances are not incentive enough for you?"

Moriarty considered. "Not while there's a chance, however slight, of leaving by more accepted means," he said. "Escaping would mean fleeing the country, giving up most of my former life. It would make it difficult to continue my various researches."

"I see," his visitor said. "Logical. You seem awfully open with me as to your, ah, potential plans."

"You don't impress me as a 'copper's nark,'" Moriarty told him, "and I imagine you have more important things to do than to run to the governor with the possibility that I might flee."

His visitor smiled. "Even so," he agreed. "Still, the time must hang heavy for a man of your intellect in here, with nothing to occupy your mind."

"Quite the contrary," Moriarty said. "Except for a few inconveniences such as the execrable food and the dampness and chill permeating these ancient walls, this is a splendid place for ratiocination and the exercise of the higher faculties."

"But with no one to talk to, nothing to see . . ."

Moriarty reached over to the small shelf by the side of his cot on which he kept the few things he was allowed: a Bible supplied by the governor of the prison, a bar of brown soap smelling strongly of lye, and a small envelope of tooth powder supplied, at the prisoner's expense, by the Newgate Hygienic Office; a bit of toweling that, whatever color it had been originally, was now a dull gray; and his pince-nez glasses, along with the small bit of flannel he used to polish the lenses. He removed the pince-nez and the flannel. "You are the second visitor I've had today," he told his guest. "The first was a journalist, and he told me it took him several days to get the required permit. Even then we could only speak in a small windowless room in the presence of two guards. Yet here you are, and alone. Another indication of the special esteem in which you must be held."

"Is two visitors a day sufficient mental stimulation for a man of your intellect?" his visitor inquired.

"The chatter of others is merely a distraction," Moriarty said. "I occupy myself in the contemplation of some of the great unsolved problems in the fields of mathematics, astronomy, and physics. I do not flatter myself that I will solve them, you understand; mathematics is a pursuit that rapidly cleanses one of hubris. But one can become lost in their contemplation."

His visitor raised an eyebrow. "Really?" he asked. "What sorts of things have you contemplated when you were pacing these stone floors in the wee hours of the morning?"

Moriarty raised an eyebrow. "First, I admit, the practical. How to depart from this place should it become necessary, for example."

His visitor pursed his lips thoughtfully. "Yes," he said. "You hinted that you had devised a way to accomplish that."

"Five different ways, actually," Moriarty told him.

"Ah!" his visitor said. "A pragmatic way to occupy your time, I admit."

Moriarty nodded. "That took up most of the first day," he asserted. "After which I fell to contemplation of the significance of certain nebulosities visible in the constellation of Orion."

"Surely that falls under the rubric of astronomy and not mathematics," the visitor protested.

"All the universe can be described as a series of mathematical equations, could we but discover them," Moriarty said. "Except perhaps for human activity. But whether *Homo sapiens* is of a higher order of complexity or merely closer to the chaotic has yet to be determined."

"So this contemplation of the infinite is how you occupy your time?"

"Occasionally, to refresh myself, I employ a system of my own devising to mentally calculate the value of pi past a hundred decimal places." Moriarty chuckled. "I had intended to stop at a hundred, but the temptation to continue was too great. Although I am often led astray into considering why the value of pi should be what we observe it to be."

There was a long pause while the visitor determined what to say. Finally he settled on "I see. Interesting. Very interesting."

"What can I do for you, milord?" Moriarty enquired. "Thank you for the cigarette and the light—my jailers don't seem to think I should be allowed to handle matches. I'm sorry I can't offer you any refreshments, but the amenities are few in this cell, and scant provision has been made for entertaining guests."

His guest raised an eyebrow. " 'Milord?' Have you caught the disease from that chubby warder?"

"Not at all," Moriarty said. "Aside from the fact that you are a retired naval officer, wounded in the service, now connected with the government, possessed of an independent fortune, and of noble birth, I confess I know little about you. But I assume nothing."

His visitor sat back and his eyes widened. Then he chuckled. "You will have your little joke," he said. "Surely you have recognized me."

"I have no idea of your identity," Moriarty assured him.

"Then how—"

"Your walk proclaims you to have been a naval man, and possesses still a hint of the swagger of the quarterdeck. Your dress marks you as wealthy—and old wealth, as your tailor certainly hasn't been taking new clients for the last half century."

"And wounded in the service?"

Moriarty smiled. "There's the slightest indication of a weakness in one leg, and there I confess I took the chance that it was acquired for queen and country."

"So the 'noble birth' was also an assumption?"

Moriarty shook his head. "If you would disguise your identity—or at least your rank—you should carry another cigarette case. I don't recognize the coat of arms embossed on the cover, but the device was not without interest. I have made some small study of heraldry. My attention was particularly drawn to the crest. The helm was surely that of the scion of a noble house. An earldom, if I am not mistaken."

"Perhaps I borrowed the case to impress you," suggested his visitor.

"Perhaps," Moriarty said.

"And that I am connected with the government?"

"You are here," Moriarty said, with a wave of his hand. "I doubt you could have obtained entry without official credentials."

His visitor sighed. "It would seem that I am not a master of subterfuge," he admitted.

"Few of us are," observed Professor Moriarty.

"My name is Clarence Anton Montgrief," the visitor said. "I am the fifth Earl of Scully."

"Ah!" said Moriarty.

"It is difficult to make small talk in the present, er, circumstances," said His Lordship. "So, at the risk of seeming rude, I'll get right to the point. There is a matter I would like to discuss with you."

"I see," Moriarty said wryly, "and here I had hypothesized that it was Your Lordship's custom to visit the condemned and bring them sweetmeats and Bible tracts."

"You are not condemned yet."

"I cannot hope for such good fortune from a second jury," Moriarty said. "Particularly as I shall be before the same judge."

"Hedge is a good man."

"He believes me to be guilty," Moriarty said, "and he doesn't hesitate to mention the fact to the jury at every opportunity."

"You're not?" His Lordship asked. "Guilty, I mean."

"Curiously, I am not."

His Lordship nodded. "Good to know," he said, "but not necessarily relevant to the present situation. I have a suggestion to make that you might find of interest."

Moriarty raised his manacled hands chest high. "I am not in a position to refuse any reasonable offer," he said. "Then again, neither am I in a position to carry out whatever actions might be required of me if they involve anything other than thought and memory."

"I will ameliorate the one if you will undertake the other," said the earl.

"Ameliorate?"

"Yes. It means—"

"I know what it means."

"Yes. Of course you do. Sorry."

"What sort of amelioration do you offer, and what must I do in return?"

"I can arrange for the crown to accept a plea to a lesser offense, say"—he waved an arm vaguely in the air—"accessory of one sort or another. A sentence of no more than three to five years, I would imagine."

"In return for this?"

His Lordship sat down again. "Ah! That is more complex. A . . . ah . . . person has disappeared. He must be found."

"You wish me to search for someone." Moriarty raised his manacled hands. "How do you propose I accomplish this?"

His Lordship shook his head. "I can certainly arrange to have the shackles removed," he said. "We wish you to use your connections in the . . . I believe it is referred to as 'the underworld' . . . to locate the person in question."

"From a prison cell?"

"If possible."

"Dubious," Moriarty said.

"You could arrange for various of your minions to visit you, could you not, and give them the necessary instructions? Effectively direct the search from here?"

Moriarty smiled grimly. "Despite what you may have heard, I have no minions, no mob, no gang, no nefarious members of some secret society ready to my bidding. I have a few associates, and I admit my range of acquaintances within the criminal classes is wide. Even so, few felons would recognize me on sight, and even fewer, I fear, would venture to visit me here—and of those, none who would be useful for your purpose."

"A pity," His Lordship said. "We had supposed—"

"Surely you must have some better way to achieve your purpose," Moriarty said. "Is this some devious malefactor you want me to unearth? What has he done to warrant such attention?" Moriarty closed his eyes for a second and considered. "No—it wouldn't be that. Scotland Yard, for all of its deficiencies, should be able to accomplish that. Or, at least, you would have no reason so quickly to doubt its reach. For some reason you can't involve the Yard; you need utmost secrecy." He opened his eyes. "Why not call upon my friend Sherlock Holmes? He's dependable and can be trusted, and I can testify to his tenacity and bullheadedness, if you consider that a virtue. Some do. Certainly if you're prepared to trust me—"

"He is unavailable," His Lordship said. "Performing some service for the king of Sweden, I've been told."

"Ah!"

"It was his brother, Mycroft, who suggested that we come to you.

He says, oddly enough considering the circumstances, that you also are dependable and can be trusted."

"Good of him, considering," Moriarty said. "Still, there's little I can do for you from the confines of this fetid dungeon."

His Lordship considered. "Mycroft Holmes is of the opinion that you are almost certainly innocent of the crime with which you are charged," he said.

Moriarty raised an eyebrow. "He thinks me incapable of murder?"

"He thinks you incapable of being caught so easily, of devising such an amateurish plan."

"I must thank him," Moriarty said.

The Earl of Scully considered for a long moment. "The task we require of you is delicate and sensitive, and demands the utmost secrecy," he said. "It is also vitally important that it succeed. It would be no exaggeration to say that the fate of the nation might depend on its success. Other avenues are being explored, but the necessity for keeping it secret restricts the number of people we dare inform, and in any case there are few we can use for something like this—and we have no one with suitable entrée into the underworld. It is there that the answer may lie."

Moriarty shook his head. "I can be of little use to you from this cell," he said. "I will gladly give you whatever little suggestions I can, but that must, unfortunately, be the limit of my assistance."

"I am sorry we cannot come to an agreement," His Lordship said.

Moriarty raised his manacled hands. "Don't misunderstand, I'd be delighted to assist you," he said. "Once I'm unshackled and free to move about, I might be able to accomplish something. But as things stand . . ."

The earl rose. "Then we are at an impasse," he said, "as I have not the authority to order your release."

"That is indeed unfortunate," Moriarty said gently. "Send an urgent message to Holmes. He can never resist an appeal from a peer.

He's something of a snob, but if he can be led away from his fixation on me, he's often very good."

"We have been in touch with the Swedish government," His Lordship said. "They claim not to have any idea where he is."

"He's probably wandering around Stockholm dressed as a defrocked Zoroastrian mobed, or some such."

"Yes, well—" The Earl of Scully banged on the cell door. "I will go now," he said. "I must look in other quarters."

"And I—I must remain here," Moriarty told him, sitting back on the cot.

CHAPTER FIVE

ONE NIGHT'S PLAY
OF FOX AND HARE

An adventure is only an inconvenience rightly considered.
An inconvenience is only an adventure wrongly considered.

—GILBERT KEITH CHESTERTON

SOMETIME, PROBABLY IN THE LATE SEVENTH CENTURY, a Saxon tribe that called themselves the Wetten built a bridge over the River Belisama, some sixty-plus miles northwest of the market town of Londinium. Over the next thousand years Londinium stretched and twisted and burst through its walls and shortened its name. The Belisama, for reasons of its own, became the Ribble, and the town that grew up around Wetten's bridge increased a wee bit in size and became Wedsbridge.

On the old Roman road on the west side of the town, cleverly situated between the train station and the river, crouched a U-shaped inn that called itself the Fox and Hare, the name a gradual shrinking and corruption of a phrase that had nothing to do with either the vulpine or lepus genus but had originally meant "Strong Place with Stone Walls of the Wetten Clan." The present building had been there for at least three hundred years, if you discount the fact that it had burned down and been rebuilt twice in that time.

So much Barnett had discovered at the British Museum, following Professor Moriarty's dictum, "An hour's research and an hour's planning saves two weeks' marching about." How much marching about would be saved by Barnett's new knowledge of the Wetten clan and their legendary leader Ogthar the Uxorious remained to be seen.

The instructions in Professor Moriarty's smuggled note were clear but left much to the intelligence and planning of Barnett:

Who is Esterman? Where from? Whence comes he to own the Fox and Hare? Why did he lie? He licks his lips when alcoholic beverages are mentioned. Ply him with intoxicants. Mention Hoxbary and see how he responds.

After the requisite hour's planning and yet another two hours' preparation, Barnett and the mummer packed up their bags and hailed a hansom cab. "Euston Station," Barnett called up to the cabbie, "and drive at a leisurely pace, if you please."

The cabbie stuck his heavily mustached face down into the trap. "Mollie and me, we been at this hoccupation for seventeen years," he said, "Mollie being but a two-year-old when she took up the 'arness. And we hain't never got a hinstruction like that, we hain't. You wants me to take my time?"

"Why not?" Barnett asked.

"To Euston Station?"

"Correct."

The cabbie shook his head. "You're an original, you are!"

"I don't want to overly excite the port," Barnett explained.

The cabbie having no response to that; they rode the rest of the way to the station in dignified silence and boarded the 10:23 A.M. Western Local, which got them into Wedsbridge in time for a late lunch.

The publican of the Fox and Hare, Archibald Esterman by name, was behind the bar polishing glasses when Barnett, two small suitcases under his arm, pushed through the door. "Good day to you, publican," Barnett called. "Are we too late for a bit of lunch? And have you rooms for my companion and myself?"

Esterman looked Barnett over suspiciously as he approached the bar, taking in the shiny derby, the bespoke brown tweed suit, and the dusty but well-polished shoes. He came to an opinion. "Good day to you, sir," he said, "but if you're another of them reporter fellows, and I fancy you are, then you can just turn around and go back out the door."

"You mistake me, sir," Barnett said, holding the door open for the mummer as the little man staggered past him lugging two large black cases. "We are traveling men. Although why you would have an animus against newspaper reporters—surely an inoffensive breed—is beyond me."

Esterman sniffed and looked doubtful. "And what, if I may ask, do you travel in?"

"Spirits," Barnett said.

"Come off it now," said Esterman, giving forth with a brief guffaw. "Gents what sell spiritous beverages don't dress like toffs, and toffs don't come around trying to sell me no spirits."

"Well said, sir, and I'm sure you're correct," Barnett told him, "but you misunderstand me." He took one of the cases from the mummer and heaved it up onto the nearest table. "My man and I travel in fortified spirits and *vins au pays,* as it were, and none of your common plonk neither. Inns and public houses are not our clientele of choice. At least not in the hinterlands, although we have some trade clients in the city. And, of course, the better gentlemen's clubs." He sprang the catch, and the case divided in two and opened like a black canvas butterfly spreading its wings. "Few public houses have a patronage who could appreciate, or would be willing to spring for, our merchandise," he continued.

Within the case, neatly embedded in wire frame and cotton batting, were eight wine bottles, four to a side, their labels facing forward for inspection.

"Here we have," Barnett began, running his forefinger over the first bottle with an air of learned professionalism, "the Royal Muscat, or Muscat Frontignan as she is properly called in La Belle France, grown in Beaumes-de-Venise within sight of the Rhone and bottled, of course, by Montiverde et Cie."

"Of course," the publican said, his left eye twitching an involuntary twitch as he licked his lips.

"This one, as you can plainly see by the label," Barnett went on, moving his finger to the next bottle, "is a Quinto do Alexandro Crusting Port. The amber liquid was poured into this bottle in the fall of 1815, shortly after Napoleon's defeat at Waterloo. Which would explain the *'Vive le roi'* overstamp at the bottom of the label. My agency has discovered forty cases that were forgotten in the cellar of a lodge in Vila Nova de Gaia, and paid a handsome price for them. These are probably the last bottles anywhere in the world of this justly renowned product."

"Justly," Esterman agreed. His eyes blinked rapidly as he peered at the bottle. His tongue ran along his upper lip as though seeking confirmation that it was still there.

"Four guineas the pop," Barnett said, swinging the case closed, "but I don't want to bore you."

"Four guineas the case is a bit—" Esterman began.

"The bottle," Barnett gently corrected him.

"The—" The publican's chin thrust out and his eyelids twitched as he fixed his gaze on Barnett's mustache. "Say, what do you take me for? Four—"

"As I said," Barnett told him, settling down on a bar stool, "the average publican could not be expected to stock such exotica, splendid a quaff as it may be." He cast a critical eye around the room, managing to raise one eyebrow in silent assessment of the ancient well-knocked and pitted tables and chairs. "I imagine your patrons are more likely to be downing porter than port. Beer at tuppence the pint is a far cry from quality port at five shillings the glass."

"True," Esterman granted, "but—"

"But not as satisfying, you're going to say," Barnett interrupted, raising a forefinger of emphasis, "and you can't say truer than that."

The mummer leaped with surprising grace onto the next bar stool. "P'raps we could let His Honor here try a tuppit of the old and mellow, gov. What d'you say?"

"Well . . ." Barnett considered, rubbing his forefinger along the side of his nose. "We have some errands to do in the vicinity," he told Esterman. "So if you'll give us a couple of rooms to throw our luggage in, we'll be off. We have people to see. Upon our return, this evening, after the last draft of lager is pumped, we'll settle down and sample our stock. Perhaps in trade for a cut off the joint and a boiled potato or two, eh?"

Esterman paused to think, flicking his tongue in and out of his mouth like a viper as he did the calculation. A shilling's worth of supper against a glass or two—three glasses?—of a three-guinea-the-bottle crusting port laid down in 1815. "Could be managed," he allowed. "Could be done."

"Done and done!" declared Barnett, sticking out his hand. "My name's Barnett, and this is my companion and adviser, Mummer Tolliver, otherwise known as Mummer the Short. And you are?"

"Esterman's the name. Archibald Esterman." He took Barnett's hand and moved it solemnly up and down twice. "Proprietor of the Fox and Hare, which I purchased these ten years ago from the Wigham clan, what has owned it, father and son, for these past four hundred years."

"Four hundred years?" Barnett marveled.

"Or more. Or even more."

"Here now," the mummer said, hopping off his chair. "We'd best be on our way, nest-see-paz? We've got a barrel full o' gentry to see afore we settles in to that joint you're cutting."

"That's so, that's so," Barnett agreed. "Landlord, if you could show us to out rooms we'll move our luggage in, and then we must be off to visit"—here he took a scrap of paper from his waistcoat pocket and peered down at it—"Lord Thornton-Hoxbary, or, as it may be, his steward or butler."

Esterman pushed himself suddenly to his feet and looked down at Barnett with foxy eyes. "And just why is that?" he demanded. "What do you want with His Lordship?"

The mummer hopped up on his chair and thrust his chin out pugnaciously. "His Lordship, is it?" he demanded. "Friend of yours, is he?"

"I had the honor to be in His Lordship's service at one time," Esterman said, pulling his face back from the mummer's sharp, inquisitive nose, "and I don't hold with people going over to annoy His Lordship, who was very good to me and mine."

"Very good, was 'is Lordship? Gave you the jolly to buy this pub, did 'e?" the mummer suggested.

"That's as may be," Esterman said sharply, "and what business would that be of yours?"

"Now-now-now-now," Barnett said sharply, raising his hand between the two. "We're all friends here, we are. We wish to see His Lordship to interest him—or his steward—in some of our fine wines and spirits. He's on our list, which was drawn up by the accounts manager himself. And Mummer, Mr. Esterman's business is just that—his business. Keep your sharp little nose out of it!"

"So that's the way the apple bounces, is it?" the mummer said peevishly, jumping off his chair. "Well, I'll just out myself into the street and await your worshipful presence, *Mr.* Barnett." The mummer put an edge on the "Mr." sharp enough to cut paper, and with that he packed up the two wine cases and stomped out of the taproom with one under each arm.

Esterman glared after the departing little man until the door had closed behind him, then turned to Barnett and smiled a jagged-tooth smile. "Interesting creature, that," he said. "P'raps you should keep him on a lead."

"I'd better go after him," said Barnett. "Sorry if he said anything untoward; he doesn't mean anything by it. He gets a bit testy when his morning dance is cut short."

"His . . . dance?"

"After he gets up and before breakfast," said Barnett, improvising furiously. "He spends about twenty minutes in his room dancing. The hornpipe, the jig, the kazatsky, whatever strikes his mood. If he doesn't get his morning dance, he tends to be disputatious all day."

Esterman nodded. "Interesting. I had an aunt who was like that. Only with her it wasn't dancing, it was—well, never mind about that now."

"So don't take Mr. Tolliver seriously. He means well."

"No problem," Esterman said, spreading his arms magnanimously.

"Hold on to our luggage, will you?" asked Barnett. "We'll be back—and there's that bit of a taste I promised you."

"I'll have the bags taken up to your rooms," Esterman said.

"We're not actually going to visit 'is bloomin' lordship, is we?" the mummer asked when Barnett caught up with him some hundred yards down the road.

"We'd best not," Barnett replied. "Supposing his lordship wishes to acquire some of our plonk? We'd have to find it somewhere."

"The professor wouldn't like it if we further denuded his wine cellar," the mummer observed. "But if we is to call ourselves traveling men, we'd best do some traveling."

"We'll knock about for a few hours," Barnett said, "and reappear at the Fox and Hare sometime late afternoon. Then, after we dine, we'll share a few drinks with the publican." Barnett turned to stare at his little companion. "What gave you the idea for that bit about Esterman and his lordship?"

"It just came to me," the mummer said, "the way Esterman reacted when you read off his lordship's name."

"I wonder if it means anything?"

"I'll be much surprised if it don't," the mummer observed.

"Well, we'll find out this evening, if our landlord is as susceptible to drink as the professor supposes. In the meantime . . ."

"I could do with a bit o' skof," the mummer suggested.

"A late lunch?" Barnett asked.

"The very same. Never too late, I says."

"There's a tearoom some ways down," Barnett suggested. "Here, let me take one of those cases."

"I won't say no," the mummer agreed, letting one black case slide slowly out from under his arm until Barnett caught the handle.

Esterman raised his glass and leered at the liquid within. "There is a divinity what shapes my ends," he declaimed, "however so much I hew them with my little ruff." He plumped down into his chair and tilted his head back so the last few drops of ruby liquor could more easily pass between his welcoming lips.

"A noble sentiment," Barnett opined. "You have a sensitive soul, Mr. Esterman, a sensitive soul." He lifted his glass and made a show of drinking deep without actually imbibing more than a few drops. There was little doubt that the landlord could drink him under the table, and probably under the whole house, if he'd a mind to. Once the drinking began, he had little mind for anything else. It was late evening of the second day of Barnett and the mummer's sojourn at the Fox and Hare. The gas lamps burned low, the other patrons were long gone, and the bottles of aged port were being sampled to extinction.

"It is unusual—I might say unique," Barnett said, "to find an innkeeper quoting the bard."

"You might say that," Esterman agreed, looking up from under his eyebrows, which seemed to have grown strangely heavy. He raised his voice.

"There is a history in all men's lives,
Figuring the nature of the times deceas'd,
The which observ'd a man may prop . . . prof . . . prophesy,
With a near aim, of the main chance of things
As yet not come to life."

He turned and squinted at Barnett. "That's Hank the Quart," he said.

Barnett mentally turned the phrase over. "Henry the Fourth?"

"The very one."

"How came you to have such an appreciation of Shakespeare?" Barnett asked.

"'Ere," the mummer interjected, "let me fetch another bottle of the '38. This one seems to have depleted itself." Bottle in hand, he trotted off.

Esterman watched the mummer's retreat with interest until the little man turned the corner. Then he ponderously moved his head and adjusted his vision to look at Barnett. "When I was with His Lordship," Esterman said, "His Lordship had the library redone. All the bookshelves, what were oak, were ripped out and replaced with other bookshelves what were cut from the Widdersign Ash, a great squat tree which were over two hundred years old when it was removed to make way for the tennis courts. He had two Italian artisans come in to do the work. On the bookshelves, not the tennis courts."

"A great improvement, no doubt," said Barnett.

"Not so's you'd notice," Esterman said, "but what His Lordship wants is what His Lordship does. At any rate, I was responsible for these big stacks of books while they was out of the shelves. And so I started reading. Shakespeare and Kidd and Marlowe and Bacon and like that. They used the most mellyfloo . . . mellifluous words, and I grew into the habit of speaking them aloud when they wasn't anybody who could hear me."

"Why did you pick the Renaissance playwrights?" Barnett asked.

"They was on top of the stack."

"Good thinking," Barnett agreed.

The mummer reappeared with another bottle of the port and carefully decanted it into the wine jug. "We're running low on bottles," he said. "Best hurry and drink it up before it's gone."

The logic appealed to Esterman, who happily refilled his glass. "A superior tipple, i' faith," he said. He held the glass to the side of his nose for a moment and then drained it. "Pardon," he said, getting up and weaving toward the back. "I think I'd best go see about a dog."

"He can put it away, can't he?" the mummer commented as Esterman disappeared out the back door.

"He'd better get more talkative pretty soon," Barnett said, "or we'll run out of port."

"Oh," the mummer said, "we ran out two bottles ago. I've been refilling the bottles from our landlord's own stock."

"Ah!" said Barnett. "I thought I detected a difference."

"Blimey if you did!" Mummer Tolliver grinned a toothy grin. "After finishing the first two bottles I could have mixed gin with horse piss and colored it red, and you both would have drunk it happily and praised it fulsomely."

Barnett smiled. "You may be right," he said. "I won't ask what you would have colored it red with."

Esterman weaved back to his seat. "As oft as wine has played the peppermill," he intoned, "and robbed me of my coat and jacket, well . . . I often ponder what the vintners buy . . . Could be as thirsty as this stuff so swell!" He sat down with a thump.

"Indeed," Barnett agreed.

"If not in word," the mummer suggested, "but close enough—close enough."

"I merely state," Esterman said ponderously, "that this is good plonk. Good plonk indeed."

"Lord Thornton-Hoxbary doesn't think so, I guess," Barnett said. "Couldn't interest his man in as much as half a case."

"I could of told you visiting Widdersign-on-Rip . . . er . . . Ribble would be a waste of you gentlemen's time," Esterman smugged. "His Lordship don't lay out a farthing till he's squeezed it bone dry, but you wouldn't have listened to me nohow, now would you?"

"Probably not," Barnett admitted, "but we're listening to you now."

"Parsimonious, is His Lordship?" the mummer asked.

"If that means miserly, mean, tight-fisted, then you might say so. Ain't no one around here what would argue with you."

"He seems to have been pretty generous with you," Barnett said, looking around.

"You mean this place?" Esterman asked. "The Fox and Hare? Well, it ain't as if he gave me the deed outright, is it? I mean, he has an interest in the place. Only he don't consider it seemly, or some such, for a peer to be a publican, so we don't talk it about."

"That explains it, then," Barnett said.

"Besides," Esterman added, "he had to, didn't he? It was only right."

Barnett leaned across the bar. "Did he, then? Why was that?"

Esterman drained his glass, blinked twice, smiled across the bar at his guests, and slowly leaned forward until he was resting on his nose. His eyes closed.

Barnett rapped on the bar. "Mr. Esterman!" he said sharply. "Landlord!"

Esterman turned his face until it was resting on his right ear. His eyes remained closed.

"P'raps we should let the man sleep," the mummer suggested. "P'raps he's told us enough if we parse it properly."

"Perhaps," Barnett agreed. "Perhaps I'll go upstairs."

"I'll do a bit of scouting whilst our landlord slumbers," the mummer said. "No telling what I might turn up."

CHAPTER SIX

THE SPANISH HOUSE

Who has known all the evil before us,
Or the tyrannous secrets of time?
Though we match not the dead men that bore us
At a song, at a kiss, at a crime—
Though the heathen outface and outlive us,
And our lives and our longings are twain—
Ah, forgive us our virtues, forgive us,
Our Lady of Pain.

—ALGERNON CHARLES SWINBURNE

THE WALLED ESTATE ON THE SOUTHWEST CORNER of Regency Square extended for forty feet along the square and twice that when it turned down Regency Street on one side and Little Horneby Mews on the other. A twelve-foot-high redbrick wall surrounded it, fronted by a thick blackthorn hedge first planted the year Nelson and his ships visited Egypt. If one stood far enough back from the wall, one could glimpse the top floor of the Georgian mansion within. Once the residence of the now-defunct Barons Wysland, it was set well inside the wall and surrounded by an impeccably groomed lawn with a gardener's cottage, gazebos, and a small frog pond. At the moment there were no frogs in residence. The wide doors of a carriage house opened onto the mews.

The property was presently tenanted by a secretive society known by those permitted such knowledge as Le Château d'Espagne, although it had no particular connection with either France or Spain. Its membership, which comprised *L'Ordre du Château,* was carefully self-chosen, each member free to suggest candidates, who would then be accepted or not according to the whim of the *chatelain,* master of the order, who was seldom seen and never spoken to directly. The name he was known by, Giles Paternoster, was certainly not the one he was born with. The stories told of him were grotesque and spoke of unnatural vices, but perhaps they were exaggerations, clever fictions crafted to be good for business. Or perhaps not.

Natyana, the dark-haired mistress of the house, her long fingernails bright scarlet but for the one ebon nail on the ring finger of her right hand, was part German, part Levantine, and part someone her mother never talked about. Most of the staff looked to be Egyptian or Moroccan, and the boys and girls who serviced the guests had been recruited from Paris, Rome, Belgrade, Vienna, and half a dozen other European cities. They were little different from the slum children of London except for their native tongue, but they quickly picked up enough English to serve, and their accents made them seem exotic. They were sent back whence they had come on or about their fifteenth birthday, when their services were no longer desired.

The members and their guests arrived in carriages or chaises with the family crests or other devices on the doors discreetly covered over. Some of the more cautious were picked up at a place of their choosing by an unmarked black four-wheeler driven by a small, thin man with a long, twisted nose and piercing black eyes set well back in his skull-like face. His top hat, cape, trousers, gloves, and boots were black, and his face was as white as though it had been dusted with the finest flour.

Both members and guests were expected—required—to have their faces masked before passing through the gate and arriving at the front door. A domino would suffice, but many of the masks were quite elaborate, and some showed more of their wearer's soul than would his naked face.

Entrance to the Château was obtained by showing the doorman a talisman and whispering a word. The word was changed monthly, the talisman yearly. This year's talisman was a gilded cock, about two inches across, pierced through the tail feathers for a small gold ring so that it could be hung around the neck on a slender gold chain and worn between shirt and chest. The word for the month was "Cybele," the name of the mother of the gods of Olympus. It is said that the ancient cult of Cybele honored her by performing orgiastic dances and unspeakable acts.

The brougham that stopped before the gate to Le Château d'Espagne just after dusk this Friday, the nineteenth day of September, was a deep maroon color trimmed in the blackest of blacks. A thin gilt stripe outlined each of the maroon panels. The driver and footman wore powdered wigs and red and gold tailcoats with oversized gold buttons over puffy black breeches terminating in a pair of white stockings just below the knee. It was a style of livery aping the court dress of the eighteenth century that the servants of the nobility seemed loath to give up.

Two men wearing black half-capes over their evening clothes emerged from the brougham, one tall and slim and elegant, the other a bit shorter and stocky, with hunched shoulders and small eyes that shifted constantly about as though looking for hidden dangers behind every lamppost. They paused to don masks: the slim man a half-mask of pressed gold with black eyebrows and a pencil-thin black mustache champlevé that covered eyes and nose but left the mouth visible, and the stocky man a black puffy-faced half-mask that covered the nose but left off at the mouth and the brown beard below it.

A third man, enfolded in a great dark blue cape with a blue muffler wrapped around his face and a squat top hat pulled low over his eyes, dropped off the brougham and settled for a long wait outside the château walls. The brougham pulled away.

Passing through the wrought-iron gate, the two masked men crossed to the heavy oaken door of the château and knocked. A small square opening appeared in the door and an eye peered out, and the tall man dangled his talisman by its gold chain in front of the eye and giggled. "Cybele," he whispered in a high, piercing whisper, and giggled again.

The door swung open, and a large man, dark hued and imposing of girth, dressed in breeches and tunic of red and gold brocade and wearing a gold turban, bowed and bade them welcome. Not quite suppressing a final giggle, the tall man tucked his talisman back under his shirt and advanced into the marble-tiled entrance way, followed closely by his companion. A cloakroom was just inside the door on the right, and behind its counter a comely young girl, unclothed except for a man's bow tie and a cummerbund, stood ready to receive their capes. The tall man passed his over with an elegant sweeping gesture and then handed the girl a white pasteboard on which had been hand-printed the word *PECCAVI*. The card was promptly put through a slot in a locked cherrywood box. Each member picked his own private word, which identified him for mundane financial purposes, and only Master Paternoster possessed the book that coupled the member with his chosen word.

Beyond the entrance was an ebon, gold, and ivory hallway, the ebony polished to a gleaming shine, lighted by a row of small gold gas lamps set along the left-hand wall, inches from the ivory ceiling. A gaily colored fresco along the ceiling depicted scenes of the sort found on Greek vases of the classical period. The vases on which these sorts of scenes were found were kept in the private rooms of museums, for viewing by serious scholars only.

There were eight rooms along the hallway, each decorated in a different style. The first on the right was a re-creation of chambers in the seraglio of an Eastern potentate, or at least what a well-read European might imagine such chambers to look like. It had red and green silk drapes descending from the ceiling at seemingly random intervals; the floor was covered with an oversized Isfahan carpet, on which round leather-covered ottomans were scattered with a casual hand. A smattering of habitués were lounging about talking softly and accepting an occasional glass of champagne, hock, madeira, or absinthe from one of the girls in their frilly white chemises, or one of several young lads clad in the uniforms of some of Britain's better public schools.

On the left was the library: easy chairs with conveniently placed lamps, desks at which to write or read, racks with current newspapers and magazines, and dark cherrywood bookshelves, ceiling high, filled with books bound in buckram, leather, linen, and silk. Books on history, religion, and natural philosophy filled the shelves, along with classical authors and a smattering of fiction, but the great majority of the works fell into that class known variously as erotica, exotica, and French. There were the works of Ovid, Catullus, Sappho, Boccaccio, Petronius, Mlle. de Sapay, Chevalier Leopold von Sacher-Masoch, and the Marquis de Sade. An unbound copy of the rare first edition of Burton's *Kama Shastra, or the Hindoo Art of Love* was in a closed case, but a dozen leather-bound copies of the later, expanded *Kama Sutra* sat on the shelves. There were multiple copies of *The Misfortunes of Virtue, Venus in Furs,* and *The Secret Manual of the House of Jade.* There were books on rough paper with flimsy covers and titles like *Six Months of Sodom, A Man and a Maid, The Naughty Schoolgirl, What Miss Flaybum Remembers,* and *The Book of Bad Boys.* On the shelves holding artwork there were erotic paintings, etchings, and prints covering a span of many centuries, and a fine assortment of penny postcards that could not conceivably have been sent through the mails.

One of the housemen, dressed all in black and wearing a domino mask, stood in the hall, and the tall man beckoned to him and murmured a few words in his ear. The houseman nodded and turned. "Follow me, please," he said.

The houseman led the tall man and his companion past the delights of these two rooms and the next two, whose doors were closed, and turned in at the third room on the left. It resembled a boys' locker room, with several rows of lockers and between them wooden benches at which the boys could change. Around the walls of the faux locker room were red and black leather couches, where the adults could sit and watch the boys at play. There were a dozen or so barely pubescent boys in the room, sporting about with towels or wrestling in a friendly manner, as boys will. Particularly if the boys have received instruction in just what sort of sporting about will please such older men as are pleased at the sight of young lads sporting about. The houseman saw his two charges in and bowed briefly to them, and then left the room, closing the door behind him.

Five men rested on various of the encircling couches, watching the young lads as they flicked each other's bottoms with towels and scampered about. Several of the men were smiling, savoring their memories and expectations. Several were staring intently, as though there were mystical secrets to be discerned in the flashing limbs and heaving torsos of the wrestling youths.

The tall man sprawled his angular body on a couch and regarded the youths with interest. His companion sat primly next to him, hands laced together, face—what could be seen of it below the mask—devoid of expression. His posture suggested a blending of vigilance and detachment.

After a time the tall man rose and beckoned to one of the lads, seemingly at random. "You," he said. "Come!" He turned around and pulled open the door, leaving the room without a backward glance, and the boy followed. The second man pushed himself slightly back on the couch, but otherwise remained where he was, motionless and unsmiling.

The tall man climbed the wide staircase to the floor above and nodded at Natyana, who sat in a heavily brocaded chair at the head of the stairs. She looked at him and his boy companion and returned the nod. "Room six is empty and freshly made up," she said. "To the left."

He nodded again and winked and giggled a brief giggle, then, taking the lad by the hand, crossed to the room and entered, closing the door gently behind him.

The hall porter, a skinny, wiry old man with a wandering eye, a twisted lip, and a freshly starched white jacket, emerged from a closet behind Natyana and stared with his good eye at the closing door. "*Peccavi*, that gent calls hisself." he observed. "I wonder which of our high-and-mighty clientele he would be when he's at home. Quite a toff, but there's sommat strange about him."

Natyana shrugged. "There's something strange about all our clients," she said. "Or hadn't you noticed?"

"I do my noticing elsewhere," the porter told her.

After a short while sounds of squealing, laughing, giggling, thumping, whipping, and high-pitched screaming could be heard faintly through the well-insulated walls of the room. No more than could be expected, given the nature of the establishment. Sometime later all sounds ceased.

Some forty minutes or so after he had entered the room, the tall man opened the door and exited, closing it behind him. Nodding to Natyana and giggling a final giggle, he went down the stairs, bouncing slightly from step to step as though unable to contain whatever emotion it was that he felt. His companion joined him almost immediately and, retrieving their cloaks with wide smiles and a more than appropriate *pourboire,* they left the premises.

It was some time before it occurred to Natyana that the lad had not emerged from the room. She crossed the hall and knocked sharply on the door to rouse him. "No shillying or shallying," she called. "The night isn't over. Come on out, Istefan." Hearing no response, she opened the door.

A sharp intake of breath, and then her hand flew to her mouth. *"Lyi tann!"*

"Pardon?" The hall porter looked up from the pastry that he had produced from one of the many pockets of his white jacket.

Natyana used the door to hold herself up. "It's . . . There's been . . . Don't look, there's no reason for you to look. I think you'd better gather the staff, and see if you can locate Master Paternoster."

The porter put the tartlet aside, pushed himself to his feet, and joined Natyana at the door. He glanced into the room and then, with a sharp intake of breath, took two steps farther in and peered at the object on the floor. Then he turned away and put his hand to his mouth. "Cor blimey!"

"I told you not to look," Natyana said.

"I wish I hadn't," he agreed. "Is he—no, never mind the question—'course he is. What are we going to do?"

Down the hall a door opened and a fat man with puffy gray side whiskers and a red nose trotted out with his arms around the shoulders of a short, very blond young girl in a red camisole. She had her arms as far as they would go around his middle, clutching on to his tattersall waistcoat front and back, and was staring up at his face. "Oh my!" he said, perhaps to the girl, perhaps to himself. "Oh, but certainly that was invigorating. Give and take, I always say. Yes indeed, give and take." He trotted toward Natyana, the girl shuffling along with him, and before Natyana thought of closing the door to conceal the horror inside, the fat man was nodding cheerfully to her and pausing to look into the room.

He froze in midstride and his mouth dropped open.

The girl turned her head to see what her cull was staring at. At the back of the room the nude body of a young boy was spread out on the red and tan Baluchi carpet, his chest and stomach splayed open, his various internal organs placed carefully around him like offerings to an obscene god. The pools of blood surrounding him had not yet begun to dry.

For a second the scene seemed not to register; then her eyes widened and the color drained from her face. Slowly, and with a sort of innocent grace, she fell unconscious to the floor.

The man screamed. Not a full-throated scream, but a sort of loud, hysterical gargle. It was enough, it would suffice.

The remaining nine rooms on the floor were soundproofed, so no one within heard anything amiss. However, there were three men on the stairs who came rushing up at the sound.

By this time Natyana had regained control, gently but firmly closed the offending door, and taken the fat man by the hand. "There's been a horrible accident," she told him. "We must call the police. Perhaps it would be wise for you to leave before they arrive, don't you think? I'll attend to the girl."

The three men from the stairs came tumbling over to them. "An accident," Natyana repeated to them. "This gentleman will tell you all about it. He's had a bad fright. You might want to help him downstairs." She paused, then went on, "It is probably a good idea for all of our guests to vacate, to go home now."

"What happened?" one of the men demanded.

"Beyond what this gentleman can tell you," Natyana replied, "you'd best not know. Downstairs, please."

The three men exchanged glances and, finding no better course of action, turned and headed back downstairs, taking the fat man with them, leaving the fainting girl lying in the corridor.

"What now, do you suppose?" asked the porter.

"Pick up the poor girl—it's Agnes, isn't it?—and lay her on the divan by the stairs."

"Yes. Of course." The porter complied, laying the girl down gently with a cushion under her head, and smoothed what there was of her clothes.

"Now," Natyana said, "I imagine, we must have any remaining guests leave. P'raps you should alert the rest of the staff and see to it. "

"What are we going to tell them?"

Natyana considered. "Trouble with the pipes should do it. Although I fancy they'll hear otherwise soon enough."

The porter nodded and then asked, "Why'd you tell those three that the fat gent would tell them all about it?"

"Because he was going to anyhow," she said. "No way to stop him."

"Ah!"

"You'd best get Master Paternoster up here. I'd go myself, but I had better stand cové over this door."

The porter shook his head. "Five years I've been here, and never nothing like this. Nothing remotely like this. What are we going to do?"

"Considering that most of our members will know about this before they leave, I fancy we have little choice in the matter."

"You ain't really nohow going to call the rozzers, are you? We ain't calling in no rozzers, are we?"

"Master Paternoster must decide, but—I don't see any way around it. Luckily there are a couple of select, ah, rozzers that we can call. Gentlemen who spend time here in a private capacity, although they spend their days at Scotland Yard. They may be willing to help us in our time of need, but our members had better be long gone before they arrive."

CHAPTER SEVEN

RELEASE

When the hounds of spring are on winter's traces,
The mother of months in meadow or plain
Fills the shadows and windy places
With lisp of leaves and ripple of rain.

—ALGERNON CHARLES SWINBURNE

THEY CAME FOR MORIARTY AT FIVE IN THE MORNING, tramping down the narrow passage, two men in mufti with the unmistakable ramrod-stiff comport of army officers. Jacobs the warder led the way, huffing, coughing, wheezing, and stomping. The sound of their coming awoke Moriarty, and he sat up and pushed the rough brown blanket aside.

Jacobs made his usual show of working the locks on the cell door before swinging it open. The beam of his bull's-eye lantern glanced about the walls of the cell and finally settled on Moriarty. Jacobs coughed and spat on the stone floor. "You're to go with these here two gentlemen, if you please," he growled. "Right away, and no discussion about it."

Moriarty blinked and squinted into the light. "Give me a moment to put on my trousers," he said, reaching for the gray prison garment folded over the cell's only chair.

"Well, and hurry up about it."

The taller of the two men peered at Moriarty over the warder's shoulder. "Here, now," he said sharply. "Take those manacles off the gentleman's hands."

"I don't know as how I have the authority to do that, begging your pardon—sir," the warder said, the "sir" stretched out and turned into an epithet .

"You have the key," the man pointed out, "and I have the authority. Go to it!"

There was a short pause while Jacobs screwed his face up in an effort to think this over. Then he said, "Just as you say, sir. It's your bleeding authority what says to let 'im loose, and that makes it your bleeding responsibility for whatever happens thereof, if you'll excuse me saying so. I washes my hands of the whole matter, as you gentlemen clearly know more about these things than I, what's been managing prisoners for these twenty-two years."

"It's been quite a while since you've last done that, I warrant," the tall man said. "Wash your hands, I mean."

"Say, now," Jacobs bristled. "I will not have my position bruted about. You may have the authority, as is your claim, but it's my responsibility. And I'm not sure as I should remove the gyves from this'ere professor."

The other man, who was not so tall but was quite wide, as a bull is wide, took two steps forward and thrust his chin toward the warder. "What's that you say?" he demanded in a high, gruff voice that was sharp as broken glass.

Jacobs caught his breath. Perhaps he had gone too far. "My mother always said that my mouth 'ud be the death of me someday," he whinged, ducking his head as though to ward off a blow, clearly expecting to be treated by those above him as he would treat those below him. "I pray your worships will excuse me. Sometimes my mouth does run away with itself."

"Get on with it, man!" the tall man said.

With a shake of his head, Jacobs maneuvered the ring of keys off his belt and sorted among them to find the proper one for Moriarty's restraints. The manacles were bolted closed, and the key was a metal tube with a slot in the end to fit over the head of the bolt. There were a number of different patterns, and Jacobs had to try several keys before he found the one that fit. Unscrewing the bolt seemed to present a serious mental problem for him; his face twisted with concentration as he made the effort. Finally it was done, and he spat and stepped back.

Moriarty rubbed his wrists and moved his hands up and down in front of him. "Interesting," he said. "My arms have grown so used to the weight of the irons that they feel curiously light."

"Finish dressing, Professor," one of the men said. "We have a way to travel."

"Of course," Moriarty said, pulling the trousers on and fastening them with the cord that served as a belt, then shrugging into the shapeless gray jacket. "I don't suppose there's any chance of my bathing and changing into clean garments before I meet with His Lordship?"

The thick man glared down at the professor. "How did you know that?" he demanded.

"What? Oh, 'His Lordship'?" Moriarty picked up the few belongings he had in the cell and stuffed them into the pocket sewed onto the side of his canvas jacket. "Who else?"

The answer was obviously unsatisfactory, but the matter was not pursued. "Come," the tall man said.

"I must retrieve my clothing as we leave," Moriarty said. "Especially my shoes. These"—he pointed to the prison-issue canvas slippers he wore—"are unfit for travel. Particularly as I believe it's raining out."

"Such garments as what you were wearing when you was incarcerated would be in the Prisoners' Personal Effects Storage and Disbursement Room," Jacobs said, "and that don't open today, this being Sunday and the day which the Lord has given unto us to rest and all."

He looked pleased as he spoke. Any inconvenience to a prisoner was an achievement for which to strive.

"We'll see what we can do about providing shoes when we arrive," the first man said. "Also proper clothing. It well may be that the need has been anticipated. What you are wearing will have to do for now."

Moriarty shrugged. "As you say," he said. "In that case, clearly, I'm ready."

They exited the prison through an obscure side door into a dark night and a cold drizzle that soaked Moriarty's slippers even as he took the five steps to the waiting carriage, a great, high-sprung traveling machine of a style Wellington might have used on his way to Waterloo, with four matched bays in the traces. Moriarty took a seat facing the rear, across from his two companions. "How long?" he asked.

The two looked at each other. "The journey?" the one on the left asked. "Perhaps two hours."

Moriarty sat back and closed his eyes. After a while the man asked, "You have no other questions?"

Moriarty opened his eyes. "Have you any answers?"

"No, not really. Not at this time."

"Then I have no questions."

Daylight found them well out of London and moving rapidly south along a well-kept country road. The rain was heavier and the puddles deeper, but the bays kept up a steady pace, untroubled by such considerations. A seemingly endless row of trees lined the right side of the road, and on the left were a smattering of hedges and fields. The small villages they passed through were stirring into life, and several of the early churchgoers paused and stared at the grand sight of a four-horse carriage racing by.

It was just shy of 7:00 A.M. when they reached a pair of high wrought-iron gates, which were pulled open at their approach, and the coachman snapped the horses into a fast trot for the last mile to the great house. Moriarty opened his eyes at the change in rhythm and stretched. He had slept most of the way, finding the jouncing carriage more comforting, if not more comfortable, than the dank cell. He twisted in his seat and examined the house critically through the carriage window as they approached, but just which, or whose, great house it was he couldn't tell, not having paid as much attention as perhaps he should to the great houses of England.

The building was a wide, three-story structure of respectable age with a four-column portico shielding the front door. In its day it had probably entertained George III, and, if the architecture of what was now the west wing was to be believed, might well have welcomed Elizabeth herself, as she traveled with her court from one noble's estate to the next to distribute among the peerage the cost of maintaining, if not running, the government.

As the carriage pulled to a stop, a man in a severe black morning coat came through the front door of the house and approached with stately tread, holding an oversized black umbrella high over his head. Two footmen accompanied him, each with an umbrella of his own. "Gentlemen," the man said, pulling open the carriage door, "I am Mobley, manager of the household staff. Please go right on in. Breakfast is laid out in the morning room."

Moriarty's two escorts left the carriage and followed an umbrella-carrying footman to the door. Mobley turned to Moriarty, who was the last to emerge. "And you would be Professor Moriarty," he said.

"So it would seem," Moriarty agreed.

"His Lordship the duke would have me welcome you to Wythender Hall," Mobley said, with an air that intimated that welcoming felons into his master's house was not a remarkable occurrence. "It has been suggested that you would like the opportunity to wash up and change your prison garb into something more suitable."

"A prescient suggestion indeed," said Moriarty.

"Allow me to show you to your room." Mobley turned and, umbrella high, led the way into the house. A young maid in a highly starched apron and a mob cap bobbed and curtseyed and took the umbrella from him as they entered.

The entrance hall was large and square and high, and seven broad tapestries hung from three walls. They depicted some great battle from its beginning on the first hanging, with two lines of knights in armor facing each other across a wide field, to the aftermath on the last, showing a field of tents and the wounded either being tended or slain, it was hard to tell. In between were scenes of the battle, with swarms of arrows arcing across a muddy sky, knights clanking their great swords against other knights, men bearing banners heading hither and thither, and general chaos. All done without use of perspective, so that men and horses seemed to be standing on each other's heads, or floating in space.

Moriarty let his gaze travel from one of the hangings to the next. The tapestries had darkened through the ages, making the battle seem as though it were being fought at night, or at least through a thick fog. Nonetheless, they were beautiful, and the images were powerful reminders of what men did to each other. Mobley stopped with Moriarty and stared at the hangings himself. "Agincourt," he said. "Some people are powerfully affected by the scenes; others scarcely notice them. No accounting, I says. The first duke was at the battle. Lost a foot. His left, I believe."

Which first duke, Moriarty wondered, but he decided not to ask. All would be revealed in the fullness of time.

"We will go this way," Mobley said, indicating a side door. "Up the service stairs, if you don't mind. The duke would prefer if his houseguests are not made unduly aware of your presence."

"Understandable," Moriarty commented, looking down wryly at the state of his apparel. He followed Mobley through the door.

"Ask for me if you require anything," Mobley said as they reached the second floor and started down a long, wide hall. "This"—he stopped by a door and pushed it open—"is to be your room. The bath is directly across. Hot water is piped up to the tub from a boiler in the basement."

Mobley stepped aside, and Moriarty entered. There on the bed were two suitcases, which seemed to be his own. They were open, and a large man was busy putting things away in a bureau next to the window.

"Mr. Maws!" Moriarty said, both surprised and pleased to find the ex-prizefighter who was now his butler waiting for him.

"The same, gov. Good to see you out and about."

"How long have you been here?"

"Minutes only. Perhaps five, perhaps ten. Some spiffy gents came to the house and said as how we should get a kit together for you of what you'd need if you was out of prison, and I said as how I'd come along with them, and so here I am."

"And it's glad to see you I am," Moriarty told him.

"I tried to visit while you were at Her Majesty's pleasure," Maws said, "bring you a clean shirt and such, but the authorities would have none of it." He sat down on the edge of the bed. "We got your communication, what you passed on to Mr. Barnett," he said. "We was wondering where the writing materials came from."

Moriarty nodded. "The 'paper' was a bit of the silk inner lining of my waistcoat," he explained. "The 'ink' was a mixture of soot and iron oxide—rust—with a taste of water and a wee bit of blood as a binder. The 'pen' was a pin."

"You're an ingenious man, Professor Moriarty," said Mr. Maws.

"Elementary," the professor said, "and did Barnett act on my suggestions?"

"O' course. He and the mummer repaired to the Fox and Hare and interviewed the publican."

"Respectfully?"

"According to the mummer, they got 'im snookered."

"Ah! And?"

"He thinks they have useful information what you can ponder," Mr. Maws said.

Moriarty nodded. "Good work."

"I've brought an assortment of garments for you to pick among once you've washed and brushed yourself up a bit," said Mr. Maws. "And a razor and such. You look as if you could put a razor and such to good use."

"Indeed I could, Mr. Maws," Moriarty agreed. "Indeed I could." He stripped off his prison grays, dropped them on the floor, and wrapped himself in his Chinese silk robe, which was laid out on the bed. "Dispose of those things," he said and crossed the hall to the bathroom.

CHAPTER EIGHT

PROBLEM CHILD

In misery's darkest cavern known,
His useful care was ever nigh,
Where hopeless anguish pour'd his groan,
And lonely want retir'd to die.

—SAMUEL JOHNSON

"THE SITUATION IS . . . sensitive . . . unique . . . without precedent," said His Grace Albert John Wythender Ardbaum Ramson, sixteenth Duke of Shorham, sinking heavily into the only chair in the room that would hold his bulk, "and presents a great potential danger to the monarchy and the empire." He shook his head ponderously from side to side. "I've never seen anything like it. Never expected to. Who could have foreseen such a thing? Who?"

"'Sensitive' is a good word," agreed Clarence Anton Montgrief, fifth Earl of Scully and hereditary holder of the baronetcies of Reith and Glendower. "Sensitive," he said again, savoring the sound. "We have great resources at our command here," he told Moriarty, "resources you cannot begin to imagine. And they are of no use against . . . whatever it is that's happening here. We need, we must have something—someone—different. Someone acquainted within the unseen worlds of mendacity, deceit, treachery, and falsehood that lurk in the corners of the realm. Someone who can travel about freely in the underworld of the illegal and illicit, and who is trusted by these men who trust no one."

"You need," suggested Moriarty, "a criminal to deal with other criminals."

"Exactly!" said the duke, thumping a thick forefinger on the arm of his chair.

"So you've sent for me," said Moriarty.

"I, ah, wouldn't put it precisely like that," said Lord Montgrief, "but to simplify the situation—to cut through to the heart of the matter—yes."

"I'm honored," Moriarty said dryly.

They sat in a room toward the rear of the ground floor, Moriarty and the four men whose influence, and whose great need, had plucked him from Newgate Prison and brought him to Wythender Hall for this meeting. Moriarty put down the cup of Soochow Special Reserve tea and leaned back in his chair. Judging by the strained expressions of his hosts, it had been an act of will for them to wait the almost two hours since he had arrived. The walls of the room were lined with bookshelves; the floor held a great oaken table of advanced age and a cluster of nondescript chairs. For reasons lost in antiquity it was known as the map room, although no maps were in evidence. One of the two men who had not yet spoken had been introduced to Moriarty as Sir Anthony Darryl, with no further elucidation; the other, a dour-looking angular man of about forty who had pulled his chair away from the table, and now sat in a corner of the room glowering at the others, had not been introduced, and the oversight had not been explained.

"You have done Her Majesty a service once before," said His Grace, "and it has not been forgotten. For this reason, and at the suggestion of Mycroft Holmes, who occupies a position unique, influential, and, ah, otherwise indescribable in Her Majesty's government, you have been called. Mr. Holmes insists that you can be trusted."

"I respect Mr. Holmes," Moriarty said, "and will try not to do anything to disabuse him of his opinion. What's to happen to me if I take your assignment?"

"What's—?"

"In regard to my present, ah, legal troubles."

"Ah! You are, as of the moment you accept the task we put to you, granted a royal pardon for the, ah, specific offense in question," His Grace said.

"And any other charges that might arise from the same offense," added the man introduced as Sir Anthony.

Moriarty removed his pince-nez and began polishing the lenses with a piece of flannel from his jacket pocket. He raised an eyebrow. "Satisfactory," he said. "I request the right to establish my innocence of the charges at some future time and present such proof to the home secretary."

"Totally unnecessary," His Grace said.

"Not to me," said Moriarty. "I will not tolerate being used in the fashion that . . . somebody is attempting to do."

His Grace nodded. "Very well," he said. "I'll see that you are able to present such evidence and have it put on the record—whatever the appropriate record may be."

"Thank you, Your Grace," Moriarty said. "Now back to the matter at hand. Describe for me, as best you can, your dilemma."

"We are doing what we can do," said His Grace. "Putting such men to work as we can do, without further endangering the situation, but I doubt whether that will accomplish anything truly useful."

"I take it that this is on the same matter that Your Lordship discussed with me yesterday?" Moriarty asked Montgrief.

"Just so," the earl agreed.

"A man has disappeared and you want my help to find him?"

"It's a bit more complicated than that," said Montgrief.

"I thought it might be," Moriarty said.

His Lordship turned to the gentlemen to his left. "Sir Anthony," he said, "perhaps it would be best if you were to tell, ah, to explain . . . to narrate the story as we know it so far. Sir Anthony," His Lordship explained, turning back to Moriarty, "has a special post within the Home Office."

Sir Anthony, a youthful-looking, slender man with a handsome face with a sharp nose and troubled blue eyes, stared thoughtfully at the far wall and took a curved and twisted briar pipe from his jacket pocket. He filled it from a pouch from another pocket, tamped the tobacco, and, thrusting a wood sliver from yet another pocket into the flame of a gas fixture on the wall, puffed the pipe into life. "The missing man," he said finally, dropping the wood sliver into a convenient cup, "is known as Baron Renfrew. He disappeared from an . . . establishment . . . on Gladston Square eight days ago. He had been visiting a young woman of, um, what I believe is usually described as 'loose character,' a resident of the establishment." He paused and looked questioningly at Moriarty.

"I see," Moriarty said. "Pray, continue."

"Ah," said Sir Anthony. "Just so. When Baron Renfrew's men came in to look for him—they estimate it was five in the morning, His Lordship being some hours past his usual departure time—it was discovered that His Lordship had indeed left some time before, but how and to where is unknown."

"Who are these 'men'?" Moriarty asked.

"Pardon?"

"These 'men' who came in looking for the baron, who are they, and why does he have 'men'?"

"Well . . ."

"I've encountered many a baron walking about entirely unencumbered with superfluous 'men.'"

"It's his grandmama, you see," explained Sir Anthony. "She is, ah, quite wealthy, and she does worry about him. So she employs several gentlemen to, you might say, watch over him."

"I see," said Moriarty.

"Then there was His Lordship's manservant, who was awaiting

His Lordship in the corridor outside the young woman's room. He had been knocked on the head, rendered unconscious, and was unaware of the manner of His Lordship's going."

"Curious," said Moriarty. "Who did the knocking?"

"He doesn't know. He didn't see his assailant. It may have been His Lordship."

"Ah!" said Moriarty.

"The woman, a respectful and industrious young woman by all accounts, whose name apparently was Elsbeth Hooten, but who called herself Rose, had been murdered most foully with a sharp implement of some sort and then butchered after her death. At least it is to be hoped that it was after her death."

Moriarty raised an eyebrow. "Butchered?"

"Indeed so," said Sir Anthony. "In an unseemly and, if I may put it this way, highly original manner."

Moriarty leaned forward, his hands laced together under his chin. "Come now," he said briskly, "this is most . . . interesting. When you say 'an original manner,' can you describe for me just what was done? Not in all the presumably repulsive details, I have no need for that yet, and I see no need to offend the sensibilities of anyone present, but in general terms."

Sir Anthony thought for a moment. "Anatomical dissection is how I would describe it, and some of the organs brought forth and laid out as it might be for inspection. I might even say it was neatly done, but for all the blood and gore."

"An apt description," agreed the Earl of Scully. "Blood and gore. Dreadful business." He winced at the memory. "As bad as anything I've ever seen, and I was at Sebastopol in 'fifty-five."

"You were there, my lord?" asked Moriarty. "At the establishment in question, I mean," he added to cut off further discussion of Sebastopol.

"I was," said His Lordship. "I arrived some hours after the, ah, event. Sir Anthony had me sent for. Decisions had to be made."

Moriarty nodded as though he understood, but what decisions, besides the obvious, he had no idea. It sounded like a reprise of the Jack the Ripper murders of two years before. Indeed, perhaps it was—the Ripper had never been caught, after all. Why, Moriarty wondered, would Sir Anthony have sent for the Earl of Scully to join him at the scene of a gruesome homicide, even if it did involve a minor member of the nobility—and one with "men" at that? What, for that matter, was Sir Anthony doing there? Just what was "a special post within the Home Office"? He refrained from asking. Let them tell it their way.

Sir Anthony took up the tale. "A search was instituted immediately to see whether anyone had seen Baron Renfrew leaving, or perhaps had just seen the baron at any time during the evening. A few had seen him enter and go to the girl's room, but no one who was there remembered seeing the baron after that. At any rate most of the, ah, visitors had long since gone home."

"What has been accomplished since?" Moriarty asked.

"The body of the unfortunate young woman has been removed to a private mortuary," Sir Anthony said.

"And the police? Scotland Yard?"

"The necessary authorities were notified." Sir Anthony discovered that his pipe had gone out and went through the process of lighting it again. "We couldn't go through the usual channels, you understand."

"Actually . . . ," Moriarty began.

"We'll get to that," said the Earl of Scully. "We'll have to, won't we?" He turned to his companions, who nodded and looked unhappy.

"Perhaps," suggested Sir Anthony, "we should let Chief Inspector Epp explain."

They all turned to the dour man in the corner.

He remained silent for several heartbeats and then looked up and said, "I'd just as soon not." His voice had the quality of coarse gravel running down a washboard.

"We've been over this," the Duke of Shorham said severely.

Epp pulled himself and the chair he sat in across the carpet and up to the table. "If there's nothing for it, then. *Ipso facto*." He turned his eyes toward Moriarty. "It's not that I object to you, you understand," he told the professor. "Although, actually, I do, from what I've heard of you, but in this case if the devil himself were able to assist us, I'd give him a cheer. It's that I don't think you—or anyone—can help us. I'm afraid that we must prepare for the worst, and pray that what befalls is something less."

"You may be right," Moriarty assented. "I know nothing to contradict you, as I know nothing of the problem you are facing at all beyond the fact that a young lady is dead and a man must be found. Also the scene of this poor girl's demise must be examined carefully to determine whether the missing baron is a murderer or a victim."

Epp shrugged a broad expansive shrug. "What do you expect to learn from the girl's bedroom?" he demanded, looking around at the others as though to say "See what I mean?"

"Something might be discovered," Moriarty said mildly.

Epp shook his head. "Two Scotland Yard men have looked at what there is to look at, and found nothing of interest," he said. "I accompanied them, and I can assure you that they were most thorough. *Quam proxime*. We must look elsewhere."

His Grace of Shorham's eyes had closed during the conversation, but at this they popped open. "Two Yard men?" he demanded. "Whom, and by what authority?"

"Inspectors Lestrade and Fitzbadely," said Epp. "Both good men. I sent for them. They know only what they had to know, and they've been sworn to secrecy."

"I suppose," said His Grace, "but the wider the circle, the harder it will be to close."

Michael Kurland

"Yet—" Epp began, pointing his chin toward Moriarty.

"It was Mr. Mycroft Holmes's idea that we bring him here," the Earl of Scully reminded them, "and Her Majesty herself concurred."

The queen herself? Moriarty thoughtfully pinched his pince-nez glasses back over his nose and stared through them at his assembled hosts. This cut deeper than he had suspected. For all the implicit urgency, for all the ugliness of the crime, he had not thought it something that affected the palace. Although during the Ripper outrage there had been rumors . . . He put off that line of thought. Allowing oneself to formulate deductions before all the facts were known could lead to avoidable misdirection.

Epp sighed and turned back to Moriarty. "As I said," he continued, "the site of the crime has been searched. The crime is done, the victim is dead, the killer has fled. The Scotland Yard inspectors looked and discovered nothing. The trail is cold."

"Nonetheless," said Moriarty, "if you wish my assistance I would examine what there is to examine. Although first—" He turned to the others. "I presume there is more to the story?"

The duke waved an arm vaguely about in the air like a walrus checking the wind. "Unfortunately there is," he said. "There has been a second killing."

"Ah!" Moriarty said, leaning back in his chair. "Interesting."

"Horrifying, rather," said the earl. "It was a butchery, like the first."

"Tell me about it," Moriarty said. "When?"

"Last night," said Sir Anthony. "Or rather the night before. I've been up so long I've quite lost track of time."

"Where?" asked Moriarty.

"At another, ah, establishment," said His Grace the duke.

"This one a rather exclusive private club," said Sir Anthony. "Catering to what I might describe as a clientele with an advanced taste in erotic stimulation."

"Another girl was killed and mutilated?"

80

"A young lad, actually," Sir Anthony corrected mildly, "and this killing was if anything, more thoroughly repulsive than the first."

"Two in a row," Epp said, smacking his right fist into the open palm of his left hand. "I worked on the Ripper murders two years ago, and what it looks like to me is Fleet-Foot Jack is back."

The others shifted uncomfortably in their seats at Epp's words and looked elsewhere, as though they had no desire to associate themselves with his remark. Moriarty took note of their reaction but again withheld comment. There was an undercurrent of . . . something . . . tugging at the people in this room, and they were going to have to acknowledge it before it swept them away.

"Mustn't say that, old man," murmured the Duke of Shorham.

"It would behoove one not to venture there," barked the Earl of Scully.

"We most assuredly must not let anyone dwell on such a comparison," Anthony said firmly. "Not for a moment!"

Epp scowled. "Seems unavoidable," he said. "The facts are there. *Ipso facto.*"

"Actually," Moriarty began, and everyone paused and turned to look at him. "The comparison with the Ripper murders had occurred to me, but based on what you've just said we can put it aside. The person who perpetrated these deeds might have had the Ripper in mind as a model, but it is highly unlikely that whoever did this is actually the Ripper."

The Earl of Scully's eyes widened at this, and he nodded. This one statement, if it could be demonstrated, would prove the worth of soliciting the aid of Professor Moriarty.

The Duke of Shorham leaned his head back until he was looking over the heads of everyone present and they were staring at the short, well-clipped spade beard that emerged from his chin. "Why do you say that, Professor?" he asked the ceiling.

"You might not find my reason very convincing at the moment,"

Moriarty said, "so I shall reserve it. Mr. Epp, tell me everything known about this second murder, if you please."

"Baron Renfrew was seen to enter the establishment in question," Epp said.

Anthony raised a hand in interruption. "A man presumed to be the baron was seen to enter," he corrected. "He was, after all, masked."

Epp pursed his lips. "If you would have it that way," he said.

"We must withhold our conclusions without further evidence," said Anthony.

"I'm afraid we have enough to convict now," Epp said. He turned to Moriarty. "The man wore a mask, as did everyone who entered the establishment. One of their quainter rules. He had the height and build of the baron, and identified himself as the baron by using the proper word of entry. No one who saw him inside doubted that he was the baron."

"And once inside?" Moriarty asked.

"He retired to a room upstairs with a lad named, ah, Istefan, leaving his companion downstairs in one of the common rooms."

"His companion?"

"Yes."

"Who was, I presume, not one of the aforementioned 'men'?"

"No, sir, this was a squat gentleman whom nobody was able to identify. He subsequently left with the baron."

"No one similar is known to associate with the baron?"

"No."

"Just to be clear, the baron's whereabouts between the two killings are unknown?"

Epp nodded. "And after. He disappeared again."

Moriarty looked around at all the serious faces. "I take it this lad Istefan was the victim?"

"Yes. The baron was in the room with Istefan for about three-quarters of an hour. About fifteen minutes after he left the lad was found, ah, as he was found."

"There's been no sign of the baron since?"

"None."

"And the body?"

"Still as it was. The room has been closed off while we decide what to do."

"We can't have these two events connected in the public mind," Sir Anthony explained.

"The public seems to have been carefully and deliberately kept unaware of either event," Moriarty said gently.

"Word gets out," said the Duke of Shorham crossly. "The great beast that is the public would seem to believe that it's entitled to know things that are not its concern. There is a great thirst for titillation, for scandal."

Moriarty polished his pince-nez. "I must speak with these people," he said, "and now you must tell me what you haven't yet told me."

The duke coughed. "Excuse me?" he asked.

"Come now. Two people are murdered, and a member of the minor nobility, who might be the perpetrator or another victim, is missing, and because of this a state of near-panic ensues among those who know, the information is suppressed, and the queen herself is consulted—and a desperate felon, if I may describe myself in those terms, is released from prison to search among the criminal classes for . . . for what? There is a piece missing from this story, and that piece will explain why you gentlemen are here and why I am sitting among you. I can do nothing useful if facts are withheld."

The Earl of Scully looked around at the others, who seemed determined to remain mute. He took a deep breath. "This is not to go beyond this room," he said.

"Obviously," replied Moriarty.

"The missing man," the earl said carefully, "the man for whom we have removed you from prison to aid in our search, uses Baron Renfrew as his incognito. His name is Albert Victor. Prince Albert Victor. *The* Prince Albert Victor, eldest son of the Prince of Wales, second in line to the throne."

"Ah!" said Moriarty. "Indeed. That certainly explains the 'men.' You have a problem."

CHAPTER NINE

THE MISSING PRINCE

Yesterday upon the stair
I met a man who wasn't there.
He wasn't there again today
I wish that man would go away.

—HUGH MEANS

HIS ROYAL HIGHNESS ALBERT VICTOR CHRISTIAN EDWARD, Duke of Clarence and Avondale, Knight of the Orders of the Garter and of St. Patrick, second in line for the British throne, tall, impeccably garbed, aristocratically slim, and handsome as a—well, yes, as a prince, and unmarried at twenty-six, was probably the most eligible bachelor in the world. All those who knew him remarked on his regal bearing, his courtly airs, his utter fitness for the role the God who looked over England had set for him.

Yet . . .

There were stories—rumors, actually—about a dissipated life and immoral habits that had to be carefully concealed from his grandmother the queen. Gambling to excess—but then, who will call in the marker of a prince of the blood? Any such debts of honor will certainly be paid. Consorting with women of a low character—but then, it is hardly possible to engage in that sort of consorting with women of a high character. Trips to Paris to engage in shameful behavior—but then, would you wish a royal prince to engage in shameful behavior at home? Surely, the wags wagged, we have here a case of wild oats being sowed before the prince must take on the somber responsibilities he is destined to assume.

Beyond these were the other rumors, whispered in shocked tones by those who had merely smiled at the first rumors. The fiend known as the Whitechapel Slasher, Jack the Ripper, or Fleet-Foot Jack had slashed and mutilated six women two years before and then had suddenly stopped. He had never been caught—as far as was known. Perhaps he *had* been, though, the whispers went. Perhaps he had been someone so important that charges could not be brought. Albert Victor's name was, for some reason, often brought up in these hushed discussions.

Ridiculous, of course.

Yet . . .

It was but a year ago, in July 1889, when the Cleveland Street Scandal had whipped through the aristocracy and evoked awe and giggles among the lower classes. Investigating a theft at the Central Telegraph office, the police questioned a lad employed as a runner who was found to be in possession of the unheard-of sum of eighteen shillings. Young Thomas insisted that he had not stolen it but earned it serving as a "rent boy" in a male brothel at 19 Cleveland Street.

Scotland Yard raided the establishment. The brothel was devoid of customers when the Yard men arrived, but they gathered in some "rent boys," who, aided by the gentle persuasion of the investigating officers, quickly identified as visitors to the establishment several army officers and an earl. The detectives traced a network of clients that soon led to the upper levels of British aristocracy, and thence it led—nowhere. A lid was clamped down on the investigation so suddenly and so tightly that it must have been someone with considerable weight doing the clamping.

Still, the story was too good to keep quiet, and the whispers soon identified Prince Albert Victor as one of the missing clients. True? False? Wishful fantasy on the part of the antiroyalists? Who could say?

The prince promptly left for India, where he was said to be having an affair with the wife of a civil engineer. The whispers had it that this rumored indiscretion was but a bit of misdirection conjured to draw the eye away from the greater evil. The whispers grew louder. The "Cleveland Street Outrage" became public knowledge. It was suggested in the press that perhaps Albert Victor was not a proper person to govern the United Kingdom and the British Empire, that perhaps his younger brother George would be more suited to inherit the throne. When asked, ever so discreetly and with due decorum, about this, the royals, together and separately, said nothing. The prince returned to England to ride out the storm.

Casting discretion aside, the newspapers took up the story and shook it as a terrier shakes a rat. Even terriers as far afield as the United States felt that they should have a say in the line of succession to the British throne. In an editorial, *The American Daily Northwestern* opined:

> Physically and mentally he is something of a wreck and not half the man in all the attributes of a manly makeup that characterizes George.
>
> Victor seems to inherit his father's vices without retaining many of his virtues, and his connection with the Cleveland Street scandal is only another indication of the debauchery which too conspicuously tinctures European royalty.

"The blasted American newspapers are bad enough," His Lordship of Scully growled, dumping the contents of a canvas dispatch box onto the table, and poking and prodding at the clutch of newspaper clippings that had spilled out, "and the Indian papers, of course," he added, spreading them widely about the table and stabbing at a long article from *The Calcutta Daily Anglo-Indian* with a stubby forefinger. This one began "It saddens us to suggest," and Moriarty read no further.

"But look at this—and this—" The earl stabbed and stabbed again. "Not even in English. German, this one, and this one's in Russian or some such."

"Polish, I believe," suggested Sir Anthony.

"Same bally thing. And look at this one. French! French, by God! A bally bunch of foreigners telling us how . . . who . . . when . . ." Words failed the earl.

The Duke of Shorham leaned his bulk forward in his oversized chair. "You see the dimensions of our dilemma?" he asked Moriarty.

"I begin to," Moriarty agreed.

"We can't ask any of the usual, the more normal, sources for assistance because, even if there were any assistance they could render, and I don't see what that would be, a secret like this cannot be kept."

"Certainly not when it involves His Highness," the earl agreed. "Too much is already suspected, or alleged. I won't say 'known,' because I don't *know* any of it and I don't believe most of it."

Moriarty frowned. "Doesn't Scotland Yard keep track of the royals on a fairly regular basis?" he asked. "Look after them when they're out and about, keep the hoi polloi at a respectful distance, that sort of thing?"

"In the regular way of business, yes," the earl said, "but when His Highness is engaged in his, ah, irregular activities, he has some retainers from the household who look after him. They were doing so, as best they could, when he disappeared and that young girl died."

"I see," Moriarty said.

"Who could have anticipated anything like this?" the earl asked the empty air, expecting no reply.

"Why did you say, Professor, that whoever did this is not the Ripper?" asked the duke.

Moriarty considered. "There are many reasons why a man might commit murder," he said, "but they seldom overlap. A man may kill for greed, lust, anger, fear, immediate gain, to eliminate a threat, or out of some sort of perverse mental derangement. Or, for that matter, for queen and country. And, once having killed, a man may find it easier to kill again. Then there are some men, born without moral conscience, who would kill you as soon as shake your hand. I have known several such."

"Dreadful!" opined the earl.

"They are usually held in by the constraints of society and the severe penalties should they get caught. As a matter of fact," Moriarty mused, "one is usually safer with them than with the other sort."

Epp stirred, looking interested. "Why is that?" he asked.

"Since their murderous urges are not occasioned by any strong emotion," Moriarty explained, "they usually find it less troublesome to solve their problems by a less drastic method."

"Ah!" said the duke.

"This is not true of spouse killers, or poisoners in general," Moriarty continued, "as after an initial success or two, they seem to think themselves immune from detection." He looked around at his audience. "But I digress," he said.

"About the Ripper," Sir Anthony said. "Surely, Professor, he falls into the category you referred to as 'perverse mental derangement,' does he not?"

"Indeed," Moriarty agreed, "but such people run to patterns. Think of the derangement as a groove cut across the mental processes of the brain. This groove can cause them to commit unspeakable acts, but its direction and, let's say, depth direct the sort of acts the madman will commit. The Ripper's pattern is quite clear. Whether his atrocities are the result of love or hate, or some emotion not shared by normal men, he clearly directs them at those we choose to call 'the fair sex.'"

"Women," Sir Anthony clarified.

"Prostitutes of the lowest sort," Epp added.

"That is so," Moriarty agreed. "Whether this is through preference, or because they are easier targets than other women, I cannot say, but there are men of the same class who would be as accessible if he chose to, ah, access them. There isn't a night when a casual eye cast over the gutters of Eastchapel won't find men sprawled in a drunken stupor or a four-pipe haze."

The duke frowned. "Four-pipe?" he asked.

"Opium," Sir Anthony explained.

"Yet your missing prince, or someone assuming his identity, has killed in two establishments catering to the upper classes, and has not restricted himself to women." Moriarty shook his head. "No, milords, gentlemen, the perpetrator of these crimes is not the Ripper, although he may hope you will think he is."

"You seem to have made a study of this," said the Duke of Shorham.

"I have, Your Grace," Moriarty admitted. "I find the repressed corners of the human mind as fascinating as some of my colleagues find flowers or butterflies, or the sorts of ash left by different pipe tobaccos."

Epp smiled a tight-lipped smile. "Or banks," he added. "Or country houses."

"Ah!" Moriarty said. "You refer to a different set of colleagues. Impetuous light-fingered colleagues."

"Villains and thieves," Epp growled.

"Mr. Epp!" the duke said sharply.

"Why, yes, if you will," Moriarty admitted. "Villains and thieves. And, to their misfortune, not nearly as good at it as the ancestors of the man for whom we search. Or, for that matter, of most of you in this room."

The duke turned his head to glare at Moriarty.

"Laws of inheritance and patents of nobility," Moriarty expanded, "exist to preserve unto the tenth generation the ill-gotten rewards of our ancestors."

"Must you be offensive, sir?" the duke asked, his voice an irritated growl.

"You disapprove of us, do you?" the earl asked. "We of the nobility?"

Moriarty raised an eyebrow. "My disapproval is easily garnered. Class distinctions based on the accident of birth are surely arbitrary and idiotic, as is easily demonstrated by the high number of idiots among the 'upper classes.' Are you seeking my assistance or my approbation?"

Sir Anthony raised an admonishing hand. "Let us get back to the matter at hand."

His Grace the Duke of Shorham continued glaring at Moriarty for some moments, but then turned his eyes elsewhere and sighed. "Even so," he agreed, "but what assurance have we that Professor Moriarty's assistance will be forthcoming once he leaves this building? Perhaps, having been released from prison, he will merely fade away, never to be seen again."

Moriarty smiled widely. "You have the word of a gentleman," he told them.

The Earl of Scully sniffed. Sir Anthony looked doubtful.

"Being gentlemen yourselves, you should have a good idea of what such a word is worth. Perhaps more reassuring is the pardon you have promised me should I undertake this. Clearly it is better to walk in the light of day with a pardon than to skulk in corners hunted by the police, however inadequate they may be to the task."

"That's so," Sir Anthony agreed.

"Add to that the fact that my first trial resulted in a hung jury, and that I fully expect to be found not guilty in the next, should there be a next."

"Is that so?" Epp demanded. "In that case, and as you disapprove of the 'upper classes' anyway, why are you bothering to listen to us at all? Why not just wait in your cell for redemption?"

"Your problem is an interesting one," Moriarty told him. "A missing man of high—the highest—station, a possible murderer and fiend, who must be located and retrieved quickly and without fuss. I can see the great danger to the government and the monarchy should he not be found."

"A noble sentiment," said Sir Anthony.

"Also, I confess that my cell is a bit too damp for prolonged occupation and a bit too chill for extended scientific meditation," Moriarty added. "Now, to the matter at hand. The questions are clear; the answers less so at the moment. If His Highness is doing this, why? If he is not, and some agency has abducted him and is making it seem that he is guilty, again why?" He turned to the Earl of Scully. "No demands of any sort have been made, I take it?"

"None."

"What has been done so far?"

The earl looked at Epp, who responded, "Given the situation, there hasn't been much we could do. The uniformed force has been instructed to report any sightings of the prince, but we've put it to them as a minor exercise in keeping peace among the royals. Her Majesty doesn't like her grandson being out on his own, him only being twenty-six, so she'd like an eye kept on him. That's the story as they've heard it."

"Anything else?"

"We've had people look in all the places he might be expected to go, including several obscure royal properties in Scotland and Wales, as well as the houses of his associates."

"Required a bit of finesse, that did," Sir Anthony commented. "I mean we couldn't just walk in and ask, 'You haven't seen the prince wandering about here anywhere, have you?' It might have started talk."

"We're looking into various other rabbit holes as well," Epp went on. "Even going so far as to send men into all the opium dens in the

East End. We couldn't actually raid them for obvious reasons." He shook his head. "So far—no rabbit."

"What assistance may I expect?" Moriarty asked.

"Whatever you require that can be managed without revealing the, ah, ultimate purpose of the requested assistance," Sir Anthony told him. "You shall report to Mr. Epp, and he or one of his men will accompany you."

"I don't think so," Moriarty said.

"What?"

"I'll pass on whatever information I glean to Mr. Epp, but I will not be accompanied by anyone, least of all a Scotland Yard man."

"You see, Your Grace," Epp said, waggling a reprimanding thumb in the air, "he has no intention of assisting. He's trying to get shot of us right off, and that's the truth of it!"

"Come now, Professor," the Duke of Shorham rumbled, pushing forward in his chair. "Surely you will grant that to be an elementary precaution in a case like this."

"Precaution against what?" asked Moriarty. "I have no objection against Mr. Epp remaining available for me to pass on whatever information I feel will be of interest. Then he can do with it whatever you gentlemen require of him."

"But surely, sir," the duke blustered, "you must understand—"

"I'm going to be requiring the assistance of people who can smell a 'copper' ten furlongs off, downwind," Moriarty said. "It would probably be best if I didn't bring one with me, and, as you don't want them, or anyone, to have any hint as to what I'm trying to accomplish, we should avoid any hint of official connivance in my inquiries. This job will be difficult enough without your attempting to shackle me to an official escort at the outset."

"I don't think you understand," said the duke. "Mr. Epp is Number Six."

Moriarty frowned and shook his head. "That means nothing to me," he said. "Number six at what?"

Epp smiled a tight smile. "I don't think he'll be impressed, Your Grace," he said.

Sir Anthony rubbed his palms together, his hands in front of his face. "You've heard of the 'Big Five'?" he asked Moriarty.

Moriarty nodded. "The heads of the five divisions—excuse me, departments—of Scotland Yard," he said.

"There is a sixth department," said Sir Anthony.

Moriarty considered. "Ah!" he said.

"It is not general knowledge," Sir Anthony explained. "Even in the Yard. As a matter of fact, its members are called 'the Invisibles' by those who do know of them. Mr. Epp is the undercommissioner in charge of Department Six. Thus he is known informally at the Yard as 'Number Six.' "

"What does this department do?" Moriarty asked.

Epp spoke up. "Whatever is required of them."

"They take the jobs that the others cannot handle," said Sir Anthony. "Particularly where it is desirable that the connection to Scotland Yard is not evident. Their men are picked for their intelligence and their discretion."

"An interesting notion," Moriarty said. "Intelligent policemen."

"Now, then," Epp said.

Moriarty considered a mole on the duke's neck for a moment. "It would seem to me that Mr. Epp must be invaluable where he is. Are you sure you should spare him from his important work merely to follow me around? Are there not other incidents or events that should occupy his attention?"

"At the moment," said the duke, "there is nothing more important than what you will be doing. What, I should say, we surmise you will be doing."

"Very well," Moriarty said, pursing his lips. "If Mr. Epp or one of his minions wants to accompany me he may, provided he makes no effort to follow me where I tell him it's inadvisable. He must take my word for that."

"Very well," said the duke. "If we're going to trust you to do this, we might as well start off by trusting you. Where do you wish to begin?"

"I shall begin by examining the sites of the two murders," Moriarty told him, "and for that Epp's assistance will be useful, and gratefully accepted. I must find some indication, however slender, of the direction in which the truth may lie."

Sir Anthony shook his head. "There's nothing of any value to be found at either place, I assure you," he said.

"Nonetheless I shall look," said Moriarty. "Let us hope you're mistaken."

"Very well."

"One suggestion," Moriarty added. "Have your people be alert for any word of this leaking out, or any rumor that is suggestive of a problem among the royals."

"Yes," Sir Anthony said. "Of course. We're doing that already."

"Then try to, delicately, ascertain where and how the rumor originated. If His Highness is, indeed, not responsible for these acts, then someone is going to a lot of trouble to make it seem that he is—and at some point they're going to want to make the matter public."

"My God!" exclaimed the Duke of Shorham. "That could bring down the government. Why, if the people thought we were concealing it from them, it could well threaten the monarchy."

"Exactly," said Moriarty.

"My God!"

CHAPTER TEN

ROSE'S ROOM

Aliorum vulnus nostra sit cautio.
(Let us take warning from another's wound.)

—ST. JEROME

THE FOUR-HORSE CARRIAGE PULLED UP in front of Mollie's establishment on Gladston Square in early evening. The gas mantle above the front door was unlit, and the few lights that shone through the windows on the upper floor were soft and subdued, the curtains drawn closed to keep out the night. The porter was long in answering the pull of the bell cord, and he looked curiously out at the two well-dressed visitors and the ornate carriage from which they had emerged as though he had no idea why they might be standing there. "Gentlemen," he said. "Miss Mollie is not entertaining clients at present. I trust this causes you no inconvenience."

"I am Epp of Scotland Yard, and this is Professor Moriarty," Epp said, pointing a bony finger at the professor. "We have come about the murdered girl, Rose. You might remember—I was here before."

"Was you now?"

"With the police," Epp explained. "I've come back to look at the girl's room."

The porter looked out at the carriage again and then back at Epp. "The police, you say?"

"Indeed."

"Scotland Yard?"

"That's correct, my man. *Idem quod*. Is there a problem?"

"Not if you say there ain't, then there ain't."

"Good. About the girl?"

"They've taken poor Rose away," said the porter. "As is no more than right. She lay there for two days before anyone thought to move her, and then I truly believe it was more the smell than the propriety of the thing. You Scotland Yard people are a thoughtless and peculiar lot, is what I say."

Moriarty stepped forward. "The room," he asked sharply, "has it been disturbed?"

"The room in what she died?"

"That room."

"Hasn't nobody been in it since they took the body out. The missus says as how we'll have to clean it up, but none of us managed to get it done yet."

"Good, good!" Moriarty rubbed his hands together in obvious delight. "Here is a stroke of unexpected good fortune."

The porter stared at him and then shook his head slowly. "A peculiar lot, I says, and a strange and peculiar lot you is—if you don't mind me saying so."

"It's no more than the truth," Moriarty agreed. "A strange and peculiar lot we are indeed. May we come in?"

"If you've a mind to," the porter agreed. "Settle yourselves down in the front room while I fetch Miss Mollie."

Mollie appeared at the head of the stairs two minutes later dressed all in black. Perhaps a bit more form-fitting than was absolutely proper for mourning garb, but all in black nonetheless. "Gentlemen," she said, holding the bannister tightly as she descended. "I'm Mollie Cobby, the proprietress of this establishment. I understand you wish to look at poor Rose's room. I don't know what sense of morbid curiosity has brought you hither—"

"I am with Scotland Yard, madam," Epp interrupted her, "and this is my, ah, colleague Professor James Moriarty. Morbid curiosity is, you might say, his *ignis fatuus.*"

"Is it indeed?" Mollie stared at Moriarty for a second and then turned her attention back to Epp. "You coppers have already thoroughly knocked about in poor Rose's room," she said. "Why would you want to return?"

"We don't wish to inconvenience you," Moriarty told Mollie. "I hope to discover some indications of the murderer: his appearance, his method, his motive, his provenance, and possibly from whence he came."

"From an empty room?"

"Even so," Moriarty said. "Depending perhaps on just how much knocking about the authorities have done. Has anyone aside from the police been in the room?"

Mollie shook her head. "I haven't had the stomach to have it cleaned up. The business is closed, and I've sent the girls away for a fortnight to give them something else to think about. I'll be using the time to paint a little and put down new carpets, and I suppose I'll have to get to that room before the girls return, but it will wait."

"With your permission," Moriarty said, "I should very much like to visit the room."

Mollie looked sharply at each of them and considered. "Very well, then. Follow me."

They climbed the stairs. The light in the upstairs hallway was low, and the bedroom doors were all closed. From behind one of the doors came the soft, insistent sound of a woman sobbing. Epp gave an involuntary shudder and tried to banish from his mind the superstitious images conjured up by the sound. Moriarty looked at Mollie and raised an interrogative eyebrow.

"Pamela, that is," Mollie told him. "Calls herself 'Heather' while she's working for some reason. Her specialty is—well, no reason to concern you gentlemen with that. She was hiding in the wardrobe in that room while Rose was . . . what happened to Rose, and she hasn't been right in the head since. She didn't see nothing, mind you. At least I don't think she did. She hasn't talked about it. She hasn't talked about anything much since . . . that night. She wouldn't leave with the other girls. Said she had nowhere to go. I told her to stay at a guest house at Bath what I know of. She said she didn't know anyone at Bath, and anyway she'd rather stay here. She's been crying like that, no loud blubbering, just quiet and steady, pretty much since it happened. She was Rose's special friend."

"What does that mean," Epp asked suspiciously, " 'special friend'?"

"I would like to speak with Pamela after I examine the room," Moriarty said.

"I wish you would," Mollie told him. "Talking about it might serve to take her mind off it, if you see what I mean. That sounds kind of contrariwise, but . . ."

"I do see, Miss Mollie," Moriarty told her. He moved down the hall. "Is this the room?" he asked, stopping in front of a door.

She said, "It is," and took a deep breath. "I will await you downstairs, if you've no objection."

"None," Moriarty said, "and I thank you."

"You ain't no copper," Mollie said. "They ain't got much thanks in them."

Moriarty pulled open the door. The room was as it had been four days before when a prince had disappeared and a girl had died. Except, of course, that Rose's body had been removed. "Light that wall sconce, if you don't mind," Moriarty said, and Epp took out a pack of lucifers and turned on the gas. "As bright as it will go," Moriarty directed.

The professor began with a slow and careful examination of the bed and the pools of dried and caked blood on the sheets and blanket. Then he transferred his gaze to the carpet by the bed, studying each fall of blood at length, as though, thought Epp, who stayed by the wall under the light, he were attempting to read from it the story of what had transpired that fatal evening.

Epp didn't hold with that sort of mumbo-jumbo. It was a waste of time that could be better used interviewing suspects, perhaps with the aid of a little friendly persuasion, in the back room of some convenient station house. The American police had developed that sort of back-room persuasion into a science, Epp had heard. However, Epp had been ordered to stay with Moriarty and let the professor do what the professor would do.

Moriarty paused to light a double-globe paraffin lamp from the bedside table, turned its wick up until it burned as brightly as it would without smoking, and then removed his pince-nez glasses and took a monocle from his vest pocket, which he settled firmly against his right eye. Holding the lamp over his head, he spent some time inspecting the wardrobe where the girl Pamela had evidently been hiding, and then he knelt on the carpet and began a minute examination of the floor, peering into corners and beneath the few articles of furniture.

"I'm afraid the most suggestive features are obscured," he said. "There have been many people in here since the event. Policemen— there's the unmistakable mark of a gum rubber sole. I noticed the tread of the mortuary cart outside the door, but I see they didn't bring it in. That's helpful. Yes, here are the footsteps of the mortuary attendant and his helper. Small feet, must have been a lad. I imagine he had something to tell them back at home that evening."

Epp grunted. "You can see all that?" he asked with a faint sneer.

Moriarty looked up. "You doubt me?" he asked mildly.

"I wouldn't say that," Epp said. "Let's say I'm withholding judgment, but I don't see how any of this—even if you can tell one footstep from another—gets us any for'rader with our, ah, problem."

"Oh, I can tell a lot more than that," Moriarty said, "and I do believe that some of it will be helpful." He put the lamp down by the side of the bed and pointed at the floor. "What do you see?"

"Blood," said Epp.

"Go on," said Moriarty.

Epp squinted at the floor. "Blood," he said again. "Dried blood."

Moriarty stood up, holding the lamp at waist level, and pointed down at the blood-soaked coverlet on the bed. "And?" He urged.

"And more blood," said Epp, his voice showing his impatience with the questions.

"What of the absence of blood in this space?" Moriarty indicated an elongated area on the bed that was largely blood-free. "How do you account for the void?"

"Yes, there's little blood in that space," Epp admitted. "I would say that it has somehow avoided the blood."

"And on the floor?" Moriarty moved the lamp to reilluminate the carpet.

"Nothing but blood—and a bit of bare carpet where there isn't no blood."

"Exactly!" Moriarty said. "How come, do you suppose, that there 'isn't no' blood in those spots?"

Epp contrived to look as though he were puzzling it out, although in truth the question made no sense to him. "There isn't no blood there," he said finally, "because it happened that no blood fell at that there spot." He smiled. "I admit to not being wise in the mysterious ways of blood."

"A pity," Moriarty said. "You could do your job so much better if you were."

"Say, now—" Epp began.

"Imagine, if you will," Moriarty said, pointing first to the coverlet and then to the floor next to the bed, "the event that caused the blood to splatter thus."

"I'd rather not," Epp offered.

"It appears that a knife was thrust into the body"—Moriarty made a thrusting motion, and Epp grimaced—"and rapidly withdrawn—

many times. Thirty-seven separate stab wounds, I believe the coroner's report said."

"I see no need to dwell on such things," said Epp. "Aside from establishing the fact that the killer was a homicidal maniac, which we already know, where does it get us? *Quidam.*"

Moriarty carefully replaced the lamp onto its spot on the table. "Everything follows from something, Mr. Epp," he said. "If you know the end result of any action or process, it should be possible to hypothesize the beginning and even, quite possibly, what set it into motion. If we plot the course of the planet Jupiter we can tell not only where it will be ten years from now but where it was ten thousand years ago."

"What has the planet Jupiter to do with this?" asked Epp. "You saying this was some sort of astro-logical crime?"

Moriarty smiled. "Thus, if we examine these stains," he continued, "we can arrive at certain conclusions as to how they were created."

"She was stabbed," Epp reiterated stubbornly.

"With considerable force," Moriarty agreed. "Some thirty-seven times. By a man who stood"—Moriarty carefully placed his feet in two blood-free gaps in the carpet by the bed—"here."

Epp examined Moriarty's pose and the blood surrounding him. "Possible," he admitted. "Those two clear spots could be where he stood, but then how came the blood splatter behind him?"

The professor took his pince-nez glasses from his pocket and held them in his closed fist like a dagger. "When he raised the blade after each stab"—Moriarty stabbed the coverlet with the pince-nez several times, throwing his hand up each time only to bring it down with greater force—"the blood sprayed from the blade, spotting everyplace except where he was standing. Look up at the ceiling and you'll see what I mean."

Epp stared for a long moment at the blood-splattered ceiling and nodded. "Ah!" he said. "So?"

"One other place remained clear," Moriarty went on, pointing with the pince-nez at the blood-free space on the coverlet.

"Where the girl lay." Epp nodded again. "Where the man stood and where the girl lay. Two voids. *Ipso facto*."

"That," Moriarty said, pointing across the bed to a different area where the blood was pooled and smeared thick and deep and free of splashing, "is where she lay. The blood gathered around and under her as she died."

Epp stared at the spot. "I could have happily lived into my dotage without knowing that. Or," he added, "seeing what difference it makes."

"The void at this spot," Moriarty said, shifting his attention back to the blood-free space on the near side of the bed, "was caused by another person, or possibly object, lying there while the girl was stabbed."

"Object?"

"I merely allow for all possibilities," Moriarty told him. "My guess is that it was a person—your missing prince, no doubt."

"So His Roya—er, Baron Renfrew didn't stab the girl himself?"

"So it would seem."

"Yet he just lay there while she was stabbed—repeatedly?"

Moriarty nodded. "Then mutilated, which certainly took some little time. I would assume that the baron was rendered unconscious first, else he would not have lain so still."

Epp nodded. "Interesting," he said, "and—I admit it—useful. Although I didn't for a moment believe that the, ah, baron could be guilty of such a monstrous act, it is good to have some sort of outside corroboration."

"This was a crime of some audacity," Moriarty said, "and I would judge that there was more than one man involved."

Epp stared down at the clotted blood, trying to see what Moriarty saw and understand how he saw it. "More than one man?"

"Clearly."

"How can you tell that?" he asked.

"That's not important," Moriarty said. "What matters is what it tells us—what it means."

"Still—" Epp began.

Moriarty took a small square of flannel from his pocket and polished his pince-nez glasses. "Re-create in you mind," he said, "the events that must have transpired here. The prince's guardian, Mr., ah—"

"You mean Fetch?"

"Fetch. Who was knocked out as he stood guard outside the door. Then he was dragged inside and thrust under the bed. Surely no matter how, ah, lustily the prince was engaged in whatever he was engaged in, he would have paused at such an intrusion—and, no doubt, attempted to do something about it. Which would have involved leaping from the bed."

Epp pondered, looking from the door to the bed and back. "You're saying as how one man couldn't have done it? Surely he could—with a little luck."

"Ah!" Moriarty said, "but he couldn't have counted on that luck. This was not a sudden inspiration but a carefully plotted scheme. The means for spiriting His Highness away would have to have been in place before the crime. That in itself implies more than one man."

I see," said Epp. "An *iunctis viribus,* as it were."

Moriarty turned around and stared at the little man. "Where," he asked finally, "did you learn your Latin?"

Epp beamed. "Noticed that, did you? I picked it up all on my own. Been studying it for some time now."

"That would explain it," Moriarty agreed.

"I carry a phrase book about with me at all times." Epp pulled a well-creased buckram-bound volume from his rear pocket: *Dr. Mortimer Philpott's Book of Latin Phrases and Sentiments.* "It is the mark of the educated man," he said. "I would like to raise the standards of the police force by requiring everyone from the rank of sergeant to study Latin, thus enabling them to make appropriate remarks when the occasion warrants. *Mutatis mutandis,* you might say."

"You might," Moriarty acknowledged.

"The educational and intellectual standards of this country must be raised, regardless of social standing," Epp espoused. "In lieu of a public school education, one can learn Latin and play cricket."

"And do you? Play cricket, that is?" Moriarty asked.

Epp nodded. "I have a bat and the leg guards and the gloves and everything."

Moriarty stared at him for a moment and then changed the subject. "Let us leave this room and go next door," he said. "I would like to talk to that girl, Pamela, now."

"Whatever for?" Epp asked.

"One never knows," Moriarty told him. "Public school teaches you that."

CHAPTER ELEVEN

PAMELA'S STORY

A philosopher produces ideas, a poet poems,
a clergyman sermons, a professor compendia, and so on.
A criminal produces crimes . . .
[and] the whole of the police and of criminal justice,
constables, judges, hangmen, juries, etc.;
and all these different lines of business,
which form equally many categories
of the social division of labour,
develop different capacities of the human spirit,
create new needs
and new ways of satisfying them.

—KARL MARX

THE ROOM WAS SMALL AND TIDY. The walls were covered in
light blue flocked wallpaper with a scattered pattern of pale yellow
English primroses. It was furnished with a bed, a washstand, a plain
pine bureau, a small table, and two wicker chairs. Pamela was sitting
on one of the chairs in the far corner of the room, rocking ever so
slightly back and forth as Moriarty entered, with Epp a step behind.
The front legs of the chair rose as she rocked back and then landed
with a slight bump as she went forward, a slow and monotonous beat
like the thumping of the human heart. The gas mantle on the wall
above the bed burned low, and the light spread cautiously about as
though it didn't want to intrude on the shadows.

The girl had stopped sobbing and was staring out through the slightly parted window curtains with no sign of interest in what she saw. Her light brown hair was done up in an untidy bun held together by three red-lacquered Japanese chopsticks thrust through the bun in seemingly random directions. Her plum-colored silk robe was tied high under her small breasts. Her face looked bland and untroubled, so that one might suppose that her red eyes and the occasional tear that ran down her cheek were the result of some mild physical affliction.

"Pamela," Moriarty said, slowly crossing the room, "may we speak with you?"

She gave no response, no sign that she had heard him or was aware of his presence.

Moriarty stopped in front of her. "Pamela? Heather?" He slipped his pince-nez into his jacket pocket and squatted by her side. "What are you looking at?" he asked.

"Come now, gel," said Epp sharply, striding across the room with great policeman's strides and stopping next to the professor, "answer the gentleman's questions. There's a good gel."

Moriarty took the girl's hand, and she neither resisted nor welcomed his touch. He pressed the back of her hand with his thumb and noted her lack of response. He took the magnifying monocle from his vest pocket and used it to peer closely into each eye. "Her mind is somewhere else," he said. "Possibly in retreat from confronting whatever it was that she saw. I shall attempt to bring it back. Although perhaps I will not be doing her a kindness."

Epp watched Moriarty's antics with resignation. His was not to reason why.

Moriarty took a pocket watch from his waistcoat and held it before the girl's eyes, letting it dangle from about six inches of chain. "Can you see the watch?" he asked, his voice soothing and gentle. "The silver face is engraved with a representation of the solar system. See this little dot here? This tiny orb represents the planet Earth. Here, I'll move the watch back and forth, back and forth, like the solar system moving through the vastness of space. Watch it and relax and consider how meaningless and unimportant our life here is: tiny specks on a tiny orb circling a tiny sun—see, that's the sun in the center— one of thousands, millions, of stars stretching for all of eternity."

"Cheerful!" muttered Epp.

"I've always found that a consideration of the futility of life is most relaxing," Moriarty said in the same soft voice. "It puts one's problems in the proper perspective."

He continued the mesmeric induction for a while, gradually adding the phrases of instruction and command and repeating them over and over in a soft, compelling tone. "Listen to my voice . . . Ignore all other sounds but my voice . . . Concentrate on my voice and let it be your guide . . . You will answer my questions . . . You will not be afraid . . ."

Then, finally, he tested. "Do you hear what I say?"

There was no response.

"You may speak," Moriarty told her. "Do you hear my voice?"

"Yes," Pamela responded, her voice flat and low.

"And only my voice?"

"Only."

"And you will listen to my voice, only my voice, and follow my instructions?"

There was a pause while she, even in her trance, thought this over.

"No harm will come to you, I assure you," Moriarty told her in the same calm tone. "My voice will lead you through the pain and the harm, and bad things will not touch you. I will protect you. My voice will guide you."

"All right," she said.

Moriarty nodded and put the pocket watch back in his waistcoat pocket. "I want you to go back in time, go back to when you were just a little girl. Can you do that?"

"Yes," she said and nodded her head abruptly up and down.

"You're a little girl now, and nobody has hurt you and you're not afraid." He turned to Epp and added in a low voice, "I'm taking a chance with this. God knows what her childhood was like."

"I wouldn't choose to return to mine," Epp said. "Much of it, anyway. *Ipso facto.*"

Moriarty returned his attention to the girl. "Tell me your name," he asked.

"Pamewa," she said. "Pamewa Dilwaddy, so it please your worship." Her voice was the voice of a little girl, hesitant and singsong.

"How old are you, Pamela?"

"Seven years old and two months, so it please your worship." She made a gesture as though she were attempting to curtsey without rising from her chair.

"Where are you, Pamela?"

"In the cottage."

"I see. Where is the cottage?"

"It's where me and my mum live."

"We're wasting time," Epp declared. "Get on with it."

Moriarty cast a mild but reproachful gaze on Epp and then turned back to the girl. "Are you happy here, in the cottage?"

"Happy?"

"Yes. Do you feel happy?"

Epp snorted.

"I ain't never thought about it, your worship." The little girl's voice held a hint of wonder. "I don't feel bad, anyways. Not about most things, anyways."

"That will have to do," Moriarty told her. "Now you will keep feeling just that way—not bad about most things—and let us move ahead in your life until you're just a little older. Let's say sixteen. You're six-teen now. It's your sixteenth birthday. Can you take me to your six-teenth birthday?"

She nodded. "Yes."

"Good. Now what's happening?"

She held out her hand, palm up, and then squeezed it into a tight little fist. "Thank you, sir," she said. "That's rightly kind of you."

"Who are you speaking to?" Moriarty asked.

"The gent what just gave me this," she replied, raising her clenched fist higher.

"What have you got there?" Moriarty asked.

"Three bob," she said. "What this gent just gave me. Just for doing it. And on a bed. And he says I can stay the night, the room's paid for."

"A nice man, is he?"

Pamela nodded. "Ain't many of them about, I can tell you."

She began to get up from the chair, and Moriarty put a restraining arm on her shoulder. "Where are you going?" he asked.

"Got to sponge out," she said. "Can't take no chances."

"Blimey!" said Epp.

"The day is over now," Moriarty told Pamela, gently pushing her back into her seat. "All that is done and time has passed. You're at Madam Mollie's house now."

"I am?" Pamela looked around, her mouth opening in what might be surprise.

Moriarty refrained from asking her what she was seeing.

She examined her arms for a long moment and then parted her robe to stare down speculatively at her legs. "I'm clean," she said.

"What's that supposed to mean?" Epp complained.

"You are very clean," Moriarty agreed.

"Mollie makes the girls wash all over." She raised one leg to take a closer look. "Even our feet!"

"It's supposed to be very healthful," Moriarty said.

"Some of the gentlemen," Pamela said, wrinkling her nose, "aren't so very healthful. Them we bathes first, if as how they let us. Most of them do."

"I imagine so," Moriarty agreed.

Pamela giggled. "What gentleman don't like having two girls in their chemises going at him with soap and sponge whilst he's tubbing? None that I've seen."

Epp made a sound that was somewhere between a cough and a snort. "Get on with it, man!" He told Moriarty in a hoarse whisper.

"Impatience is not regarded as a virtue," Moriarty said, "even in our hasty society. Do you want speed or do you want results?"

"I doubt there are any results to be had," Epp replied testily.

"We'll see," said Moriarty. He turned back to the girl. "I want you to think of Rose now. Can you do that?"

Her face tightened and her chin quivered.

"Not as you last saw her," Moriarty continued, "but as you remember her. Your friend. Your good friend. You're back with her now."

"Rose," Pamela said softly.

"Your good friend," Moriarty suggested.

"She's the best," Pamela agreed.

"Tell me about it."

"We stay together," she said. "We go to the shops together. Of a time we see gentlemen together, when the gent wants such. Of a time we sleep together and hold each other when the one of us is sad or otherwise upset or hurt."

"Do you ever go to plays or entertainments?" Moriarty asked.

Epp gave an exasperated sigh and stepped over to a wooden chair across the room and sat down.

"We go to the music halls," she said. "The Palace, and the Empire, and the Alhambra. We get all dressed up and fancy, we do."

"Fancy indeed!" Epp mouthed.

"Like regular ladies," she said.

Epp snorted.

"Well, now we're going to go to the day at the end of the week before when you were hiding in the closet and Rose got . . . hurt," Moriarty told her. "But you're not really going to be there. You're going to be looking down at it from a distance, as if it were a performance at the Alhambra. It can't affect you. You're just a spectator. It's just a play."

"In the audience," Pamela whispered.

"That's right—just in the audience."

"Just a play."

"Just so. The play's beginning now. What do you see?"

After a long wait, Pamela said, "Heather is hiding in the wardrobe."

"Wait a sec," said Epp, leaning forward. "That's her name, ain't it? When she's, um, working."

"Yes," Moriarty agreed. "She's looking down at herself and that room from a safe height."

"Interesting," Epp admitted. *"Verbum sap."*

"Why, Pamela?" Moriarty asked the girl. "Why is Heather hiding in the wardrobe?"

"It's a game we plays with the baron," she said. "When I don't have a gentleman of my own I hides in the wardrobe, and then when Rose and the baron have been at it for a while, I sneaks out and comes up next to the bed. The baron always acts as like he's surprised. Then he says, 'My two flowers,' or something of the sort, and I joins them."

"And this night?" Moriarty asked. "This last night? You are— Heather is—hiding in the wardrobe when the baron comes in?"

The line of her mouth tightened and turned down, and she clenched and unclenched her fists.

"You're in the audience, Pamela, watching the story unfold," Moriarty told her. "Just in the audience. Just watching."

"I see it," she said. "Rose and the baron is coming in, and Heather is squatting in the wardrobe peeking through the keyhole."

"Then what?"

"The baron sits on the side of the bed, and he says, 'Come here, my little princess,' like always. Well, it's always something of the sort. Sometimes 'little duchess,' and once it was 'my slender rani.' I remember that one because I had to go ask what it meant. Mollie says it's like an Indian princess. So I says to Rose that she should ask the baron if he'd ever been to India." She looked down, and her voice changed to a husky vibrato. "But she never did. Never did."

"So the baron said, 'Come here, my little princess'? And Rose went over?"

"She dances over to him," said Pamela. "Dances. Kind of, you know, twisty-like. What men like to watch."

"Does the baron like it?"

"Seems to. He gets this silly smile on his face, and his little mustache starts twitching like it does when he's pleased. Very pleased, if you see what I mean."

"I do," Moriarty told her. "Then? What happens next?"

Pamela's eyes grew wide, and both hands came up to her mouth. A soft, high-pitched keening sound began somewhere deep inside her thin frame and slowly got louder until it filled the room.

"Now, now," Moriarty said sharply. "You're outside the event looking in. It may be hard to look at, but you've no part in it. You're sitting with me in the audience! The two of us together looking at the scene as though it were on a stage."

"Looking," she said.

"That's right."

"From the orchestra."

"If you like. Or we could be in the balcony, or in a box."

The keening stopped. "It's a frightful thing, it is," she said. "A frightful thing. All sudden-like, and it don't make no sense."

"Tell it to me," Moriarty said. "Describe it to me as it happened. We'll sit here together in the audience, and you'll tell me what you see."

"Bam!" she said. "Like that. Bam! The door throws open and these two men jumps in like. All in black they is. And the baron, he cries out, 'What the . . . ,' and starts to leap out of bed. But the tall, thin one, he coshes him across the head, and the baron falls down like a sack. Then Rose, she starts in to scream, but before it can come out of her mouth, the other one, he coshes her, too, and she falls flat on the bed."

"Can you describe the two men?"

"The tall, thin one is . . . tall. Even taller than the baron, and thin. He moves like a—" she thought about it for a second. "Like a cat—all sort of smooth and slicket and pleased with himself. The other was shorter, but not real short or nothin', and thick and wide and sort of solid-like. He had this thin, wide mustache as well."

"What happened then?" Moriarty asked.

Pamela turned her head sideways and cast her eyes up so that she was looking at the ceiling. She said nothing.

Epp, who had been standing aside for most of this, came and bent over the girl. "Come on, now!" he said sharply. "What did you see? What happened next?"

Pamela's mouth formed into an O. Of astonishment? Fear? Horror? It was impossible to tell.

"Describe it for me," Moriarty said, "what you see happening up there on the stage. Remember, you and I are here, and the stage is way up there. Very far away. And nothing happening on it is real. It's just playacting." He paused and then said, "What do you see?"

"They drags in Mr. Fetch and pushes him under the bed. I guess they must've coshed him too, 'cause he was all loose-like."

"What happened next?" asked Moriarty.

"Then the shorter one, he goes over to the door. And the taller one, he goes over to the bed, and he takes out a knife . . ." Her eyes got large and round, her face turned white, and tears formed in the corners of her eyes. "And he laughs . . . giggles . . . like sumfing funny was happening—" She choked up and began gasping for breath. "And—"

"That's enough," Moriarty told her. "Really, it's all right. That will do. We won't watch what happens anymore. Let's go past that to what happens next."

After a pause her breath became regular, and a few seconds later she was able to raise her head. "Next?"

"After the tall one finishes with . . . what he's doing on the bed. What happens next?"

Pamela thought it over for a few seconds, and a look of great pain passed over her face before it became once again impassive. "Next," she said.

"Yes," Moriarty agreed.

"Next what happens is the thick one, he pushes the window open and sticks his head out," she said.

"Ah!" Moriarty said. "The window. I should have thought of that."

"Thought of what?" Epp demanded, sounding aggrieved.

"The window. If the, ah, baron was not the perpetrator of these horrors, and it looks now as though he was not, they, whoever they are, had to get him out, didn't they? And without chancing being seen."

"So they just flung him out the window?"

"I fancy they used a rope of some sort."

Pamela nodded. "A rope," she said. "They tied a rope around his middle and lowered him out the window. Him in his silk underdrawers."

"Did they say anything, these strange men? Anything at all?"

"The shorter one. He says, 'Feet, feet!' a couple of times. The taller giggles a bit more, but he says nothing."

"Feet, feet?"

" 'Feet, feet!' he said. Then he said again, 'Feet, feet,' and that's what all he said."

"Interesting," said Moriarty.

"Nonsense!" said Epp.

"Let us just look at the taller man—at his face. Can you see his face?"

She nodded.

"All right. Look at his face. Pay no attention to what he's doing. It doesn't concern you now."

Pamela's face twisted into an ugly grimace. "What he's doing . . ."

"No, Pamela, he isn't doing anything," Moriarty said in a soft, insistent voice. "He's frozen where he is. He isn't moving at all."

"Not moving." Her face relaxed.

"Now," Moriarty said, "can you see his face?"

"His face? Of course."

"Good. What does he look like?"

Pamela was silent for a minute, her nose wrinkled with concentration. "He looks a bit like the baron, don't he?"

"I don't know," Moriarty said. "Does he?"

"A bit. Yet his nose is bigger, isn't it?"

"Why, so it is," Moriarty agreed. "What else?"

She squinted into empty space, seeing a tableau of the past. "His ears."

"What about his ears?"

"They're kind of flat at the bottom. Not like the baron's, which are round."

"Very good, Pamela. Now, would you know the man if you saw him again?"

"See him again?" Pamela started crying softly, but she seemed to be unaware of the tears coming down her face. "Yes, I'd surely know him if I see him again. I surely would."

"Now, the other man. What did he look like?"

"The other man?"

"Yes. The one who said, 'Feet, feet.'"

"He was shorter, and kind of round. Not fat, as you might say, but round. About the face, you know."

"Round face?"

"That's it."

"And his hair?"

"He had hair okay. It were sort of pasted down on his head, all straight-like, but there were a bit of it."

"What color?"

"Black, I'd say."

"Would you know him if you saw him again?"

She thought it over. "I would," she said finally.

Moriarty nodded. "Thank you, Pamela. You're being very helpful. We'll go to sleep now. Just close your eyes and go to sleep. Clear your mind of the past and sleep."

"Sleep," she said. Her eyes closed slowly, and her head lowered.

Moriarty lifted her out of the chair and carried her to the bed, where he gently placed her, her head on the pillow. "You will sleep through the night," he told her, "and let your mind cleanse itself of these memories. When you awaken they will seem a distant dream, unable to hurt you any longer. You will be refreshed and happy, or reasonably so, and no longer troubled by the past."

He rose. "I think we can leave now," he said. "I'll have to speak to Miss Mollie and have the girl sent around to my house tomorrow."

"Come now, Professor," Epp said. "I don't see why—"

"One treatment will hardly be enough to relieve her of these memories," said Moriarty. "I owe it to her to finish what I began. Then, of course, there's the more important reason."

"What might that be?" asked Epp.

"She's the only one who knows what our villains look like."

Epp snorted. "A big nose and flat ears? A round head? Not much of a description."

"I have no doubt that it can be improved on," Moriarty said.

"And what was that 'feet' nonsense?"

"Feet, feet," Moriarty said musingly. "It doesn't tell us much, but it does indicate where the answer might be found."

Epp turned to look at him. "Does it now?" he asked.

"Ipso facto," Moriarty told him. *"Veritas curat."*

CHAPTER TWELVE

THE MUMMER CREEPS

Whoe'er has travelled life's dull round,
Where'er his stages may have been,
May sigh to think he still has found
The warmest welcome at an inn.

—WILLIAM SHENSTONE

BENJAMIN BARNETT SAT AT EASE in his accustomed chair in Professor Moriarty's study. It *was,* he reflected, his accustomed chair, even though it had been some two years since he had last settled into it. That part of his life he had spent as the professor's associate had not been walled off in his memory or faded away into the past; it had been set aside like a pair of once-worn shoes, ready to be stepped into when the occasion arose.

A pair of ill-fitting shoes, his wife, Cecily, would say. Barnett's association with the professor had brought him into danger many times and face-to-face with true evil more than once, but always with the knowledge that he himself fought on the side of good. Possibly not always "good" as his stiff-necked Anglican parson brother-in-law would have it, but good nonetheless. A melodramatic way to think of it, he admitted, but there it was. He refused to think of life as a tragedy and couldn't quite bring himself to think of it as a comedy— although he suspected that Moriarty saw all human activities as an unending source of humor—so he was left with melodrama or farce, and little to choose between them.

"So it would seem," he told Moriarty, winding up his story of the excursion to the Fox and Hare, "that Esterman was not merely mistaken, but was certainly lying when he testified that he had seen you at the inn—and that he was doing it at the behest of his former employer, the baron."

"Interesting," said Moriarty.

"That ain't the half of it," the mummer added from his perch on the corner of the leather couch. "Baron what's-'is-face was busy robbing himself that night, is what I sez."

Moriarty removed his pince-nez and raised an eyebrow. "Is that so?" he asked.

"Just so." The mummer hooked his thumbs into his green braces and struck a rhetorical pose. "You can fool some of the people all of the time, sez I, and all of the people most of the time, but you can't nohow fool me. Not much, anywise."

Moriarty nodded. "Indeed," he agreed. "Just how are Baron Thornton-Hoxbary and his minions not fooling you this week?"

"Well, stands to reason, don't it?" The mummer gesticulated with his right thumb, waggling it about in front of him. "Here are the facts what I will lay in front of you what I uncovered in my search through yon publican's private and personal belongings while he were in a state of sublime insobriety. First, it's the baron himself personally what actually owns the Fox and Hare."

"How do you know that?" Moriarty asked.

"Simple enough," the mummer said. "He has a ledger book, don't he—"

"Who has? Esterman?" Barnett interrupted.

"Himself," the mummer affirmed.

"I didn't know that!" Barnett was miffed. "You didn't tell me anything about a ledger. Is that what you went looking for while I was plying Esterman with the professor's expensive port?"

"I would have settled for less," the mummer said. "Anyways, I comes upon this ledger book, as I says, and I gloms onto it for long enough to take down some numbers."

"What made you think they'd be of interest?" asked the professor.

"The very simple fact that the book was, as it were, hidden," answered the little man. "You hides swag, you hides or locks up valuable knickknacks what you don't rightly have the lawful possession of, you hides your professional tools and appurtenances if you happens to be a coiner or a cracksman, but whatever for would you hide a ledger book?"

"Where was it hidden?" asked Moriarty.

"It were behind a false panel under the counter," the mummer told him.

"You got it open with us both sitting there?" Barnett asked.

"You wasn't exactly paying attention to what was going on under the counter," the mummer told him. "You talked and talked, and did a marvelous job of keeping him busy while I crept along on my hands and knees beneath your notice and found the panel. When yon publican laid his head on the table and entered the land of snore I went back under the counter to take a glim at whatsoever might be crouched inside the thing, and it were that there ledger book."

"And in it you found?" Moriarty prompted.

"Every month Esterman pays out coin to one BTH."

"Baron Thornton-Hoxbary?" suggested Barnett.

"Who else?"

"Well, the baron gave him the money to buy the place," Barnett said. "Maybe part of it was just a loan and he's paying it off. Or maybe the baron owns the building itself, but not the business, and it's rent. That would still indicate a degree of familiarity in their relationship that didn't come out at the trial. "

"It wouldn't have meant anything if it had," commented Moriarty. "The baron wasn't suspected of anything. We need something of which to suspect him."

"Well, I hadn't finished telling you what's what," griped the mummer, "had I?"

"Ah!" Moriarty exclaimed. "I apologize, Mummer. We shouldn't have interrupted you."

"Nobody has no respect for little men," the mummer objurgated, "but I shall go on."

"Oh, please do," Barnett said.

The mummer gave him a glance that would wither lupin and took a breath. "The payments weren't for a loan or rent because they were never for the same amount. Besides, they was monthly, and rent is usually paid quarterly."

"Still," Moriarty said. "That makes them the baron's share of the profits, but it's not illegal to go into business with your ex-valet. Suggestive, but not illegal."

"There's more," the mummer said. "Wait for it—wait for it."

"Go on."

"Some men take rooms at the Fox and Hare, and they don't nohow pay for the rooms."

"I don't see—" Barnett began.

"The baron pays for 'em. Like, I'd say, half the going rate." The mummer paused and looked around him. "Don'tcher see? The two of them, the baron and Esterman, must be a pair what delights in squeezing pennies till they squeal. Can'tcher picture the conversation? 'I'm going to have me men staying here on occasion,' says the baron. 'Fine, but they're going to pay like anyone else. I has me expenses, after all,' says Esterman. 'I'll pay for them blokes as I sends here,' replies the baron, 'but no more than sixpence a bed.' 'Eight pence,' says Esterman. 'Seven,' replies the baron, 'and that includes dinner.' 'All right,' says Esterman, 'but just the ordinary. They wants a cut off the joint, they pays extra.' 'Done and done,' says the baron. They shakes hands on it, and then counts their fingers."

"So?" asked Barnett. "What of it?"

"Two of the blokes what I found in the ledger book, what the baron paid for, are 'Groper' and 'Piggy.'"

Barnett shook his head. "So?"

"Cast your thoughts back," said the mummer, "to the events surrounding the robbery. Two of the supposed robbers got themselves killed, and their monikers, according to the rozzers, were Gerald 'Groper' Swintey and Albert 'Piggy' Stain. And it's the baron himself who's paying for their rooms the night before the robbery."

Moriarty pressed his hands together and rested his chin on the outstretched fingers and spent some seconds in thought. "Interesting," he allowed finally. "Did you find any other sobriquets in the book for that evening?"

"Monikers, you mean? I thought of that," said the mummer, "and indeed there were a few other names what were not those their mothers gave them, unless their mothers was trodding heavily on the gooseberry bush."

Barnett looked puzzled but, as he opened his mouth, Moriarty raised a hand. "Don't ask," he told Barnett. "Let it pass."

"There was 'Yennuf Yob' and 'Cobow,'" the mummer said, "and 'the Swede.'"

"Clearly persons of interest," Moriarty said. "We'll have to unearth these individuals and see what they have to say."

"I hope they ain't buried too deep," the mummer observed.

"What sort of names are they?" asked Barnett. "Cobow? Yennuf Yob?"

"One of 'em's a funny boy," said the mummer, "and the other's a bastard."

"'Yob' is East End reverse slang for 'boy,'" Moriarty explained. "Much favored among the villainous classes. Evidently someone with a sense of humor created 'Yennuf Yob' for 'Funny Boy.' Whether referring to the gentleman's appearance or his antics or his mode of conversation, I couldn't say. 'Cobow' is one step more complicated. It's reverse for *w-o-b-o-c*, 'without benefit of clergy.'"

"Which is better, ain't it, than calling him a bastard?" asked the mummer rhetorically.

"A distinction that should not be made," observed Moriarty, "and that certainly shouldn't be inflicted on the children."

"So I says meself," said the mummer. "I fancy these are the other lads what participated in yon robbery which went so spectacularly astray."

"There are many other possible explanations," said Moriarty, "but I'm rather fond of yours, so we'll assume it is so unless further information proves it false."

"Why would the baron be robbing himself?" Barnett asked.

The mummer raised his arm, his fist clenched except for the forefinger, which was pointed at the ceiling. "That question," he intoned, "may be divided into two parts. The first part: 'Why?' Me father, a God-fearing man, used to say, 'Never ask why, for it may come to pass that you will be answered, and you probably won't like what you hear.' The second part: 'Would the baron be robbing himself?' Well, it certainly seems that way, don't it?"

"I doubt the baron was robbing himself," said Moriarty. "Find out who his guests were for the weekend, and what at least one of them was carrying that the baron might covet. We might also profit by a closer look at what the morning papers called the 'rash of robberies' at the great houses in the baron's neighborhood. Determining what was taken in them might give us an idea of just what it is that the baron covets."

"How do we go about doing that?" asked the mummer. "We going to grow us a plant in the baron's household?"

"I fancy that Mr. Barnett can find someone to handle it," Moriarty suggested. "Perhaps one of his employees at the news service. I'll pay his salary and expenses, of course."

Barnett nodded. "There are certain advantages to being in the newspaper racket," he said. "One of them being the implicit permission to be horribly nosy."

"I'll leave it to your people to find out what can be found out," Moriarty told him.

"I'll put young Blake on it," said Barnett. "He's a natural-born ferret."

"Good," Moriarty said. "Tell him to be a bit cautious in his inquiries. We don't want them to get the wind up, and, in the fullness of time, we shall do something about the larcenous baron. For now there's something else that may require your assistance."

"You running about with them toffs what Mr. Maws told me about?" the mummer asked. "Dukes and duchesses and the like?"

"They took me out of prison," Moriarty said, "in return for doing a little job. One that presents an interesting intellectual challenge, as it happens."

"All about the missing prince, is it?" the mummer asked.

Barnett suddenly looked interested. "What missing prince?"

"Who told you about that?" Moriarty asked, frowning.

"Mr. Maws again," the mummer said. "He heard it from the duke's valet."

"No secret is safe from the servants," Moriarty said.

"Which poses a puzzle," said Barnett. "If I may turn back for a moment to the problem of the prevaricating baron. Why did Thornton-Hoxbary's servants not know of the impending robbery?"

"I imagine they're mostly local people," Moriarty surmised. "Not up to robbery and murder. Then, too, it adds to the verisimilitude to have them trussed up during the robbery and free to tell stories about the experience ever after. Besides, if they'd known about it, the whole county would have known about it right quick enough. No—the baron had to import his talent from the city, and trusted no one local except the innkeeper."

"What was in cahoots with him," the mummer expanded.

"That hangs together," Barnett agreed. "Now: What missing prince, and how long has he been missing? Missing from where? And who took him? And why?"

Moriarty raised an eyebrow. "Ever the journalist," he said. "Sit back, my children, and I'll tell you a story."

CHAPTER THIRTEEN

THE PROFESSOR EXPLAINS

*"Mine is a long and sad tale!" said
the Mouse, turning to Alice and sighing.
"It's a long tail, certainly," said Alice,
looking down with wonder at the Mouse's tail, "but
why do you call it sad?"*

—LEWIS CARROLL

PROFESSOR MORIARTY LEANED BACK AND PRESSED his palms together under his chin. "My story involves several gruesome murders that we know of," he began. "They seem to be part of a complex plot against the government conducted by an unknown antagonist for an unknown purpose. The facts are barely believable and, at the moment, constitute a secret of the first water. It would not be mine to tell, but I am deeply involved in the investigation now and certain possibilities have crept to the fore. Your assistance, I believe, would be invaluable."

"My, 'e do talk pretty, don't 'e?" the mummer said. "'Ave you any idea of what 'e's talking about?"

Barnett shook his head. "You're dropping your *H*'s," he said.

"Leave them lie," said the mummer.

"I shall explain," said the professor. "But first—understand that what I tell you is to go no farther than this room."

"Mum's the word," Barnett said.

"Like 'e says," added the mummer.

Moriarty leaned back. "There is an exclusive, ah, gentlemen's establishment on Gladston Square known as Mollie's," he said.

"Mollie's?" Barnett interjected. "I've heard of the place, but I didn't know where it was."

"Oooo! And you a married man," chided the mummer.

Barnett turned to glare at the little man. "In my capacity as a journalist I hear many things," he said. "Many of the, ah, unusable stories that come to my attention concern the demimonde and its relationship to the upper classes."

"How the rich and titled despoils themselves, eh?" said the mummer.

"How the poor take their pleasures—such as they may be—is of little interest to anyone," Barnett said, "possibly not even the poor themselves." He turned back to Professor Moriarty. "This place— Mollie's—has been mentioned."

Moriarty nodded. "It's where all this began, as far as we know." He told them the story of murder and abduction, skimming over the fine details but letting them know what there was to know. Then he stopped talking and looked at them both, his eyebrows slightly raised.

"Gorblimey!" said the mummer.

"What a story!" Barnett said, smacking his fist into his hand. "What a story! Incredible! The audacity! Who could be responsible for such a monstrous thing?"

"That's what I've been released from durance vile to discover."

"They couldn't just let you out because you had nothing to do with the robbery and the subse-bloody-quent killings, and that baron and his cohorts are a gang of lying, thieving, conniving swine, now could they?" asked the mummer indignantly.

Moriarty grimaced. "Much as I'd like to hie over to Wedsbridge this very evening and speak with His Lordship, it will have to wait," he said. "We'll take care of the baron and his cohort subsequently. My job right now, and yours if you're willing to assist me, is to unravel the affair of the missing prince."

"If that girl hadn't been hiding in the closet . . ."

Moriarty nodded. "Were it not for Pamela we'd be running around in circles trying to discover why the prince had run away and whether he had killed these children. Although there were sufficient indications that he had not. "

Barnett pursed his lips. "Poor girl," he said. "What she saw . . ."

Moriarty looked at him thoughtfully. "Tell me, Barnett," he said, "how does your wife feel about 'fallen women'?"

"She feels that they should be helped to their feet and given a decent job," he said. "She thinks that there wouldn't be so many women selling themselves on the streets of London if employment of a decent sort could be found for them. She thinks all men are selfish beasts. She can go on for quite a while about it, too. Why?"

"Pamela is here—staying with me."

"Whatever for?" Barnett asked. Then he felt himself blushing for the first time in two decades. "That is, if you don't mind my asking."

"She's the only person who knows what our mystery man looks like."

"Looks a lot like Prince Albert, I'd be thinking," said the mummer.

"Not him," said Moriarty, "but his companion. His keeper, I would imagine, since anyone with his sort of bloodlust can't be let out on the streets alone."

"Specially if they don't want to blow the gaff before they're ready to have it go up," the mummer added.

"Even so," Moriarty agreed. "Thus Pamela may prove invaluable to us—and since our villains seem to move about in the upper levels of society, we may need to take Pamela into circles in which a woman of her class would stand out by her every gesture and be lost entirely if she opened her mouth."

"And?" Barnett prompted.

"And Mrs. Barnett has had some experience in teaching people how to move about in society, if I am not mistaken."

Barnett nodded. "Foreigners, mostly. She learned the skill from her father, who is a philologist and phonetician of some repute."

Moriarty nodded. "Professor Henry Perrine," he said. "The developer of the Perrine Simplified Phonetical Alphabet. Quite remarkable, actually. I've read his book."

" 'E teached me everything what I knows," said the mummer, nodding and cocking his head to one side with a crooked little grin.

"So will you ask your wife if she's willing to come over here for a few hours a day and tutor the girl?" Moriarty asked Barnett. "I'll see that she's handsomely remunerated from the public purse."

"It will take more than a few hours a day if it's done right," Barnett said, "but I think she'll be fascinated by the project. I'll speak to her as soon as I get home."

"Very good," Moriarty said. "Speaking on behalf of queen and country, something I doubt that I'll ever be able to do again, I thank you."

Barnett leaned back in his chair and stared at the ceiling. "So," he said, "what do we have here? Prince Albert Victor, grandson of the queen and second in line to the throne, is going around cutting people up. Only he isn't, but someone wants us to think he is. Why?"

" 'To the matter that you mention I have given much attention,' as Mr. Gilbert has it, and I have a possible answer. Of course, as is the way with answers, it only leads to another question."

"Answer away," said Barnett.

"Consider what would be accomplished were Prince Albert Victor to be accused of the savage killing and mutilation of an innocent girl—and boy. The accusation itself, unless immediately and forcefully refuted, could set in play a chain of events that could, the Duke of Shorham assures me, topple the throne. Or come damnably close."

"Couldn't hurt," the mummer observed. "After all, what 'as the 'Widder at Windsor' done for us lately?"

"Ah, but you wouldn't like the near results of such a collapse. Trust me."

"Somehow," said Barnett, "I never fancied you as a monarchist."

"The human race has not solved the problem of governing itself yet," Moriarty said. "Nor is it likely to in the near future, but a constitutional monarchy is as good as anything we've come up with yet." He paused and then went on. "It's not that I particularly favor the present form of government. The nobility in particular, in this country and, indeed, all others that I'm aware of, are intrenched, intransigent, inflexible, for the most part unintelligent, and control an inordinate amount of the country's wealth. However, what would follow the monarchy, if it were to be toppled in such a crisis, would not be an improvement. Most likely we'd see chaos for the near future."

"I'm not sure I follow, Professor," Barnett said. "What would be throne-toppling about Victoria's grandson, who's believed to be not quite right anyway, turning out to be a murderer? Quite a scandal I daresay, but put the monarchy itself in danger? I don't see it."

"You're an American at heart," Moriarty said, "for all that you've lived here for—what?—eight years now. For you the monarchy is a quaint relic that's outlived its usefulness, and the queen and all the royals are an archaic holdover from another age."

"I couldn't have put it better myself," Barnett confessed. "Have I got it wrong?"

"No," said Moriarty, "not at all. But you're not allowing for the intangibles of the institution."

"How's that?" asked Barnett.

"It completely leaves out of account the question of the royal will and the interesting problem of regal intransigence."

Barnett thought this over. After a lengthy pause he reprised, "How's that?"

"The queen, through losing her direct power, has become, in a perverse way, the voice of the people. If Victoria accepts a law, then the British people accept it. They look to her to keep the government honest. Not that they think of it that way, most of them."

"Now that's what I would call an interesting notion," the mummer said. "I ain't sure you're right, but I ain't sure you're wrong neither."

"Think of her as the nation's mother," Moriarty said, "and our national mum is scrupulously, even excessively, proper and moral."

"Granted," said Barnett.

"'Er Majesty's a proper prude, all right," the mummer agreed.

"So what would the reaction of the British people be if it were suddenly revealed that she'd been concealing a horrible secret—that one of her own children was a fiend, an insane killer, and she'd known about it and did nothing, or worse, actively hidden it from the authorities?"

Barnett thought this one over, and after a minute he slowly shook his head. "It would certainly bring the government to a halt," he offered. "Nothing much else would get done while the various organs of the government tried to decide how to act. They'd certainly have to do something—something serious and something fast."

"What I has observed," added the mummer, "is that the more the need for haste, the less haste is achieved."

"I've noticed that myself," Barnett agreed.

"So here's what we have," said Moriarty. "Someone has devised a way of discrediting the British monarchy and has found a tool to help him achieve this end."

"By 'tool' you mean the killer?" Barnett asked.

"That's right," Moriarty agreed. "The murderer himself is clearly mad, but someone, or I think rather some organization, is using his insane proclivities and his chance resemblance to Albert Victor to attempt to disgrace, and perhaps even bring down, the British throne."

"Whatever for?" asked the mummer.

"Ah!" said Moriarty. "That's the question that arises from the answer. Whatever for? Certainly to cause the aforementioned chaos. But out of the chaos they intend to bring—what? And when and how do they intend to raise the curtain on Act Two?"

"Act Two?" asked Barnett.

"Indeed. Act One is a series of murders; two that we know of so far. Act Two will be the startling revelation that HRH Prince Albert Victor is the culprit—that the royal family is harboring, and probably hiding, a monster. The curtain will come down on a lot of screaming and running about."

"And Act Three?" asked Barnett.

"Ah!" Moriarty took his pince-nez from the bridge of his nose and commenced earnestly polishing the lenses with a bit of flannel. "That is the denouement that we must do our utmost to prevent. Whatever it is our unseen antagonists have in mind, I fear we will not like it."

"I don't like it already," said the mummer.

Mr. Maws opened the door and took two stolid steps in. "The Epp gentleman is here," he said.

Moriarty rose. "I must go," he told them.

"What are we to do?" asked Barnett.

"You, if you will, visit your brethren of the pen and see if there is any news, or hint of news, regarding either Albert Victor or mysterious murders being kept from the public. Be extremely circumspect. If you do find any such hints, try to ascertain whence they originated. Be even more discreet about that."

"Fair enough," said Barnett. "There are always rumors and fanciful stories floating about concerning the royal family. I'll gather them in under the pretext—the altogether plausible pretext, now that I think of it—of doing a piece on what the British think of their sovereign for some American magazine."

"Excellent," agreed Moriarty.

"I'll mosey about amongst the costermongers and their ilk," offered the mummer. "They always seem to see and hear things afore the general population."

Moriarty nodded. "Good idea," he said. "If either of you comes up with something, report back here. Mr. Maws will take any messages."

"Where will you be?" Barnett asked.

Moriarty pursed his lips. "Following in the footsteps of a monster," he said.

[CHAPTER FOURTEEN]

GILES PATERNOSTER

Buttercup:
  Things are seldom what they seem,
    Skim milk masquerades as cream;
    Highlows pass as patent leathers;
    Jackdaws strut in peacock's feathers.
Captain:
  Very true,
  So they do.

—W. S. GILBERT

THE WALLS OF THE NARROW BASEMENT ROOM at the south end of Le Château d'Espagne were of an ancient-looking red-gray brick and had a recently scrubbed look, as of an operating theater or an abattoir. The single window high on the west wall provided a narrow view of an overgrown thorn bush with hints of sky. Six gas sconces on the walls spread an inadequate yellowish light throughout the room. A heavy oak table surrounded by five massive oak chairs squatted a few feet out from the east wall. Scattered about the rest of the room were a marble baptismal font, a four-foot-wide, six-foot-high cast-iron safe with no known combination, a standing eighteen-branch wrought-iron candelabra, a glass-front cabinet holding sexual esoterica, much of it of delicately blown glass, and a solid oak whipping post. On the wall above the table framed in black silk, a great silver cross hung inverted.

Giles Paternoster, master of the château, sat across the table from Moriarty and Chief Inspector Epp. He was a tall, gaunt man with a long, bony, cleft chin and prominent ears, one of which was pierced for a large gold earring in the shape of an eight-pointed star, and he appeared to be somewhere between forty and ageless. He wore a loose-fitting black suit with a thin clerical collar, highly polished black shoes, and a red fez with a gold tassel. A massive gold ankh hung from a thick gold chain around his neck.

Leaning back with his arms folded across his chest, Paternoster surveyed his two guests. "It would be fitting for me and my organization to receive a modicum of credit for calling in the gendarmes without so much as touching the poor lad's body," he said, his voice deep, his words measured, and his accent thick, broad, sibilant, and nasal. "Most of my helpers were of the opinion that, were we to just toss the wretched thing in the Thames or leave it in a dustbin in Eastchapel, all our troubles would disappear. Yet I said no, that would not be just or, as you say, proper. We should treat the lad's earthly remains with as much dignity as possible under the circumstances, and we'd best call in the constabulary. So, thusly, we did that."

"You didn't exactly call in the Yard," Epp pointed out. "You called in Inspectors Danzip and Warth, both, as it happens, members of your little club."

"And both," Paternoster amended, "officers in the Yard's Criminal Investigation Division."

"You thought they'd hush it up, now, *anguis in herba*. Didn't you?"

Paternoster looked around, a puzzled expression on his face. "What right have you to be displeased?" he asked after a moment. "I assumed Danzip and Warth would do whatever it was that they properly had to do. I had no way of knowing what that would be."

"But you had hopes," Epp insisted.

"Every man's entitled to a little hope," replied Paternoster, "or I ask of you, what's a heaven for?"

Moriarty leaned forward and tapped the table with his forefinger. "Come off it," he said.

"Excuse?"

"Your accent is quite delightful, but it does not owe its intonations to any language that I am familiar with."

Paternoster raised his head and looked at Moriarty down the length of his nose. "Truly?" he asked. "This is what you think? And of how many languages do you profess the familiarity?"

"I speak nine languages fluently," Moriarty told him, "and can understand perhaps half a dozen more."

"Really?" Paternoster asked. "Whatever for?"

"A fair question," said Moriarty.

"A waste of time," said Epp.

Moriarty looked at him. "Perhaps," he said and then turned back to Paternoster. "I believe that the use of any language forms a pattern—a matrix, as my friend Reverend Dodgson would call it—in the brain that makes it possible to gather and retrieve other information more easily. The pattern formed by each language is different, and thus the brain acquires subtly different information depending on the language in which an object or event is described. Or perhaps a better way to put it is that it allows one to examine the facts presented to it in a subtly different way. Thus a Frenchman, a German, or a Spaniard, presented with the same information would form a different mental image of it and would react to it in a different way. It has yet to be rigorously determined whether a man fluent in all three of those languages would react differently depending on in which language the information was given him. I'm gathering notes for a possible monograph on the subject."

"Really?" Paternoster reiterated.

Moriarty took out his pince-nez and affixed them to the bridge of his nose. "A familiarity with the tonal distinctions of various languages—the pitch of the vowels, the snap of the consonants—

also makes it possible to ascertain with fair accuracy what the native language of the speaker is regardless of what language he is currently using."

"So?" Paternoster asked.

"So, despite the fact that you speak English with what you fondly regard as an Eastern European accent, your speech patterns make it clear that your native tongue is, indeed, English. I daresay, you were brought up somewhere within the sound of the Bow Bells. Only a Cockney treats his vowels with such disdain."

Paternoster leaned back and stared at the ceiling while he thought this over.

"It's a fair cop," he said finally, his speech now sounding more East London than Eastern Europe.

"Go on!" Epp said. "You mean you ain't—whatever it is you're supposed to be? Well, I never. *Non liquet,* as they say."

"And your, um, society," Moriarty said. "Something about this house, these surroundings, inspires in me a lack of confidence as to their authenticity. There is a certain theatrical quality in all of this. Would I be right in assuming that Le Château d'Espagne is neither as ancient nor as exotic as it seems?"

Paternoster transferred his gaze to the professor. "Say," he said, "you ain't *the* Professor Moriarty, are you?"

Moriarty looked upon him mildly. "I am certainly *a* Professor Moriarty," he said. "Professor James Moriarty of Russell Square, London."

"Well, fancy meeting you here, like this. I've heard a bit or three about you. About your work."

"I hold doctorates in mathematics and astronomy," Moriarty suggested. "Although I haven't lectured in either for a number of years. Are you interested in the sciences? Perchance you've read my little monograph on the relation of the Moebius Band to the Chrysopoeia of Cleopatra?"

Paternoster shook his head—perhaps just to clear it. "Well, what I've heard—well. It surprises me to see you gadding about with the rozzers, is all."

"Ah, *those* stories," Moriarty said with a sigh. "They will follow me about. I assure you there's no more truth to them then, ah, say, some of the things I've been hearing about you."

"The Napoleon of crime," Paternoster said, an inescapable overtone of awe in his voice.

"Really?" Moriarty asked. "That's what you heard?" He leaned back in his chair and laced his fingers together under his chin. "There is one man who calls me that. How did you come to hear it?"

"Well, now—a fella came by here, must have been six or eight months ago, looking for work. A lascar by the look of him. Claimed he jumped ship and daren't go back. Said he was a cook by trade, skilled at the sort of Indian dishes favored by the British pukka sahibs.

"Well, he wasn't no cook, that became clear pretty quick, and he wasn't no lascar neither. A bit of the nut-brown color of his skin rubbed off on the back of his shirt. I didn't mind that too much—we all got secrets—but I had taken him on as a cook, and it was a cook I needed. So I gave him the sack."

"I have no doubt that I know the gentleman in question," Moriarty said. "Do you have any inkling as to what he was actually doing in your establishment since, as you surmised, he assuredly is no cook?"

"He came here looking for you," Paternoster said. "That is, if you is indeed the Professor Moriarty he was gabbing about. He didn't say nothing about astronomy or any moby's band."

"Looking for me?" Moriarty took his pince-nez from his nose and began polishing the lenses with a scrap of red flannel. "That's odd. He certainly knows where I live. He has spent countless hours loitering about my house in some puerile disguise or another."

"Well," Paternoster considered. "Before he found his way out the door he gave me to understand that he was 'wise' to my 'nefarious schemes,' and that they could have been devised by no one other than Professor Moriarty. I said as how I didn't know any Professor Moriarty, and he said not to try his patience."

"And what were these nefarious schemes of yours?"

"He never did say."

"Perhaps something about how you run this establishment?"

Paternoster snorted. "There ain't nothing nefarious about this place. Just a bit of the old slap and tickle, and a little mumbo-jumbo and some fancy costumes for, as it were, atmosphere."

"And the name," said Moriarty. "Le Château d'Espagne."

"Yes, well. I had to call it something, didn't I?"

"You chose well, it would seem by your membership list."

"Well, the château's oh-so-patrician membership wouldn't have been so eager to sign up if I'd called it the Bubble and Squeak, or if they'd known that the mysterious master of the establishment was plain old Charley Washburn of Canning Town, would they now?"

"It would have been a bit off-putting," granted Moriarty.

"What piqued their interest was the odor of the mysterious East," said Washburn. "Metaphorically speaking, as you might say. So that's what I gave them. That and the ritual and appurtenances, which I dragged in to add that air of verisimilitude, as Mr. Gilbert might put it. And of course the smut. Nothing draws a toff in like high-class smut, or so I've found."

Epp sniffed. "And children," he added.

"Ah, well," said Washburn. "Most of the lads are not as young as they look, some of them by quite a bit. The lasses, too, for that matter. Slum kids tend to be smaller and younger-looking for some years due to the wondrous nutritional opportunities they are afforded, and then, all at once, into their twenties, they look older, much older. It's the way we have in this civilized country we inhabit."

Epp gave him a stern glare. "You sound bitter, my man."

"Not I," Washburn said. "I, who was given the splendid opportunity to travel around to various parts of the world, courtesy of Her Majesty's forces, and even remunerated for my troubles at the rate of one and six a day, minus reimbursements for this and that. And all I was required to do in exchange was shoot at people I didn't know while they were shooting back at me."

Epp stiffened. "That, sir, is hardly the way to describe honorable service to queen and country," he said with a sneer in his voice. "*Ipso facto*. You must have been something of a credit to your regiment, I have no doubt."

A smile flickered across Washburn's face and disappeared, briefly revealing a row of uneven, discolored teeth. "They thought so," he said. "I was awarded a medal for what I would now describe as extreme stupidity in the face of the enemy, another for obeying the orders of the idiot who was my superior officer—he got himself killed in that one—and a third for saving the life of the idiot who took command after the first idiot was killed. Then a jezail bullet took a nick out of my femur, and a grateful government declared me unfit for duty and kicked me out."

"So you found—no, created—a new line of work for yourself," suggested Moriarty.

"I did that," Washburn agreed. "By a series of fortuitous circumstances, and a bit of timely assistance from here and there, I worked my way up the ladder of the demimonde of the erotica until, two years ago, I set up this establishment."

"And the 'odor of the mysterious East'?"

Washburn shrugged. "Mostly just a smell. A hint of the Levant can be found in many of London's less distinguished areas, along with a touch of Egypt, a heady dose of the Celestial Empire, and a smattering of Balkan this and Russian that. Many of my children are, indeed, from strange and exotic corners of the earth, but for the most part I found them much closer to home."

"What of the child that was killed?" Moriarty asked.

"Istefan," Washburn said. "He was, I think, sixteen. Looked fourteen perhaps. I wondered when you were going to get around to asking about him. He may have been a child of the Jago, but nobody deserves to die like that."

"My sympathies for the lad," Moriarty said. "Tell me about the gentleman he was with."

"The one what sliced him apart?" Washburn grimaced. "I've been wondering about him, too."

"What about him?" demanded Epp.

"Well," Washburn said, "you should know, shouldn't you? What with your people in and out of here for the whole day, looking here, sniffing there, peering into this and opening that."

"A murder investigation, my good man, is no respecter of privacy," Epp told him.

"Up to a point it ain't," Washburn agreed. "Then, suddenly, everything changes, and privacy is what we got too much of. We ain't to talk to anyone about what happened, and there's a gent in plain clothes and flat feet at the door, which ain't so good for custom, all things considered. Ain't no member come through the door in the past two days."

"We have our reasons, my man," said Epp, "and they ain't for you to question."

"What can you tell me about the killer?" Moriarty asked. "Who was he, if you know, and how long had he been a member?"

Washburn grimaced. "I told the Scotland Yard blokes all this already."

"Yes, well, then," Epp said, "you should have it fresh to mind, shouldn't you?"

"I just don't like talking about it," Washburn said. "I mean, with what happened and all."

"You want us to catch the man who did it, don't you?" Moriarty asked.

"Of course," Washburn asserted, "but are you sure you want to do the catching?"

Epp leaned forward pugnaciously. "What does that mean?" he demanded.

"Well, it stands to reason. If you wanted to catch him you'd have done it already. Just marched up to his house, wherever it may be, and knocked on the door and taken him away. And if you'd done that, you wouldn't be here asking me all these questions, now would you? It stands to reason."

"So you told the inspectors who the man was?" Moriarty asked.

"Not me. I didn't see him, did I? It could have been any of our guests for all of me. It was Natyana who got a glom at him when he came out of that room."

"Natyana?" Moriarty asked.

"She's the chatelaine, as we call her. Same title as me but with an *e* on the end. It's a way the French have with names. My partner, she is, and I was lucky to find her. In truth, she pretty much runs the place."

"Really?"

"Oh, yes. I strut about and impress the clientele with my dark secrets and manage any squabbles that come up, and I see to admitting new clients and make sure that we get our proper remuneration for services rendered. Natyana actually keeps the books and manages the household and such."

"A Russian name, is it, Natyana?" Moriarty asked.

"Could be, could be," Washburn agreed. He reached behind him and tugged several times at a bell pull hanging from the wall. "She'll be here directly and you can ask her yourself."

A short, slender woman with high cheekbones and piercing dark eyes in a narrow face, Natyana wore a mask of complete composure, effectively covering any emotions she might be feeling. She knocked, entered, crossed the room, and settled into a chair with the placid look of a duchess arriving at the local vicarage for tea. Only the white knuckles of her clenched left fist gave an indication of the emotional strain she was feeling. "Yes, gentlemen?" she asked. "How may I assist you?"

Epp looked sternly at the woman, his eyes taking in the dark, severely cut dress, the maroon shawl, and the button shoes. "Natyana?"

"That is my name."

He scowled. "Natyana what, if I may ask? You have a surname? And what was your name before it was Natyana?" The words came out sharply in the harsh tone of an interrogation.

She looked at him mildly, showing no anger or resentment at his tone, but her left hand clutched convulsively at the folds of her skirt. "The name Natyana is on my certificate of birth," she said, "of which I have a copy. You'll have to go to St. Petersburg to see the original, I'm afraid. I am told that in one of my past lives my name was Sharima, and that I was an odalisque in the hareem of the great Kublai Khan, but of that I'm afraid I can provide no documentation."

"Chief Inspector Epp does not approve of you," Moriarty told her. "I'm afraid there is much of which Mr. Epp does not approve. He is a policeman. My name is Professor Moriarty, and I am not a policeman. May I ask you some questions?"

Natyana looked at Washburn and then back at Moriarty. "There you are, and here I am," she said. "You might as well ask what you like."

"To satisfy Mr. Epp's curiousity," Moriarty said, "what is your patronym?"

"I couldn't say," Natyana answered. "My mother had no idea who my father was. She believed he was probably one of the men I grew up calling 'uncle,' but it might have been someone else entirely. On my birth certificate it says, *'Otets nyeizvestnyh.'*"

"A bit severe, isn't it?" asked Moriarty. "'Father unknown.'"

"The tsar's bureaucracy tends to be rather precise and inhuman," Natyana said. "*Otets nyeizvestnyh*. And so, I'm afraid, he shall remain. You speak Russian?"

"Sufficiently," Moriarty said. "Let us now, if you don't mind, speak of what transpired here two days ago."

"If we must," she said. "I could go for a long time without bringing that back to memory."

"Of course," said Moriarty. "Let us go through the event this one last time, lightly touching on the salient facts. It would assist me greatly, and perhaps after that you'll never have to think of it again."

Natyana sighed deeply and stared at the wall. For perhaps a minute she was silent. And then she spoke. "Peccavi and the lad went up to the room at around three, I think it was. His associate remained in the greeting room. It was some time after Peccavi left that I realized that the lad had not yet come from the room. I don't know how long."

"Peccavi?" asked Moriarty.

"Each of our gentlemen has a name that he assumes while here. For our records, you understand."

"You keep records?" asked Epp, sounding somewhere between astonished and disbelieving.

"Certainly," Washburn interjected. "Have to know who purchased what service, just when, and for how long."

"We don't know the true identities of many, perhaps most, of our members," Natyana said. "A new initiate is put up for membership by an existing member, seconded by another, and approved by the chatelain. It lets the members feel more secure and free from possible outside entanglements if they don't know one another and we don't know who they really are."

"By 'outside entanglements' you mean blackmail?" Moriarty suggested.

Natyana nodded.

"That's about the size of it," Washburn agreed. "When a bloke comes up for membership I give him a look over, give him the thumbs-up, and he's in. Never do ask him what his real name might be."

"On what basis do you approve new members if you don't know who they really are?" Moriarty asked.

"Mainly on my finely honed instincts and whether they can come up with the membership dues."

"Ah," said Moriarty. "And what does it cost to become a member?"

"Two hundred for most of them," Washburn said.

"Two hundred pounds?" asked Epp, sounding startled.

"Guineas," Washburn corrected.

"Guineas? For membership in this organization?"

"Yes, well, gentlemen will pay for their little entertainments, won't they?" said Washburn. "And they wouldn't have no respect for you if you didn't charge them in guineas. A hundred and twenty is the membership fee, and the other eighty is put on the books for expenses. Whenever the account gets below twenty guineas, they ponies up another eighty. That's why we don't have to know who they are in the outside world; they have paid in advance for their little pleasures. The fact that a member puts them up and they have the requisite nicker goes a long way—and then once they passes my glom, they're in. Of course, special members what might be useful to have around, like the two aforementioned coppers, get a special rate."

"What did your finely honed instincts tell you about Peccavi?"

Washburn looked up at the ceiling and thought for a moment. "He joined us about six months ago. Put up, as I recall, by a member who signs himself 'Saint Jerome.'"

"Interesting," Moriarty said. "Jerome. Anglicized from the Greek Hieronymus."

Epp snorted. "Greek, Egyptian—that's all very good, but just where does knowing that get us?"

"The utility of any fact cannot be ascertained in the absence of that fact," Moriarty said. "It may do us no good whatever to know that 'Jerome' took his name from an early Christian saint, or that St. Hieronymus used to visit those places in Rome that would most remind him of the terrors of Hell. *'Horror ubique animos, simul ipsa silentia terrent,'* as you might say."

"How's that?" asked Washburn.

"The horror and the silence terrify the soul," Moriarty translated. "Isn't that right, Mr. Epp?"

"Might be," Epp conceded.

"I quote St. Hieronymus," Moriarty explained. "Of course, he was quoting Virgil. Assuming that your Jerome has a classical education, was he commenting on this establishment when he chose his nom de guerre? Does it matter? If it has any bearing on his introducing Peccavi to membership, it may. It is in such obscure and seeming unimportant details that people often give themselves away."

He removed his pince-nez and began polishing the lenses with the ever-present square of red cloth. "Let us return to what you recall of the gentleman who called himself Peccavi."

Washburn nodded. "Squat and wide he was, as I remember," he said. "Prominent nose and ears. Well dressed. Brown sack suit and old-boy tie. Just which old boys I couldn't say. Well groomed. Military bearing. Typical public school pitch to his voice. If you'd been here you could probably have told me which one."

"No doubt," Moriarty agreed.

"But a bit whiny-sounding for all that. And shifty. Wouldn't look you in the eye."

"Pardon," Natyana interrupted. "But that gentleman is not the Peccavi I've seen."

"Ah!" said Moriarty, rubbing his hands together. "Now we may be getting somewhere. Pray describe the man as you saw him."

"Tall and slender," Natyana began and then paused to consider. "Well, perhaps not so much tall, now that I think of it, as elegantly slender. Not that he was short, but his slimness of body and his posture—quite upright and regal it was—gave him an impression of added height. If you see what I mean."

"Quite so," Moriarty said. "Anything else strike you about him?"

"He laughed quite a bit."

"Laughed?" asked Epp. "At what, may I ask?"

"Well, not so much laughed as, I suppose, chuckled. No—giggled. At everything. He giggled when he came up to the room, and he giggled when he left the room. With that poor boy—the way he was." She shuddered and averted her eyes, as though speaking of it had brought the scene into her thoughts, and she was turning away from looking at it again. "What sort of man could do such a thing?"

"That's what we must find out," said Moriarty. "The gentleman you describe as his associate—he waited downstairs while Peccavi went up?"

"That's right, sir."

"But they left together?"

"That's so."

"Tell me about him—this other man."

"I only saw the top of his head. That was when he joined Peccavi downstairs. He was wearing a wide red-and-black domino mask tied at the back with a red ribbon. I remember that a little round spot at the back of his head was devoid of hair. The remaining hair was black, parted at the middle and brushed or combed very flat to his head."

"What name did he use when he came in?"

"He entered as Peccavi's guest," Washburn said. "No name was used."

"Come, come," Epp said. "Surely someone must have seen something. This could be important. *Ipso facto.*"

"He spent his time in the boys' locker room, but he didn't show much interest in the lads," said Natyana. "I asked about him after . . . after." She sighed and shook her head from side to side as though trying to clear troublesome images from her brain. "Was it our fault—what happened? Could we have known?"

"There have been organizations like this in London since the seventeenth century," Moriarty told her. "Perhaps before, but I have found no earlier records. Some pretty unwholesome things have happened in them over the years. But the wanton and pointless murder of a young boy and the dissection of his still-warm body . . ."

Natyana made a soft screeching sound and brought both hands, balled into fists, to her mouth. Her eyes seemed to grow larger, wider, and more distressed.

"I apologize, madam," Moriarty said. "That was unnecessary and thoughtless of me."

"If you'd seen it—" she began.

"Ah, well," he said, "distressing as it would have been, I wish I had. It might have given me some useful insights. I must deal in facts, not surmises, if I am to sort this out. But I'm sorry that you had to witness such a sight."

Natyana closed her eyes and put her balled fists in front of them. "I thought I had seen horror," she said. "In Constantinople, in Cairo—but like this? No—never like this."

Washburn got up and moved over next to Natyana, taking her hand. "Is there anything else?" he asked them.

"One thing," Moriarty said. "Was anyone close enough to overhear anything either of the men might have said?"

"I've asked that," said Natyana. "The domino mask said nothing the whole time he was here. A few murmured comments to his, ah, friend, perhaps, but nothing to anyone else. The giggling man—the murderer—said a few words to the girl in the cloakroom on his way out."

"The girl in the cloakroom?"

"Yes. She told me so, but I did not think it important. They were the sort of words one says to a cloakroom girl—devoid of content."

"Perhaps so," Moriarty said, "but I would like to know what was said."

"I don't know what he said, word for word." Natyana stood. "The girl's name is Wendy. I will go fetch her."

"We are wasting our time," Epp muttered as Natyana left the room. "For the love of—what possible use could it be to know what the man said to this girl?"

"*Acta non verba*, eh, Epp?" Moriarty said. "Well, who knows. Perhaps he told her his name and address."

"Bah!" said Epp.

Wendy was a petite blonde with delicate hands and what the French would call a pert face. Unlike on the evening when she worked the cloakroom, she was clothed in a pink wraparound cotton peignoir with a fluffy collar. "You wanted to see me, sir?" she asked.

"Yes, indeed, young lady," said Moriarty. "Wendy, is it? Thank you for coming."

Her eyes widened slightly at that. "I didn't know as I had a choice," she said.

"Well, thank you anyway." Moriarty smiled his most disarming smile, which under other circumstances had caused strong men to suddenly realize that they had urgent business elsewhere. At this moment it was devoid of menace, and Wendy smiled back, shyly and tentatively, as though she were afraid his smile might be withdrawn without notice.

"The man who caused all the trouble a few days ago," Moriarty said. "You remember him?"

This time her eyes did widen, and her lips quivered. "Oh, sir," she said. "He went right by me, he did. And I smiled at him and bobbed as I gave him his cloak and hat, and he gave me a shilling, he did. His eyes all bright and his mouth all giggly. How was I to know?"

"Now, Wendy, don't blubber!" Natyana said sharply.

"That's all right," Moriarty said soothingly. "How were you to know? Let's not think about that part of it for now. Let's think about the man and his friend. Can you describe them—the giggly man and his friend?"

"The chubby one had this long mustache with the ends like twisted into points, but that's all I could see."

"And the other?" asked Moriarty. "Can you describe him?"

"The elegant-looking gent—I should think so. Besides, I've got his picture, don't I?"

Epp sat up with a sudden jerk. "Here now, what's that?" he demanded. "His picture?"

"What do you mean?" Washburn asked, almost leaping to his feet. He leaned forward over the table. "How did you get his picture? What are you talking about?"

Wendy put her hands in front of her face. "I didn't mean nothing, I didn't. It ain't my fault." She broke into earnest tears.

Epp stood up and pointed an accusing finger at her. "You have his *picture*? And you said *nothing*? Stop that blubbering, girl, and explain yourself!"

Which caused her to sob even louder until, in a few seconds, she was gasping for breath.

"Now, Wendy," Natyana said soothingly, going over and putting her arms around the girl. "Nobody's blaming you. We just need to know what happened."

"Close your eyes and take a deep breath," Moriarty suggested, "and then another. That's a good girl. And now one more. Don't try to talk for a moment. Just breathe in and out . . . in and out. All right. Now another deep breath—like that. Better now?"

She opened her eyes and thought it over for a second and then nodded.

"Good. Now tell us about it. Just what did the elegant-looking gent do?"

"He left it—his picture—behind, tucked inside this little silver case thing what he left on the counter. He did. I tried calling to him to give it back, but he just about ran out so's I couldn't nohow."

"Ah!" said Moriarty. "I should have thought of that, of course."

"Should you?" Epp asked, sounding aggrieved as he sat back down. "Of what, may I ask?"

"That he would leave something behind to establish his, ah, alternate persona." Moriarty turned to the girl. "Can you show us what he left?"

"It's in me cubbyhole," Wendy said, standing up. "I'll go fetch it if you please."

"We do," Moriarty told her.

Nobody spoke while the girl was gone, and when she returned, standing in the doorway with a flat silver object in her hand, there was a collective releasing of breath.

Epp reached over and took the object from the girl's hand. *"Decus et tutamen,"* he said, turning it over and over, "if it ain't a cigar case."

Moriarty put his pince-nez in his vest pocket and retrieved his magnifying monocle. "May I?" he asked, extending his hand.

"Magno cum gaudio, Professor," Epp said, making a minor ceremony of handing him the case.

"Certainly," Moriarty agreed, taking the object and peering at it through his glass.

"What have you got there?" asked Washburn.

"It is, indeed, a silver cigar case," Moriarty said, displaying it, "with a coat of arms embossed on the lid, and inside"—he opened it—"a photograph of the, ah, gent in question stuck under the lid, and, um, two cigars." He took one out and rolled it in his hand. "Cuban. *El rey del mundo,* I believe. Very fitting." He replaced the cigar and closed the case, leaving the photograph inside.

"It is . . . him—for certain?" asked Epp.

"No question," Moriarty affirmed, "and the coat of arms adds verisimilitude."

"A coat of arms?" Epp asked suspiciously. "It's not, by any chance . . ."

"Small and tasteful," Moriarty said, examining the lid. "A white shield with a simple red cross in the center, surrounded by a blue belt. Done in cloisonné, I believe, with the motto of the order on the belt in gold."

"Order? What order?" Epp demanded.

"It's the crest of the Most Noble Order of the Garter," Moriarty explained. "The motto is *Honi soit qui mal y pense.* 'Evil to him who thinks evil' is the usual translation."

"The Garter, eh?" Washburn mused. "So he really was a toff."

"Indeed," Moriarty agreed. "The owner of that case certainly was a toff."

CHAPTER FIFTEEN

THE WHICHNESS
OF WHAT

Hearest thou the festival din
Of Death and Destruction and Sin . . .

—PERCY BYSSHE SHELLEY

"I CANNOT YET TELL YOU WHAT IS GOING TO HAPPEN, although I am making some progress in that regard," Moriarty said. "I can, however, describe for you in some detail what has already happened."

The four others in the small room shifted in their chairs. "What sort of progress?" asked Lord Montgrief.

"I can tell you that the killer is not a lone madman, and that the people behind him are well organized, well financed, and in some fashion highly motivated. There's nothing random or haphazard about what they're doing. They are operating from a detailed plan. Also I would say there is one guiding hand behind the whole escapade, perhaps one of those fabled 'master criminals' that I personally am so loath to believe in. And that whatever is planned as the culmination of this scheme is going to happen soon."

Sir Anthony Darryl leaned forward. "On what basis can you say that, and when you say 'soon,' how soon?"

"Probably not today or tomorrow, but some day in the immediate future," Moriarty responded. "My guess is they plan one or two more 'incidents' with hints reaching the public ear, passed on artfully to the press by their agents, and then one final happening of some kind, which will result in the prince being captured *in flagellum delicto*, as Chief Inspector Epp would say."

His Grace the Duke of Shorham slammed his fist down on the table, rattling the teacups. "This is damnable," he said in a hoarse whisper. "Damnable!"

They were meeting in a small private dining room in the third floor rear of the Diogenes Club. Moriarty sat on one side of an oblong dining table of some rich dark wood and considerable age, and ranged around him the Duke of Shorham, the Earl of Scully, and Sir Anthony Darryl. In an overstuffed chair in the corner of the room, his hands folded across his ample belly, a look of detachment on his face as though he were here for some other event entirely and just happened to be overhearing these proceedings, sat Mycroft Holmes.

"There is one thing," Sir Anthony said. "Epp says that it is definitely established—beyond any shadow of a doubt—that His Highness is not in any way involved in these, ah, events." He pushed his tortoise-shell glasses farther forward on his nose and peered over them at Moriarty.

"Not that we believed for a moment that he was—that he could be," added the duke.

"Is that so, Professor?" Sir Anthony asked. "Do we know for certain that His Highness is not guilty of these crimes?"

Moriarty nodded his head slowly. "Yes," he said. "At least, certain enough to satisfy us, although whether it would satisfy the general public is doubtful. A young lady who fortuitously witnessed the first murder, or at least the first we know about, from a concealed position says that the prince was knocked unconscious before the killing and removed from the room afterward by being lowered out the window. And that two men—one greatly resembling the prince—were involved."

"Well!" The Earl of Scully pushed his chair back and looked around him. "We heard about that. Epp grudgingly admitted that you have added to our knowledge of the events. I can tell you that he was pretty surprised that you discovered anything. Also mesmerizing that girl. Who would have thought that sort of thing actually worked." He gave Moriarty a hard, straight look. "It *does* actually work, doesn't it?"

"The accepted term in the scientific literature today," Mycroft's gruff voice pronounced from the corner, "is 'hypnotism.' 'Mesmerism' refers to a form of charlatanism involving magnets and auras and suchlike nonsense. Hypnotism itself is not highly regarded, but there is some evidence that it works when employed by a trained practitioner for uses where it is suitable."

"Makes one cluck like a chicken, is what I've heard," volunteered Sir Anthony.

Moriarty raised an eyebrow. "The method can be used to suppress pain, to induce sleep, to recall or suppress memories, or to encourage one to cluck like a chicken, if that is the desired result. Which of these ensues depends on the inclination of the practitioner and the circumstances of the hypnotic induction."

"It worked with this girl, eh?" the duke said. "Brought out her memory of this horrid event, eh? Fortuitous that you know how to do it, eh? That you thought of using it."

"It seemed like a good idea at the time," Moriarty said.

"Indeed—indeed. So, frankly, I don't see what the problem is. That's certain enough then, isn't it? I mean, whatever happens, whatever these people do, we can merely produce the young lady and she can, er, explain what happened. That it wasn't His Highness. Yes?"

"No!" came a rumbling voice from the corner chair. Without looking up, Mycroft Holmes continued, "It won't do, unfortunately. Explain it to them, Professor."

Moriarty looked at Mycroft and then turned his gaze back to the illustrious men gathered before him. "The girl wouldn't be believed," he said. "Her age, her background, her profession; all would militate against her and any story she might tell."

"Yes, that's so," said the earl. "I understand that she is one of the employees of the establishment. That would certainly put her veracity at risk."

"Although why a harlot's word should be more suspect than that of a duchess—pardon me, Your Grace—I'm not sure I understand," said Sir Anthony.

"I find that ladies of the demimonde," said the duke expansively, "are quite accomplished at telling you what they think you want to hear." He considered for a moment and then added, "But then, so are duchesses."

"Then there's the fact that she was hypnotized," Moriarty added. "I was using it to recall memory, but it could be said by those who would want to say such things that I was instead creating memory."

"Not very well understood yet, hypnotism," said Mycroft. "Even by those who practice it."

"So what are we going to do?" asked the earl.

"There are certain signs to look for here in London," Moriarty told them. "I think it's a reasonable assumption that the final show, whatever it turns out to be, is going to take place here. I'm going to put eyes and ears in the most likely places."

"Many eyes and ears?" asked Sir Anthony. "Would you like some help in that regard?"

"I think I can arrange for a few dozen, er, agents to cover the ground," Moriarty told him. "Although we can use a select few more since there are some places into which mine do not have easy access."

"I thought you told me that you had no 'gang,'" the Earl of Scully complained. "You were very firm about that."

"I assure you that I command no followers," said Moriarty. "However, there are those who do, and the assurance that it's in a good cause—along with just a bit of gold—may influence them to aid us."

"Just who would these 'helpers' be?" asked the duke.

"A chap named Twist, who's the head of the Mendicants Guild, for one," Moriarty told him. "He has his, if I may use the word, 'agents' all over London."

"Really, now?" the Earl of Scully interrupted. "It never occurred to me that the beggars might have a guild."

"Ancient and honorable, or so their charter says," Moriarty told him. "Dates back, I believe, to the mid-seventeenth century. The membership varies in size according to the social conditions in the country."

"Fascinating!' said the earl. "Who would have guessed? A guild. Beggars. Sort of reminds one of *The Beggar's Opera*, what?"

"What will they be looking for?" asked the duke.

Mycroft Holmes stirred in his chair. "Any unusual activity," he growled. "Hummm," he said. "Anything French," he added.

They turned to look at him. "French?" demanded the duke.

Mycroft waggled a finger at Moriarty. "Tell them, "he said.

Moriarty looked at him. "Your regard for my omniscience is refreshing," he said.

"You and my brother are well matched," said Mycroft.

"Yes . . . well . . ." Moriarty turned to the others. "Do you recall what the man who accompanied the murderer said as they absconded with the prince?"

"Something about shoes, wasn't it?" asked the Earl of Scully.

"'Feet, feet,'" Sir Anthony recalled. "Something of the sort."

"That's what the girl heard," Moriarty said, "but it seems probable that what he was actually saying was *vite, vite*. He was telling the other man to hurry. *Vite, vite*—quickly, quickly. In French."

"French," said the duke. "I should have guessed. French."

Mycroft Holmes leaned forward and tossed something on the table. "After speaking with Professor Moriarty yesterday," he said, "I sent a cable to the prefect of police in Paris. Here is a copy of that cable and of the response, which arrived shortly before this meeting."

The two papers were pinned together. The first one read:

ARE ANY CONVICTED KILLERS OF MULTIPLE VICTIMS INCARCER−
ATED ON FRENCH SOIL IN PAST FIVE YEARS NOW MISSING ARE ANY
STILL AT LARGE MYCROFT FO

The second, on a Post Office Telegram form, read:

WE HAVE NON SUCH AWARENESS OF PERSONS ALIVE OF TODAY
LECLERK PREFECT

"So to their knowledge they have no madmen running around killing people in France at the moment," Sir Anthony said after reading the two cables.

"It doesn't mean there wasn't one," Mycroft said.

"Just so," said Moriarty. "I believe it might be of some use to send a trusted agent to Paris."

"Why?" asked the earl. "There may be some French, ah, people involved, but they would seem to be over here, *n'est-ce pas?*"

"So it would seem," Moriarty admitted, "but a babe does not spring from his mother's womb fully clothed and, in this case, with a knife in his hand. There must have been a maturation period. Or, to look at it from another angle, if one is looking for a killer—that is, if one needs to obtain a murderer for some reason—one looks among those who have already killed. It is possible to create a murderer, given sufficient time and a truly evil turn of mind, but it is more efficient to find one ready-made, as it were."

"But finding one who's a dead ringer for Prince Albert—" His Grace began.

"True," Moriarty said. "I rather think that in this case the existence of the 'dead ringer' with murderous proclivities is what formulated the scheme, whatever it turns out to be."

"You mean if this murderer hadn't existed—" began the earl.

"Then," interrupted Mycroft Holmes, "these people would have devised some other heinous strategy to accomplish their ends—whatever these ends may turn out to be."

CHAPTER SIXTEEN

AN OUTRAGE AT COVENT GARDEN

Hell hath no limits, nor is circumscribed
In one self place; where we are is hell,
And to be short, when all the world dissolves,
And every creature shall be purified,
All places shall be hell that are not heaven.

—CHRISTOPHER MARLOWE

ON FRIDAY, THE TWENTY-SIXTH OF SEPTEMBER, 1890, the Prince of Darkness spent the evening at the Covent Garden Opera House. The performance that evening was Boito's *Mefistofele,* an Italian look at the Faust legend written some twenty-five years before. Mephistopheles was being sung by Vespaccio Garundo. The fifty-six-year-old basso, who weighed in at twenty-three stone, was at the height of his long and successful career and, as several reviewers insisted on pointing out, was surprisingly agile for a man of his girth.

The management of the theater had been pleased when an impeccably dressed young man with a faint squint and a notable sneer appeared at the box office an hour before the performance, announced that he was a royal equerry, and requested seats for Prince Albert Victor and a small entourage. The theater staff were urged not to make a fuss, as the prince desired that no fuss was to be made. His Royal Highness merely wanted to see the opera, and not to be seen, the equerry said, so he wished to avoid the music, the waving to the audience, and all the attendant pomp that usually accompanied the circumstance of a royal presence.

Of course, word *did* go forth from the box office to the house manager to the cast to the stage hands to the ushers to the audience members as they were shown to their seats. How could it not? All eyes were on the slim, tall, elegant figure with the thin mustache and the black suit that was not quite a uniform, and all mouths were whispering as he took his seat in the royal box, accompanied by two servitors who were probably, the whispers decided, merely barons or earls.

There were none there who knew that Albert Victor had been missing for over a week, that he was suspected of several heinous crimes, that no one in the royal household had any idea where he was. None there to ask the young man in the box if he was really the prince and, if so, where he had been.

The house lights went down, pulling the audience's eyes away from the royal box, the electric arc spotlights burned and hissed, and invisible trumpets bleated as the curtain opened on fluffy clouds and chubby cherubim. Mefistofele entered in his red costume and black cape, looking like a giant overripe tomato with a black bib, and complained to God, who was somewhere in those clouds, about the wretched behavior of men, who had sunk so low that it was no longer any fun to tempt them.

As Act One progressed Faust, sung by a spry young tenor named David Spigott, and Margaret, sung by thirty-four-year-old Mathilde van Tromphe, whose slender body, said the reviewer from *The Times*, held a surprisingly rich and full soprano voice, joined Mephistopheles in singing of Heaven and Hell, of beauty and truth, of desire and despair, while, aptly enough, the Prince of Darkness sat, silent and watchful, in the royal box at the far left of the first balcony.

Toward the end of the second act Constable Bertrand Higgins stopped by the stage door for a cuppa and a bit of a chat with Bix, the stage doorman, who was in the way of becoming Higgins's father-in-law when his daughter Nancy, who had already said, "Of course I'll marry you, Jock," decided just when she would allow the event to transpire. First she wanted to, as she told her mother, finish sowing her wild oats.

"Can't stay long," PC Higgins told Bix. "The sergeant's putting in a command performance at the call box by Tavistock Street. Keep us on our toes, that's what he's all about."

"Speaking of a command performance," said Bix, "we's got a royal personage in the box tonight."

"Coo," said Higgins, "and who might that be, if I might ask?"

Something in Bix's answer rang a faint bell in Constable Higgins's mind, and he closed his eyes to recapture the memory. One of the standing orders from a few days ago, it was. Her Majesty's household someone-or-other requested of the Metropolitan Police that the whereabouts of Prince Albert Victor should be communicated to the palace from time to time if one should happen to become apprised of said whereabouts. Perhaps not precisely in that wording, but that was it.

So, when this and that had been discussed and the cuppa had been downed, PC Higgins outed into the street with something to tell his sergeant.

Margaret died and was welcomed in Heaven at the end of Act Three, and Mathilde van Tromphe retired to her dressing room to rest her voice, kick off her shoes, pull off her wig, drink a cup of weak tea with honey, and lie back on her chaise longue for half an hour to await the curtain calls.

As Act Four began, a bevy of beautiful young maidens danced about the stage to amuse Faust, who awaited the entrance of Helen of Troy. Sometime during the dancing the Prince of Darkness left the royal box and went down the long corridor connecting the boxes to the backstage area.

Sid Scuffin, the stage manager, saw the prince arrive backstage, and even pointed the way to Mademoiselle van Tromphe's dressing room. "Up that there flight o' stairs and to your right, Your Majesty— second door—mind your head." If a royal wanted to engage in a bit of backstage, er, conversation with a prima donna, who were we mere mortals to intervene?

Sergeant Cottswell was waiting at the call box when PC Higgins turned the corner to Tavistock Street. Tapping his feet, the sergeant was, and mouthing words, and the smile on his face was a tight little smile that did not indicate pleasure. Higgins was sure that the words concerned him and, when spoken aloud in a few moments, would not be words that PC Higgins would be anxious to hear. A constable should not keep his sergeant waiting. A constable should walk his rounds in a timely manner and arrive at the appointed place at the appointed time and not a moment before or a fraction of a moment after.

It would behoove PC Higgins to give Sergeant Cottswell something else to consider in a timely manner. If possible, in a very timely manner.

"Sorry I'm a mite late, Sergeant," Higgins began, "but I thought you should know His Royal Highness is at the Opera House this evening."

Cottswell frowned. "Of which royal highness are we speaking?" he asked. "Why wasn't the Yard informed that he was planning to attend? The Palace Guard surely would have sent along an information had they known." Along the corridors of the Metropolitan Police stations those assigned to the Special Household Branch were known as "the Palace Guard," although their duties did not in any way encompass guarding any of the royal palaces but only keeping a watchful eye on the royal family while out in public.

"Albert Victor," Higgins said. "He didn't tell anyone as he was coming until he arrived, it would seem," he added, "but there was an information come along over a week ago, if I remember rightly, say-ing as how we should keep note of His Royal Highness's comings and goings if he should happen to come or go in our purview."

"Purview, is it?" Sergeant Cottswell muttered. "Have you seen His Royal Highness yourself?"

"No, sir," Higgins told him.

"You should have taken a glim," Cottswell said.

"Well now, Sarge," Higgins said, doing his best to sound aggrieved, "I had to come along and meet you here, didn't I?"

Cottswell took a deep breath and blew the air out through pursed lips in an almost silent whistle. "Well, I suppose there's nothing to it but I should come back with you and take a look at his Royal High-and-Mightiness." Cottswell had vague republican tendencies, which never got much beyond using mild epithets to describe members of the royal family and occasionally threatening to uproot his own fam-ily and move, bag and baggage, to Baltimore, where he had a cousin in the luggage business.

Higgins nodded and held back a sigh of relief. "If you think so, Sergeant Cottswell, then p'raps we'd better. This way, Sarge."

It was force of habit that took Higgins around to the stage door, Sergeant Cottswell following. Bix welcomed them with a smile and a kettle. "A cuppa?" he suggested.

"We have come," Sergeant Cottswell told him, "to have a glim at His Highness, as which I understand to be in this here theater." He accepted the mug of tea that was thrust upon him. "This is in the way of being an official viewing, you understand, at the request of our superiors." No way was he going to let the possibility hang about that he had any interest in regarding royalty, or nobility, or anyone but other hardworking yeomen and yeowomen.

"There's a corridor that runs from offstage right to behind the royal box," PC Higgins offered. "We can just tiptoe along there and the sergeant can see who he has to see."

"No need," Bix told them. "His Royal Highness is backstage at the moment. His Highness is, um, visiting Mam'zelle van Tromphe in her dressing room."

"Mam'zelle van Tromphe?"

"The diva."

"The principal lady singer," Higgins explained. "The star, as it were."

Sergeant Cottswell lifted his head from his mug. "Well, really!" he said. "A royal consorting with a woman of the theater. I never!" He contrived to look simultaneously shocked and satisfied, as though pleased to discover that his worst suspicions had been justified.

"And the opera not over yet," said PC Higgins, listening to the muffled sounds of the orchestra.

Mr. Bix cocked his head thoughtfully to one side. "Theater people are not as you and me," he said. "They has their own way of doing things. As for royalty—" He sniffed. "I could tell you some things. Though I've no doubt you've heard them yourself, in your line o' work."

"In France, it may be," Cottswell told him, "but not here in London."

Bix looked up at the big clock on the wall that regulated the comings and goings backstage. "Twelve minutes to final curtain," he estimated. "Maybe fifteen. I believe they're running a mite slow tonight. Mam'zelle van Tromphe will be coming down for her curtain calls right after the final curtain. No lady of the theater will miss a curtain call, no matter 'oo she's entertaining in her dressing room. Certainly no principal player." He considered. "And never no soprano. No gentleman of the theater either, if it comes to that."

"I can't wait fifteen minutes," said Sergeant Cottswell. "I should be on my way back to the station house. I should be there already as it is."

"Well." Bix considered. "If you want to pop in on Mam'zelle van

Tromphe and His Highness, and interrupt their, um, discussion of artistic what'll-you-'aves, 'op to it my lad."

"I am not your lad," Cottswell pointed out.

"Well . . ."

Cottswell put his mug down and slapped his knee. "By God, I'll do it! I have orders to see His Highness, and His Highness is who I'll see." He rose to his feet and thrust forward his jaw. "And if I happens to discover His Highness *in flagellentay directo,* as they say—"

"You'll lose your pension," offered Bix.

"That's as may be. I has my duty." Sergeant Cottswell adjusted his jacket, checked his buttons, smoothed his collar, ran his finger alongside his nose, tucked his helmet firmly under his arm, and headed for the iron staircase that led to the dressing rooms.

"It's the second door on the right," Bix called. "Mind you knock first!"

"P'raps you'd like me to approach the door on my knees, as befits an humble policeman," Cottswell muttered just loud enough to be heard. "'Course I'll knock. I doesn't enter a lady's room without I knock first."

"Well, how was I to know?" Bix replied. "You are a copper, after all."

"Now, now," Higgins whispered, making a shushing gesture with the flat of his hand.

Cottswell would have knocked, he planned to knock, he was prepared to knock, but just as he reached the door and paused to raise his knocking hand, a high-pitched scream began and was as instantly squelched, as though somebody had clamped his hand over a screaming mouth.

All thoughts of whose room it was, or who might be inside, fled as he twisted the knob and bellowed, "All right then, what's all this?"

The door wouldn't budge.

"I'm a policeman, ma'am. Are you all right?" he called. Taking a step back, he kicked out, slamming the door with the heel of his thick policeman's boot. The door sprang open.

A slender, elegant-looking man in what might have been a uniform boiled out of the room, slammed Sergeant Cottswell in the chest with his arm and in the stomach with a knee. Cottswell was thrown back against the iron railing and recoiled off it, hitting his assailant in the nose with his own head. The nose spurted blood, instantly soaking the trim mustache below it, and the man screamed, *"Merde!"* and vaulted over the railing to the floor below. Cottswell was thrown onto his back.

In another five seconds the man had dashed past Bix and PC Higgins, two stagehands, and three sopranos of the chorus and was out the stage door and away. By the time Higgins made it through the door he was able to make out the rear end of a black carriage as it rounded the corner, and for the next few moments he could hear the sound of galloping horses receding in the distance.

Cottswell pushed himself to his feet and went into the room. Mlle. van Tromphe was lying on the floor, her back propped up by the couch against the right wall. Both her hands were clutched around her own throat. Blood seeped between the fingers.

"Here now, mam'zelle," he said, dropping to his knees. "How bad is it?"

She opened her mouth and made a slight croaking sound. Blood dripped from the corner of her lips. She closed it again.

Cottswell looked around wildly and spied a makeup-stained towel on the dressing table. He reached up for it and pulled it down. "Come now," he said, prying her hands away from the wound, "let me wrap this around your neck, it will stop the blood. You can't afford to lose too much blood."

Her eyes grew wild with panic for a second until she understood what he was trying to do. Then she loosened her grip on the wound enough for him to wrap the towel around.

"Keeping as much blood in your body as possible is the key to pulling through this. We see a lot of wounds like this of a Saturday night in Cheapside. You'll be all right if we can keep the blood in you. I won't ask you just what happened because you shouldn't talk now."

He stood up. "I'll get help!" He dashed from the room and scrambled down the stairs. "The mam'zelle is wounded," he yelled. "We need a doctor. Now!"

Bix ran down the short corridor to the stage and grabbed the stage manager, who was standing behind the nearest tormentor staring at the oversized pocket watch in his hand. After a few whispered words and emphatic nodding from Bix, the stage manager gave the signal to bring down the curtain. The duet *"Ah! Amore! misterio celeste"* had just begun, and it took three firm repetitions of the stage manager's order for the curtain to start down. Faust and Helen stopped singing, looking bewildered and annoyed. The orchestra dribbled into silence.

The stage manager entered stage front and motioned the audience to quiet. "I apologize for the interruption," he yelled. "We've had a bit of an accident backstage. Nothing to worry about. We'll resume shortly. Is there a doctor in the house?"

CHAPTER SEVENTEEN

CASTLE HOLYRUDD

It is in truth a most contagious game:
HIDING THE SKELETON shall be its name.

—GEORGE MEREDITH

IN 1738 THE TWELFTH BARON of Wittle and Palmsy died without an heir, and the ancestral lands, but not the title, went to a Scottish third cousin on his mother's side. Most of the baron's holdings were in Scotland, but Castle Holyrudd, a long-abandoned pile of stone, was in Ruddshire, in the north of England, along with some farmland that raised mostly nettles and a few dozen sheep. Cousin Angus wanted nae to do with the Sassenach land, so he drove the sheep north and sold the rest off—all but the castle, which even the English were not daft enough to buy.

A hundred and fifty years later a man who called himself the Earl of Mersy, a title that Debrett's believed to be extinct, made an offer to buy Castle Holyrudd from Angus's great-grandson Angus. The younger Angus made a hasty trip south to visit his family's long-neglected property and see whether the extinct earl was mad or whether he had stumbled upon some overlooked value in the neglected stone walls. He found naught but drafty halls, gray dust, cobwebs, and crumbling stone, but almost decided not to sell the property anyway. The earl must have some use for the castle, and the fact that Angus couldn't discover what it was he found very irritating. He finally decided to sell when he heard that the earl was looking at another castle in, if anything, worse shape on the Devon coast. If what the earl wanted was to *live* in a castle, then let it be Castle Holyrudd.

Two years later Albreth Decanare, who called himself the Earl of Mersy, looked around him and was content. He sat in what he was pleased to call his throne room, although at present it held only a side-board too massive to move, an oversized fireplace with a pair fire irons in the shape of great lumpy dogs, and an ancient four-legged stool, and was as yet devoid of anything resembling a throne. Through the window he could see the workmen hammering at wooden forms and troweling gobs of what he assumed was concrete. He really should learn more of the arcane argot of these sturdy yeomen so that he could chastize and reward them using the proper terms.

The construction was a bit, but only a bit, behind schedule. In a month the moat would be finished and Cathcaril Rill would be diverted to fill it, and that bunch of laborers could go home. A herd of skilled artisans and artists were still working inside the great house, setting the tile, carving the wood beams, and completing the frescoes. But skilled artisans seemed to have no sense of the passage of time. The tapestries from the mill in Flanders were to begin arriving within the month, but he'd believe it when he saw them unrolled.

In a month. In a month, if nothing went wrong and the Great Plan stayed on course, the whole world might change, shift sharply sideways and set off in a new direction, like a ship with a new steersman. In a month, those who had forgotten him and his line would have cause to remember. Commons, and perhaps even peers, would be banging at his doors—the massive oak doors that had just been installed to replace the original castle doors, absent since the seventeenth century when the castle had been plundered and abandoned by the Roundheads or the Squareheads or a band of passing jugglers. Accounts varied.

Or, more probably, they would bang at the doors of Westerleigh House, his manse in London, which had sixteen bedrooms, two kitchens, and a ballroom big enough to hold a full orchestra in one corner while a few hundred people danced.

Maisgot, his lordship's seneschal, approached and bowed. "My lord," he said, "Prospero is here with news from London."

"Good news or bad?"

"I did not presume to ask," Maisgot told him. "If I may, I'll send him in." Albreth nodded his permission, and Maisgot bowed again and glided from the room, closing the door behind him.

It was at moments like these that Albreth felt taller than his scant five feet three inches, older than his thirty-two years, imbued with the wisdom and strength of the ancestors whose blood flowed through his veins. He sat on the oversized oak stool that, although by no stretch of even his imagination a throne, was itself three hundred years old and had supported the bottoms of many a prince and king, and waited to hear the next stanza in the saga of his destiny.

Maisgot opened the door. "Prospero, Your Lordship," he announced.

The hefty, ratlike man who came through the door bowed and scurried and bowed and scurried until he reached the oak chair. "Your worship," he intoned in a scratchy voice.

We have to be more selective when we choose our noms de guerre, Albreth thought. *Names from Shakespeare, yes. Names plucked from a helm at random, no. Bottom the Weaver for this one, perhaps, or Andrew Aguecheek. This man is no Prospero.* He leaned back in his chair and fixed his gaze somewhere to the right of the man. "What news have you?" he asked.

"The night at the opera went well, Your Excellency. There was an unexpected interruption, but Macbeth thinks it may have actually heightened the desired effect."

Albreth's gaze shifted to fix on the man's nose. "Unexpected how?" he inquired gently.

"A copper interrupted Henry just before he achieved, um, climax, as it were. Henry fled successfully."

"What was a policeman doing there?"

Prospero managed to look aggrieved. "Well, I don't know, do I?" he asked. Adding, "Your Lordship," after a slight pause.

"But Henry removed himself in a timely manner?"

Prospero thought that over for a second before venturing a "Yes."

"And maintained the illusion?"

"He did that. They was calling him 'Your Highness' and such. That was before the altercation. On his way out they was yelling, 'Stop!' and 'Oy!' and suchlike."

"What about the woman?"

"He took a slice at her throat, but he didn't have time to do any other cutting about here and there, if you see what I mean—and she lived."

"She survived?"

"Right enough, but she won't be singing for a while."

The Earl of Mersy mused. He slouched on his stool and put his thumb under his nose and stared off into the middle distance. He didn't like this part of it. Not at all. Macbeth said it was necessary, though, and Macbeth took the responsibility. You can't make an omelet without breaking eggs. He didn't, he realized, much like omelets.

He straightened up on the stool and squared his shoulders. "What must be done must be done. It might," he decided, "be to the good. When she is questioned, assuming she can speak, she will have a tale of horror to tell."

"She can write notes, if it comes to that," Prospero observed.

"And Henry? How is he?"

"A bit disappointed, I'd say. He was going on about how he didn't complete the design."

"What design?"

"He didn't say. You talk to him if you want to know just what he's talking about. I'd rather not, if it comes to that." The earl glared at him until he added, "Your Lordship," and relapsed into a sullen silence.

"He's under control? Macbeth is having no trouble handling him?"

"Macbeth won't nohow have trouble with nobody, never," said Prospero the Rat. "I don't know where you found him, Your Lordship, but there's a gent what knows how to take care of himself. And everybody else, if it comes to that."

He found me, the quondam Albreth Decanare found himself thinking. Were it not for Auguste Lefavre, henceforth known as "Macbeth," there would be no earldom, no castle, no grand scheme. Macbeth had set all this in motion. Macbeth pulled the strings. Macbeth had found the madman known as Henry whose appearance and whose proclivities were at the heart of the grand scheme. Albreth, by himself, had grown up knowing who he was—his mother had drilled it into him from the cradle—but neither he nor his mother, nor any of his male or female relatives out to second or third cousins once or twice removed, had any idea of what to do about it aside from shaking their fists at blind providence and cursing the fates. All the wealth his great-grandfather had accumulated selling tinned smoked beef to Napoleon's armies and smuggled cognac to the British couldn't buy him a throne.

But Macbeth had connections, and had an implacable desire to take down the British monarchy. The *present* British monarchy. So when he found Albreth and discovered that he was a direct descendant of Edward Plantagenet, the seventeenth Earl of Warwick and rightful heir to the English throne, if four hundred years of inconvenient history could be overlooked, he decided to support the claim—a claim that Albreth had no idea that he could actually pursue until Macbeth had shown him how.

"Macbeth says as how he thinks it's time what you should come down to London," Prospero said. "The Residence on Totting Square is staffed and ready for you and the Word is being spread."

"What?" Albreth squinted at the man. "Westerleigh House is ready? Good God, man, why didn't you say that before?"

"Well, I just did, didn't I?" asked an aggrieved rat. "I was getting to it, and then I did get to it, and there you are . . . Your Lordship."

Albreth leapt from his stool and began pacing back and forth across the width of the room. "So the time has come," he muttered, "but am I prepared—truly prepared?"

"Pardon?" asked Prospero.

Albreth ignored the interruption. "Can any man say he is truly prepared?" he asked the oak doors in front of him. "You must seize the moment when it offers itself." He made a seizing gesture with his right hand that caused Prospero to take two sharp steps backward and out of his way. Then he raised the arm and declaimed, "That which cries 'Thus thou must do, if thou have it'—and that which rather thou dost fear to do than wishest should be undone." He punctuated the words by slamming his fist down on an oaken sideboard *en passant*.

"Whot's that?" asked Prospero.

Albreth paused for breath. "Macbeth," he explained.

"Whot about 'im?"

"Not our friend. The play. *Macbeth*. The Scottish play. By the bard. Those are his words."

"Oh. Is it then? . . . Your Lordship."

Albreth waved a finger at him. "You must to London with all due haste," he said, "and tell Macbeth that I shall follow anon!"

"Whatever you say, Your Lordship," Prospero agreed, backing toward the door. "Whatever you say."

CHAPTER EIGHTEEN

THE FRENCH CONNECTION

Nature, in her indifference,
makes no distinction between good and evil.

—ANATOLE FRANCE

"GO, THEN," PRONOUNCED CECILY, prodding with an oversized hairpin to subdue a few strands that had somehow worked themselves loose from the coil of long auburn hair that was her workday coiffure. With one last twist and push of the hairpin, she raised her head and continued, "I shall not stand in your way."

Barnett paused, a pair of socks in each hand, and considered. "If you want me to stay——" he began.

"No, no," Cecily insisted. "You've already decided. If the professor needs you in Paris, then to Paris you must go."

"*We've* decided," he reminded her.

"True," she conceded.

"You know I wouldn't——"

"No, no, really," Cecily interrupted. She sighed. "I'm sorry. You're right. Professor Moriarty is right. You must go. And since this latest outrage . . . There should be a better, stronger word. That poor woman—will she recover?"

"They think so, but she may never be able to speak again, much less sing."

Cecily shuddered. "You must go. This must end, and if your going to Paris brings that one day closer—you must go. For queen and country, and all that. But I don't have to be pleased about it."

"You could come with me," Barnett suggested for the third or fourth time.

"*Au contraire*, I must stay," Cecily said. "After all, I have my own tasks here. The girl Pamela Dilwaddy must learn how to appear in public and not look like . . . what she is. What she was. And it must be achieved quickly, if it's to be any use. So says Professor Moriarty, and, given the situation, he's clearly right. For queen and country." She looked critically at the way Barnett was stuffing clothing into the leather traveling bag. "Here, let me do that."

"Ah, Pamela," Barnett said, stepping aside to let his wife continue the packing job. "How are you doing with her? I haven't seen her but once in the, what, ten days you've been, ah, tutoring her."

"Nor shall you," Cecily told him, "until she's ready."

"How long is it going to take you to turn her into a lady?" Barnett asked.

Cecily laughed. "A lady, no. Although give me a year . . . but I can teach her to be a passable lady's maid in a few weeks." She picked a starched, folded white shirt from the bureau drawer and compared it critically with a second starched, folded white shirt.

"Really?"

"I think so. Provided she doesn't have to open her mouth, past saying 'ma'am' and 'pardon.' The girl is a surprisingly quick study, but ridding her of that dreadful accent . . ."

"Just stand and curtsey in an apron and mob cap? Is that it?"

"Just so," Cecily agreed. "Turning her into a truly useful lady's maid would require a bit longer—perhaps even a bit longer than turning her into a lady. Being a 'lady' is, after all, largely a question of picking the right parents." She put one of the shirts into the traveling bag and returned the other to the drawer.

"Society then pummels one into shape, whatever one's own inclinations," she continued on her theme. "One does not really *learn* to become a lady, one is molded into the shape of a lady by constant external pressure."

" 'There is a destiny that shapes our ends,' " Barnett suggested.

"Indeed so," Cecily agreed, "and our manners and our carriage and our speech and the clothes we wear and our friendships, and even the books we read, the places we visit, and the food we eat. And eventually, as we are young ladies, our beaux and our husbands."

"You don't seem to have been strongly affected by any of this," Barnett observed.

"I was not raised to be a lady," she told him, "nor to ape them. I was raised to be the daughter of an eclectic professor of philology who believed that my mind was more important than my gender or my social class."

Barnett smiled. "What a dangerous idea."

"Indeed," Cecily replied seriously.

"So one becomes a lady by a process of osmosis, is that it?"

"I would say so. Also if one, or one's parents, are insecure as to how much of the knowledge has seeped in, there are always the Swiss 'finishing schools.' After a year or two at one of those it could be said that a young lady is well and truly finished."

"And a lady's maid?"

"Usually starts her career as a lowly domestic and, after some years in service, may achieve the rank of upstairs maid. If she is quick and fortunate and suits the needs of the mistress of the house or one of the daughters, and a position opens up, she may attain the exalted status of lady's maid. But, as I say, I can teach Pamela how to stand and curtsey and such in a week, if she's a quick study. She does seem to be quite bright once she allows herself to be."

Barnett watched as Cecily held two more identical white shirts up to the light, selected one for his suitcase, and put the other back in the bureau drawer. "Will that suffice?"

"It will have to, won't it? The idea is to be able to take her into places and situations where the miscreants—if that's a sufficiently harsh word for these evil men—might be found, and see if she can recognize anyone. All we'll have to do is find a lady whom she can seem to be tending, and I assume that the professor's new friends should be able to accomplish that."

"Ah!" said Barnett. "And did the professor say in what sort of places or situations he expects the villain to be found?"

"I assume that's what you're going to Paris to find out," his wife told him.

He nodded. "I suppose it is," he said.

She selected two cravats from the rack, rejecting a third, and folded them over the bar in the bag placed there especially to fold cravats over.

"I like the red one," he said.

"No you don't," she said. "Not with either of the suits you're taking."

"I don't?"

"No." Firmly.

"Ah! Clearly I was mistaken. Good of you to point these things out to me."

"What," she asked, smiling sweetly, "is a wife for?"

When he was completely packed to Cecily's satisfaction, he kissed her firmly and completely and stood back. "I have to leave," he said. "Catch the train."

She suddenly clutched at his sleeve and pulled him to her. "Take care of yourself," she said. "Please. Be careful."

"I shall be very careful," he assured her. "Besides, I'll have the mummer to look after me. He spent a few years in Paris and Marseilles before he came to work for the professor. His French is better than mine."

"*My* French is better than yours," she told him, "and I've never lived there."

"There is that," he admitted.

"Do your best to stay out of trouble, my dear," she said.

"I shall, you have my word. Besides, you know I'm a confirmed coward."

"I know what you are," she said. "Please take care."

He hugged her close. "How could any man," he murmured into her hair, "with you to return to, risk losing one moment of the future?"

She said something muffled into his shirt front.

"I shall," he replied, hoping that was the proper response. "I'll be back as soon as—as soon as I can."

Only a few decades earlier it would have taken a traveler ten days or more to make the journey from London to Paris, Barnett mused as he and the mummer settled themselves into their first-class seats on the Continental Express in Victoria Station, and the coach ride would have been fraught with the possibility of peril or at least minor adventure. Today, with a bit of luck, one could leave London in the morning and eat dinner in Paris. Three hours from Victoria to Dover, an hour and a half on the ferry to Calais, and another three hours to the Gare du Nord. If the train isn't delayed. If you make all your connections. If the Channel isn't too rough. If the French customs man doesn't spend too much time poking about in your luggage.

Barnett pulled out his pocket notebook and jotted down these notions as they came to him, pausing as the prefatory jolt of the train getting under way rocked the compartment, and then continuing as useful images came to him: difference between British coach and American stagecoach; the cry of "Stand and deliver!" and the perils of the highwayman and bands of outlaws on one side of the Atlantic and the other compared; the hazards of crossing the Channel under sail; the idea of digging a tunnel from Dover to Calais—and then the fear that Napoleon was actually having one dug, causing the British Army to post men in Dover to listen for the sound of tunnel digging and *Punch* magazine to get several useful cartoons from the image.

Barnett wrote an occasional column, "Mutterings from the Continent," for the *New York World*, and this topic looked as if it could be mined for a cluster of them. "Only Fifty Years Ago: London to Paris in Two Weeks." Two weeks sounded about right. He would have to do some research to pin down facts. There was always some pedantic curmudgeon who knew the exact times and distances, and essayed an erudite letter of shocked indignation if you got it wrong. Usually with the phrase "everybody knows" somewhere in the missive. "Everybody knows that the *carosse de diligence* from Calais to Paris took an average time of three days and four hours, except for that time in May '64 . . ."

The crossing was, indeed, uneventful, and Barnett and the mummer checked into the hotel Pépin le Bref in Montmartre in time for dinner. It wasn't a fashionable area of the city, being infested with artists, writers, poets, playwrights, actors, models, Bohemians, and other untouchables. But it was close by the flat Barnett had for two years as a correspondent for the *World*, before the trip to Constantinople to witness the sea trials of the Garrett-Harris submersible had put him in prison, introduced him to Professor James Moriarty, and forever changed his life.

After a light dinner of *ris d'agneau Provençal avec this and that* for Barnett and an omelet *avec* smelly cheese for Tolliver in the Café Figaro around the corner from the hotel, which reminded Barnett once again that the English, for all their other virtues, can't cook, the mummer took off to renew his acquaintance with *les méchants d'antan*. Barnett, lingering over his cassis, decided that now was as good a time as any to begin his own quest. The journey had been tiring, but the air of Paris was invigorating, and the memories that came flooding back to him at his outdoor table, the very one where he had spent countless hours in those bygone days, were almost overwhelming. Old friends: journalists, artists, novelists, poets, playwrights, perpetual students; earnest intellectuals to a man and, yes, to a woman, solving the world's problems and trying to figure out how to get next month's rent. Was it really eight years ago? He had half expected them to be waiting, frozen in time, to appear ambling down the street or popping from a doorway, to join him at his table.

Benjamin, mon ami, it is good to see you. It has been too long.

It must be—no!—eight years? It can't be. You haven't changed not a bit.

Benjamin, Benjamin—I heard you had gone to Constantinople. For so long? It must have all the delights of the other world to have kept you away from Paris! Oh, London, I see. But—London is so cold. And the British—they are so cold.

Since no one from his past appeared, from doorways or otherwise, he was left to sip his cassis and ponder. What was wanted was information, and he knew just the sort he would be looking for, but he had only the vaguest idea of where to find it. Professor Moriarty's thesis was that the madman, whoever he was, came from France, and thus the plot had originated in France. There were other places in the world where they spoke French, but only in France was the enmity against Britain strong enough to have spawned a plot of this complexity and expense. Ergo it was in France that traces of it might be found, and if it originated in France, then it probably came from Paris.

Barnett took out his pocket notebook and reexamined the notes he had made during the journey. Presumptions: The killer was recruited for this job because he looked sufficiently like the prince to fool at least anyone who didn't know the prince personally, and because he was a killer—that is, he had previously shown some interest in and prowess at the murder and gruesome dissection of his victims. So somewhere in France—assuming Moriarty was right—there should be some record of a tall, thin, aristocratic-looking homicidal maniac.

Where to look?

"It is usually futile to speculate," the professor had said, "when you don't have all the facts, but if there's no way to assemble the needed facts, a bit of speculation might at least point you in a favorable direction." The professor had ventured, admitting that it was a step into the dark, that the trace of the killer might be found in the demimonde—the world where the faux prince would have found his first victims. If he had aimed higher, among respectable women, the outcry would have been huge. The city—or whatever area of France in which he perpetrated his horrors—would have crept about in fear, and the headlines in *les journaux* would have spoken of nothing else for weeks. If he had merely attacked random women in the streets, whether streetwalkers or the bourgeoisie, the resulting panic would have been the same, as witness the impact of Jack the Ripper on the streets of London a few years before.

So his victims, Moriarty surmised, would have been women—or men—who took men home for fun and profit and who had a flat to take them to, since whatever happened didn't happen on the streets. It was estimated, by the authorities that estimate such things, that there were well over ten thousand such women in Paris, and if on occasion one got sliced up the *flics* would not be eager to call attention to the event.

There were several possible sources of information about these women: the doctors who treated the various ailments common to such women, the police who kept an eye on such women, the reformers who went among the ladies of the evening to entreat them to turn their footsteps from the paths of sin and vice and spend their days knitting and starving to death in a genteel and ladylike manner, and the women themselves, if they could be enticed to talk. *Les filles de joie* told their customers what they thought the men wanted to hear, and it would be difficult to elicit from them the secrets that they whispered and shuddered at among themselves.

Barnett pulled the gold pocket watch from his vest pocket, and his eyes went to the motto engraved on the face before he clicked it open. *Tempus fugit non autem memoria: Time is fleeting but memories remain.* The watch had been given to him by the widow of a British officer who had died in the massacre at Khartoum some five years before. She said that he'd be doing her a favor by taking it, as the watch, with that motto, was not what she chose to remember her husband by.

It was a bit past ten o'clock. Barnett rose, threw some coins on the table, and headed in the general direction of Pigalle, where the night's activities were just beginning and a man could find a friend at a reasonable price. Or, often, merely a kind word, a meal, and a place to sleep.

Three hours later he returned to the hotel, having resisted temptation in its manifold forms and learned nothing of any use. Perhaps in the morning something would suggest itself. He lay in bed tossing and turning fretfully for perhaps a full thirty seconds before sleep overtook him.

At nine the next morning, feeling very virtuous for having managed to shower, shave, and dress before noon, he headed downstairs to find some quiet nook where he could have a spot of breakfast and a café au lait or two and read a morning paper.

As he rounded the final bend in the staircase he came upon a man, or at least the tall, thin, angular back of a man, dressed in good Scottish tweeds and an air of ineffable correctitude, accosting the concierge at the front desk, and heard the unexpected words, "My name is Holmes, Sherlock Holmes."

Barnett paused.

"Send a boy up to Monsieur Benjamin Barnett's room, *s'il vous plaît,* and tell him I await him in the lobby."

"I shall have Monsieur Barneet informed of your presence," the concierge agreed.

"Fine. I shall sit over there." The tall man pointed to one of a pair of overstuffed chairs in the corner and proceeded to cross the lobby and sit.

For a moment Barnett wasn't sure what he should do. Holmes and Moriarty were, to put it politely, not the best of friends. What was Holmes doing in Paris? Was Barnett once again to be accosted and charged with being a minion of the professor in some undefined nefarious scheme? Had Holmes suddenly appeared to put some barrier in the way of Barnett's efforts, not understanding what was actually happening?

There was nothing to it, Barnett realized, but to confront Holmes and see what he had to say. Barnett couldn't go skulking around Paris for the next few days avoiding the man and at the same time trying to do his job. He put on his best nonchalant expression and strode across the lobby. "Well, Mr. Holmes, what an unexpected pleasure."

Holmes rose. "Ah, there you are," he said. "Good morning." He extended his hand.

Well, at least it wasn't to be open warfare. Barnett exchanged a firm but brief handshake. "What on earth brought you here," he asked, "and how did you know where to find me?"

"Easily explained," Holmes said, waving Barnett to the seat next to his and sitting back down. Barnett noted that the detective was thinner than he remembered, and his face was drawn, as though he had not been eating well.

"I returned from the little task that has occupied me for the last few months," Holmes told him, "and determined that I would relax in Paris for a fortnight before getting back to the chores of London. I sent a cable to Dr. Watson to inform him of my reemergence and enquire as to the state of things at home. An hour later—an hour later, mind you—I received a response from my brother, Mycroft.

"The speed of the response was enough to tell me something extraordinary was afoot. My brother is noted for his quickness of mind, but not for his fleetness of foot, and somebody had to do a bit of rushing about to get the reply out that rapidly. Not to mention quite a bit of prodding of the telegraph company."

"I would think so," Barnett agreed, having had some experience with the overseas cable office.

"As for the cable itself—" Holmes took the form from his pocket and thrust it at Barnett. "Extraordinary."

Barnett read:

SEE BENJAMIN BARNETT STAYING AT HOTEL PEPIN LE BREF HE
WILL EXPLAIN DO WHAT IS REQUIRED WELCOME BACK MYCROFT

"Extraordinary," Barnett agreed.

"At first I thought it might be some scheme of Moriarty's, so I cabled Mycroft, 'What was the name of our dog?' He replied—within the hour, mind you: 'What dog don't be asinine.' So I knew it was truly from Mycroft."

"Someone might have guessed that you didn't have a dog," Barnett suggested, just to be troublesome.

"True," Holmes admitted. "It was the 'don't be asinine' that convinced me."

"Ah!" Barnett said.

"So I eagerly await your explanation," Holmes said. "Have you, perchance, left the service of Professor Moriarty, who I assume is still safely in durance vile?"

Barnett opened his mouth and then closed it again. Holmes had been told to ask him something—but Barnett didn't know just how much of the story he could, or should, tell the eager consulting detective. "I think—" he began.

"Monsieur Barneet—Monsieur Barneet—" The chubby concierge

came plumping across the lobby waving a sheet of paper like a signal flag in front of him.

"Yes?"

"This gentleman wishes to see you," the concierge said, coming to a stop and pointing a finger at Holmes.

"Really?"

"Indeed. And"—he offered the sheet of paper—"this cable has come for you."

"Ah!" Barnett said. "I thank you."

"It is of nothing." The man nodded and returned to his station behind the front desk.

The telegram was brief:

MY BROTHER SHERLOCK IN PARIS WILL CALL ON YOU TELL
HIM ALL MYCROFT

Well. That simplified things.

Holmes jumped to his feet and pulled at Barnett's sleeve. "It seems that you must have quite a tale to unfold," he said. "Come, let us go in search of breakfast, and you can tell me everything over a couple of croissants and some potted *confiture de fraises*. And a coffee or two, of course. Or do you prefer tea? No—surely coffee."

Barnett laughed and followed Holmes out of the hotel lobby. "Is that one of your famous deductions?" he asked.

"Famous deductions? Really?" Holmes looked bemused for a moment and then responded, "No. Merely that you are a Yankee. I, myself, have a preference for coffee, as it happens. I find it stimulates the mind."

They found seats outside a café that called itself Les Deux Puces and had tables stretching for yards along the street on both sides of a small black door. The croissants were warm and fresh, and the crocks of sweet butter and assorted jams were naive and unprepossessing but held hidden pleasures.

The story of the murders and Moriarty's involvement took a while to tell, and Barnett was on his third cup of café au lait by the time he was done. Holmes let him run through the narrative once without comment and then went slowly back over the details to clarify what could be clarified and to get the whole story fixed in his mind.

"Hmmm," Holmes said. " 'Feet, feet,' eh? Small porridge on which to base a meal, I would say."

"You disagree?" Barnett asked sharply, loyally unprepared to have anyone challenge the professor's conclusions.

"No, no. I quite agree. French they are and therefore France it is. And a tremor anywhere in France is felt somewhere in Paris."

"Exactly what the professor thought," Barnett said.

Holmes frowned at that, but then looked up and tapped on the table with his forefinger. "So your little friend Tolliver is off scouting the underworld? He has, so I am given to understand, quite an extensive knowledge of the underworld."

"So he claims," Barnett agreed. "It is certainly true in London."

"Ah!" Holmes commented. "Not surprising. After all, he is in the employ of Professor Moriarty."

Barnett stared at him steadily for a moment and then said, "You also, I believe, have an extensive knowledge of the London underworld."

Holmes leaned back and smiled. "A touch, Mr. Barnett," he said. "A distinct touch."

They were both silent for perhaps a minute, and then Barnett said, "Well, Mr. Holmes, what do you propose we do?"

"What were you planning to do before I arrived?" Holmes asked.

"I had some nebulous notion of approaching the, ah, ladies of the demimonde hereabouts and asking whether they or any of their friends—"

"Had been murdered and artfully dissected by a homicidal killer?" Holmes finished. "It won't do, you know."

"When you put it that way," Barnett said, "I'm forced to agree. So, I repeat, what do you propose we do?"

Holmes laced his fingers together under his chin and twaddled them restlessly, staring off into space. "I know," he said finally, "of one person who may be able to help us. If she'll talk to us on this subject at all."

"Who might that be?" Barnett inquired.

"She is known as *l'abbesse grise*," Holmes told him. "Perhaps you've heard of her?"

"The gray abbess?" Barnett shook his head. "Never. Surely I would have remembered even a mention of anyone with such a title."

"Ah, well," Holmes said. "She is someone whom the streetwalkers of Paris turn to when they're in trouble."

"What sort of trouble?"

"With the *flics*, with their clients, or money, or losing their domicile, or"—he waved a hand in the air—"whatever. She prefers to work in the shadows, but an occasional mention of her does surface in the mundane world. Which is how I happened to hear of her. I met her about two years ago, in relation to a case involving a rather highly placed Englishman who found himself in a spot of trouble. Curiously it transpired that I had met the lady before she took holy orders and I've had occasion to see her several times since."

"So she is really an abbess?" Barnett asked.

"Indeed so. She is Sister Superior of the Paris chapter of the Holy Order of the Sisters of Mary Magdala, an order of the Moldavian branch of the Catholic Church. One that the Church proper does not recognize, as far as I can tell. Although things occasionally get a bit murky when it comes to what the Catholic Church does or does not recognize."

"Sister Superior?"

"For some reason she dislikes the title 'Mother Superior' and refuses to use it. She works from a small building on rue Montrose that I believe used to be what we would call a 'gin mill.' I'm not sure of the French equivalent."

"I'm sure they have a word for it," Barnett said.

"They have a word for everything," Holmes agreed.

"From this former gin mill," Barnett speculated, "she guides young ladies of the street away from their paths of sin? Teaches them knitting and good works?"

"Quite the contrary," said Holmes. "She makes no attempt to turn the young ladies away from their chosen vocation. Although if any of them wish to take up some other form of gainful employment, she is ready to help. She dispenses helpful advice when asked and material and financial assistance when needed, although where she gets the money from is a question, since she doesn't solicit funds for her good works in any way that I have been able to discern. Most of the nuns of her order are former women of the streets."

"You've investigated her?" Barnett asked.

"I was curious. As I say, I had known her before."

"Well. Shall we go visit her?"

"Finish your coffee and I'll get us a fiacre."

The vehicle that responded to Holmes's hail was an aging one-horse, two-passenger fiacre with a collapsible top. They settled into the lumpy seat cushions, and Holmes gave the *cocher* directions.

As they rounded the corner at the rue la Fayette, the top of the great tower of M. Eiffel came suddenly into view in the distance, poking through the morning mist. "My God!" said Barnett. "So that's what it looks like."

Holmes squinted up. "It's what the upper third of it looks like, anyway."

"Quite a sight," Barnett said.

"You haven't been here since they put that thing up?" Holmes asked. "What do you think?"

"Damn! So that's the tallest man-made structure in the world."

Holmes nodded. "So I believe."

"It's awfully bare—skeletal."

"That, I believe, was the idea."

"Progress!" Barnett snorted. "Now, I believe, someone somewhere will find it necessary to construct something even taller."

"Probably," Holmes agreed.

The fiacre took another turn, and the top of the tallest man-made structure disappeared behind a hotel. Ten minutes later the *cocher* pulled his horse to a stop. "We're two blocks away," Holmes said. "I don't think she'd like to have carriages pulling right up to the door." He handed the coachman a few coins, sprang from the vehicle, and headed down the sidewalk, with Barnett a few steps behind.

The building was a grimy three-story affair that fit in well with its neighbors. Its only distinguishing feature was a sort of turret that began at the second floor and ascended past the roof, ending in a conical top with a pronounced tilt like a dunce's cap. Holmes rapped at the door, which was opened by a short, stout middle-aged woman in a severe gray dress who glared up at him.

"*Oui?*"

"*Je voudrais voir l'abbesse, s'il vous plaît,*" Holmes ventured.

There was a pause, and then the woman's face contorted into what she probably meant as a smile. She was, Barnett decided, unaccustomed to smiling. "Ah!" she said. "You are ze Ainglishman who visited among us previously, is it not?"

"*Oui,*" Holmes agreed. "That was I."

"Ze lady, she is upstairs. Come weeth me."

L'abbesse grise was younger than Barnett had thought she would be and—was it sacrilegious to think?—extremely pretty. *No,* Barnett corrected himself. *Comely.* It meant the same thing, but somehow it was a more decent way to put it when referring to a woman in religious orders. *Exceedingly comely.* She was dressed in gray, not in the robes of a religious order but rather in a severely cut silk jacket with puffy sleeves and a skirt that looked to his untrained eye to be in the latest fashion, or certainly not far behind.

She turned and stretched her hands out. "Sherlock," she said. "How good to see you again."

Sherlock? Nobody ever called Holmes "Sherlock." His brother, perhaps, but nobody else, and the French in particular were punctilious about correct speech, even more than correct behavior. A lot more than correct behavior, if it came to that, Barnett thought. Holmes and the *abbesse* must have developed a particularly close relationship in what must have been a very short time. Or perhaps . . . he decided not to take that train of thought any farther along the track.

"And is this," the abbess asked, extending her hand to Barnett, "the elusive Dr. Watson, whom I hear so much of but never get to meet?"

Holmes chuckled. "May I present my, ah, friend, Mr. Benjamin Barnett," he said. "Mr. Barnett, may I introduce the Princess Irene, abbess of the Paris chapter of the Holy Order of the Sisters of Mary Magdala."

Barnett bowed slightly and shook the slender hand. "A pleasure, ma'am," he said.

"No, the pleasure is mine," the abbess said. "If you are a friend of Sherlock Holmes, then you are a friend of mine. But," she added, turning to Holmes, "I hope someday to meet this mythical Dr. Watson."

"I will bring him when next I come," Holmes told her. "If I can convince him to leave the comforts of wife and home for long enough to embark on such a discomfiting journey."

"He does not like to travel, then, this doctor of yours?" asked the abbess.

"Watson has traveled extensively," Holmes said, "but I admit he doesn't seem to be overly fond of the experience. It's pipe and slippers and a well-done cut off the roast, with his good wife to look after him, that makes him happy these days."

"So," the abbess said. "What is it that brings you to visit me this day?"

"A series of mysterious murders," Holmes told her.

Her eyes widened. "Really? What would I know of such things?"

"We can but hope," he said. "If I may explain?"

The abbess sat herself on a delicate-looking chair by an even more delicate desk and waved the two men to sturdier wooden chairs at the side of the room. "Please begin," she said.

"The situation is this . . ." Holmes briefly and concisely explained what there was to explain. The Abbess Irene followed the narrative intently and interrupted but twice to ask relevant questions. To the first Holmes turned a querying eye to Barnett, who replied, "A production of Arrigo Boito's *Mefistofele* I understand. The victim was a singer named Mathilde van Tromphe."

The abbess nodded. "Lyric soprano," she said. "*Lirico-spinto,* as they call it. Impressive vocal technique. Wide range. I hope she recovers."

To the second question Holmes again deferred to Barnett, who shook his head. "You're right. There must be an aim—a purpose—to all of this, but what it is we do not know."

A prolonged silence followed Holmes's completion of the narrative while the abbess thought over what he had told her. "I may, just may, be able to help. Or at least add to your store of information. There is a girl . . ." She turned to her desk and took one of the new Waterman fountain pens and a sheet of paper from a drawer. Lowering her head to stare at the floor, she held the pen tentatively over the paper. She was, Barnett noted, left-handed.

After a minute she wrote a few sentences on the paper, folded it several times, and sealed it with a bit of gummed tape. "Margarete!" she called.

A young woman in a white smock and the sort of hat one associates with hospitals appeared in the doorway.

"Take this," the abbess said, holding out the paper, "to Mademoiselle. Deschamps. You know where she lives?"

"Yes, Sister," said the girl, holding the sides of her skirt and bobbing her head in an abbreviated curtsey. "And if she isn't in?"

"She's almost always in, but if she's absent, leave it under her door."

"Very good, Sister." The girl repeated the curtsey and tiptoed rapidly out the door.

CHAPTER NINETEEN

THE MENDICANTS GUILD

The law, in its majestic equality,
forbids the rich as well as the poor
from sleeping under bridges,
begging in the streets,
and stealing bread.

—ANATOLE FRANCE

OF THE FOUR SCORE OR SO GUILDS OF LONDON, some dating
back to the twelfth century, most represent craftsmen who perform
some useful service, create utilitarian and even beautiful objects, and
possess learned skills that are passed down through the generations.
Over the years these guilds have devised banners with odd devices
and pithy sayings, and strange and singular raiment for their members to wear when appearing in pageants, at fairs, or behind the closed
doors of their guild halls. Royal charters from this king or that queen
are displayed under glass in their halls, and they are on occasion visited by the Lord Mayor or a royal duke or duchess.

Then there are those guilds that are seldom spoken of and may or
may not still exist—some of which may indeed never have existed.
The Worshipful Order of Leeches and Bleeders disappeared without
a backward glance sometime in the eighteenth century. The Respectful Guild of Spokeshavers was subsumed by the Carpenters and Cabinet Makers Guild within the living memory of some very old craftsmen,
although that useful instrument the spokeshave, in all of its infinite

varieties, is still with us. The Exemplary Order of London Pudding and Duff Makers turned out to be an elaborate hoax, which persisted through the last half of the seventeenth century.

The Poisoners Guild is mentioned in several fourteenth-century manuscripts and court records. Its members performed a useful service for wives wishing to demonstrate their devotion to overbearing husbands and young men desiring to ease the mundane burden of their rich fathers or doddering uncles. White arsenic, the guild's instrument of choice, became known as "inheritance powder" in certain select circles. Individual poisoners were apprehended and convicted from time to time, and hanged or burned at the stake depending on the temper of the times, but the existence of an organized guild was never proven.

The Guild of Assassins is surely apocryphal, and the flurries of assassinations, political or otherwise, that occasionally break forth are merely symptoms of particularly willful or deranged men and women living in particularly virulent times.

The Doxies Circle, also known as the Pavane d'Odalisques, which name is believed to be an oblique inside joke, certainly existed in the seventeenth and eighteenth centuries and is probably still around today, although references to it are few and obscure. Its members are said to support each other financially and morally in times of distress, and to apprise each other of clients whose needs are specialized, or who should be avoided altogether. The ladies of the guild occasionally work together to influence social legislation.

The Mendicants Guild, we are assured, does not really exist. What would be the point of a society of beggars, who would collect the dues, and what possible benefits could accrue to the members? Where would a gathering of the homeless gather?

An old, hunchbacked man with a twisted arm, a gimpy leg, and a leering expression frozen on his withered face, one eye larger than the other under bushy white eyebrows, fondles a thick brass-knobbed hobbling stick and peers at you as you approach the doorway where he sits at the end of Entwhistle Mews, off Poultry Lane in Cripplegate. If you ignore him—for he will do nothing to hinder your approach—you will find the door open, and a long hallway with walls fashioned of ancient bricks will lead you, with sharp twists to the right and left, to a flight of stairs going down, terminating in a closed door, which will open grudgingly if you push at it and enter. It will close behind you when released and will not reopen.

When you have gathered your courage to continue, a narrow hall that smells of things long deceased will take you to a small room, lit by a naked gas fixture, which may contain a wizened old man who will be polishing his wooden leg as you enter, but will more probably be deserted. The man, if he is there, will not answer questions or, indeed, utter any sound beyond the squeaks of his rag on the glossy wood of his leg. Passing that room you will ascend a second flight of stairs and emerge into a stone and brick chamber illuminated by daylight, if it happens to be day, passing through slits some ten feet above you. You will probably not recognize the chamber as being a part of an ancient Roman fort that was incorporated into the city wall in the twelfth century. Pushing open the narrow door in the far wall of the chamber, you will find yourself in a small yard some ten feet below street level on the north side of the church of St. Mary-in-the-Fields, Cripplegate, some two blocks away from where you began.

If the hunchback recognizes you at your approach, or if you murmur the word of the day to him and perhaps drop a small coin in his cup as you pass, your experience upon entering the doorway will be quite different.

It was two in the afternoon of an overcast day when Sir Anthony Darryl followed in Professor Moriarty's footsteps as the professor, swinging his silver-owl-headed ironwood cane rhythmically in time with his step, strode down Entwhistle Mews. Moriarty nodded at the beggar at the doorway and raised his right thumb. The old man tapped his nose twice and returned the nod. Moriarty entered the hallway and paused; Sir Anthony barely avoided bumping sharply into him, the stop was so sudden and unexpected. After a few seconds there was a muted *click-click,* and a section of the brick wall on the right-hand side swung open, revealing the bricks to be mere facings set into a wooden door.

"Well!" said Sir Anthony. "This is getting interesting. Into what secret conclave are you taking me?"

"You shall soon see," replied Moriarty.

The doorway led to a staircase, which went up, turned to the left, and continued up again, ending at a corridor framed in brick, lit with three gas mantles spaced along the wall, and permeated with the musty smell of ancient decay. At the end of it a large man with a twisted lip, wearing brown trowsers and a wool pullover of indeterminate color made for a gent even larger than he, was leaning against the wall, speculatively cleaning his fingernails with a knife of the sort made popular by the late American Colonel Bowie. When he saw who was headed toward him, the knife disappeared with the suddenness of the Great Blackstone's Vanishing Birdcage Illusion, and a great smile centered itself on his face. "Well, if it ain't the perfesser," he said. "What brings you here, if I might ask, amongst the hoi and the polloi?"

"I have come to speak to Twist and ask something of him and your, er, organization," Moriarty said.

"And who you got with yer?" asked the large man apologetically. "You know I has to ask."

"This gentleman is Sir Anthony Darryl," replied the professor. "I vouch for him."

"*Sir* Anthony, is it?" the large man repeated. "My, isn't we getting toney." He stuck his head through the doorway and bellowed, "The professor what is Moriarty and one coming in," and turned back to them. "Enter," he said. Raising his right hand and putting his left hand over his heart, or at least the upper part of his belly, he added, "May no evil befall you whilst you is among us, so we pledge."

"And I pledge for myself and my companion," Moriarty said, duplicating the large man's gesture, "to harbor no evil thoughts or designs against this honorable society."

The room was surprisingly large and well lighted by a row of windows high on the north wall. It bore a variety of threadbare drapes and ancient tapestries along the walls, depicting maps of faraway places, some of them real; exotic fauna, little of it bearing a strong resemblance to any animal known to science; and pictures of castles and manor houses, some with mottoes over or under them in Latin or Greek that would serve to identify the great family who had dwelled in the house to someone conversant with the mottoes of the extinct lines of the nobility.

The floor was covered with rugs of all sizes, shapes, and conditions, and the rugs were inhabited by people; misshapen, grotesque, incomplete people, and the contrivances with which they pulled, pushed, dragged, rolled, stumped, hopped, or simply limped through London while making their daily rounds. A man rose from the middle of this mélange as Moriarty and Sir Anthony entered. He hobbled over to them, pausing to stare up at Moriarty with his one good eye— the right one had a great patch over it—and then either bowed or doubled over in great pain, Sir Anthony wasn't sure which. The flourish of the battered bowler hat that the man achieved with his left hand in the next second made it more probable that the gesture was meant as a bow. "Good morrow, Professor," he said.

"Twist," Moriarty said, with a slight inclination of his head in the direction of the man. "A pleasure to see you again."

"It's been a dog's age," said Twist. "Indeed it has. Who's your friend?"

"Ah! Mr. Twist, may I present the Honorable Sir Anthony Darryl. Sir Anthony, Mr. Twist, chief factotum of the London Maund, largest chapter of the Mendicant's Guild."

"Just Twist, if you please," said the man, peering at Sir Anthony with his good eye. "No 'Mister' and no 'Sir,' and no 'Lord,' and not very honorable, if I do say so meself." He stuck out his hand, which was balled into a fist with the thumb sticking out the side.

"It's their version of a handshake," Moriarty told Sir Anthony. "The thumb touch. As the name suggests, just touch thumbs."

"Um," Sir Anthony said and complied, feeling a bit foolish. Twist seemed satisfied, nodding and turning back to Moriarty. "To what does we owe the honor of this visit, Professor?" he asked.

Moriarty fixed his pince-nez in place and spent a few moments looking around the room, then turned back to the man. "Nice digs," he said.

Twist straightened up. "'At's right," he said. "You ain't been here since when we moved."

"I ain't," Moriarty agreed.

"We was forcibly ejected from the place in Godolphin Street, what they is planning to tear down and in its place erect a government building, or some such. What they ain't started yet and it's going on two years now, but nonetheless we was outed—and here we are."

"Actually, I'd say it's an improvement," Moriarty told him.

"Took a bit o' mopping and dusting and suchlike," Twist said, looking about him with a proprietary air, "but it is beginning to shape up right enough." He waved a hand in the general direction of the far wall. "Come along over here where we can transact our business. We do have some business to transact, I would say. You've not come after all this time just to get a gander at me phiz, pleasant a prospect as that may be."

"Your face is, indeed, a work of art," Moriarty agreed as they moved together in the general direction of the indicated wall. "Rembrandt would have treasured you. Raphael—not so much. But, as you say, we may have a bit of business at hand."

When they reached the wall, Twist poked at the tapestries, each poke raising a little puff of dust, muttering, "Never can find the bloody thing," until a bit of the tessellation of a castle wall sank in under his probing finger.

"This must be the place," he said and lifted the tapestry to reveal the doorless entrance to a small room beyond. "Come into my sanctum," he said, "and we'll jabber."

The room was lit by a high window through which the spire of a church, presumably St. Mary-in-the-Fields, could be seen. The walls were covered by ancient velvet hangings with red-and-gold-flocked representations of tulips in different attitudes. The room held a desk and chair that Henry VII might have sat at, some overstuffed chairs of indeterminate ancestry, and a mahogany bookcase crammed full of books. Sir Anthony leaned over to get a look at some of the titles. There was a partial set of the works of Dickens, a complete set of the Waverley novels, a *County Guide to Nottinghamshire*, a few bound volumes of *Punch*, and several of the novels of Anna Katherine Green.

"Interesting, ah, variety of books you have here," Sir Anthony said when he noticed that Twist was watching him.

"Eclectic is what," Twist offered. "They are brought to me from all over this great metropolis by my fellow guild members, most of whom does not read. So they does not choose the books for their content as such, but they does, on occasion, come across them in what may be described as interesting circumstances. That one, for instance," Twist said, indicating a volume lying sideways on the shelf, "was hurled out of a hansom cab by an elderly gent who snarled, 'Bah! What utter rubbish!' as it left his hand. Flew right by the nose of young Nobby the Gimp, who brought it here. I ain't had a chance to peruse it myself, so I can't comment on the gentleman's judgement."

Sir Anthony peered at the spine of the book. *The Descent of Man, and Selection in Relation to Sex,* it read, *by Charles Darwin.* "Perhaps the gentleman who hurled it," he suggested, "was expecting, based on the title, something other than what he got."

"P'raps," Twist agreed. "Now." He rubbed his hands together as though he were warming them before a fire. "Let's get down to it. What can we wretched mendicants do for you two gentlemen?"

Moriarty considered. "How many of your, er, members do you suppose can understand, or at least recognize, French when they hear it?"

Twist's good eye widened a bit, and he turned his head to get the professor directly in his view. "Now, I wouldn't have any way of knowing that, would I?" he asked. "It ain't the sort of thing what comes up in the passing back and forth of normal chitter or chatter, now is it?"

"Do you think you can find out?"

" 'Course I can find out, who says I can't?"

"Fairly rapidly?"

"By this time tomorrow."

"Then here's what I want," said Moriarty.

THE LAST PLANTAGENET

SPECIAL TO THE EVENING CALL

IT IS NOT EVERYDAY that an ancient and honorable patent of nobility which has fallen into disuse is reclaimed by its rightful heir. Mr Albreth Decanare, who has recently moved to Britain from his domicile in France, has assumed the title of Earl of Mersy. Mr. Decanare claims to be the direct male descendant of Reginald Phipps Calworthy Bonneworth, the last Earl of Mersy, and has presented documents to support his peerage claim to the Crown Office of the House of Lords, which is looking into the matter.

The last Lord Mersy fled England in 1588 when evidence was presented involving him in the so-called Babington Plot, which as every schoolchild knows was an attempt to displace Queen Elizabeth with Mary, Queen of Scots. He is believed to have died in Grenoble in 1604. The peerage itself was never revoked and has remained vacant these last three centuries.

The prospective Lord Mersy has also brought with him documents that prove his ancestor innocent of the charges which were brought against him by Lord Walsingham, Queen Elizabeth's personal secretary and, it is popularly believed, her spymaster.

If his claim is upheld, then Mr. Decanare may also regard himself as the rightful heir of the Plantagenet kings, as the Earls of Mersy had always claimed direct descent in the male line from Richard III's nephew Edward, Earl of Warwick, who was executed in 1499.

Of course it is all moot now. The presumptive Lord Mersy could scarcely find any support in a bid to reclaim the British throne for the House of Plantagenet in this staid and settled century of ours, but it is interesting to speculate on what could have been. ∎

CHAPTER TWENTY

THE BELLEVILLE SLICER

Nobody ever does anything deliberately
in the interests of evil, for the sake of evil.
Everybody acts in the interests of good,
as he understands it.
But everybody understands it in a different way.
Consequently people drown, slay, and kill one another
in the interests of good.

—P. D. OUSPENSKY

MLLE. LOUISA DESCHAMPS WAS A tall, slender young woman of perhaps thirty. Her thick bun of brown hair was meticulously done up atop her thin face, and her wide brown eyes looked unflinchingly upon the world and expected nothing from it. She sat stiffly on the front edge of the straight-back oak armchair that Holmes had pulled out for her, her feet together, her arms tight against her sides, as though not to encourage her body to take up more than the least necessary amount of space. Her high-waisted brown dress was without ornamentation but for a wide white lace collar that circled her neck. She carried, clutched firmly in her right hand, a long white parasol with an ivory handle in the shape of a parrot's head.

"This is not something of which I enjoy speaking," she said in French, looking from Barnett to Holmes and then turning her gaze to the abbess, "but you must know that. Why am I here?" Her voice was deep with a barely perceptible burr that softened the consonants.

"Because I asked you to come?" the abbess suggested.

"Yes. Why?"

"Because you have a story to tell, and these men want to hear it."

"Why?"

"This," the abbess said, gesturing with her hand, "is my friend Mr. Sherlock Holmes, and this is Mr. Benjamin Barnett. They are British."

"So I gathered," Mlle. Deschamps said, "by their shoes."

"They have come over here for our help, Louisa," the abbess said. "There is a madman loose in England. He is murdering women and cutting them most horribly. According to Mr. Holmes, the man was described by one who saw him as tall, slender, regal-looking, dressed as a gentleman. He laughs while he mutilates. Not a robust laugh but a childish giggle. They believe he is French. In order to better ascertain where he might be now, they need to discover his history."

Louisa Deschamps had been slowly rising as the abbess spoke. She was trembling all over. A moment after the abbess ceased speaking, Louisa's parasol clattered to the ground in front of her, her eyes closed, and she fell back into her chair.

"*Mon Dieu,*" said the abbess, rising quickly. "I should have thought . . . I am so sorry."

Before the others had a chance to do anything, Louisa's eyes opened and she looked around the room. "Silly of me," she said, sitting up in the chair with an attempt at a tiny smile.

Holmes was on his feet. "Mademoiselle, are you all right?"

Louisa's eyes went to Holmes and then to Barnett. "Is it he?" she cried. "Could it be? I thought he was dead. They told me . . ."

"Here!" The abbess passed Holmes a small glass. "Cognac. Give it to her."

Holmes took the glass and cupped Louisa's hands around it. For a moment she stared at the glass as though unsure what it was and then, in a quick motion, brought it to her lips and emptied it.

"Ah!" Holmes said, rubbing his hands together. "Come, this is promising!"

"Holmes!" exclaimed Barnett. "Really! The lady is seriously distressed."

"Indeed," said Holmes. He leaned toward Mlle. Deschamps, his eyes fastened hawklike on her face. "I take it this description has some meaning for you?" he asked. "Is that why you carry the parasol?"

"Yes," she told him, reaching down to retrieve the object from the floor by her feet. "I am never without it."

"Holmes," Barnett said, "what—"

"Come now," Holmes said. "You heard that dainty little sunshade clatter as it hit the floor. Surely to give such a satisfying thunk its shaft contains either a flask or a blade. Circumstances favor the blade." He turned back to the young woman. "Of whom are you afraid?"

"Of the man who did this," she said, pointing a finger toward the high collar surrounding her neck. "I had thought him dead, but I couldn't be sure. Now—what you say . . . There couldn't be two such monsters."

"Monsters?" Barnett asked. "You mean . . ."

She raised her hands to her neck and undid the small buttons that held up her collar. "Two such men as the one who did this," she said, pulling the collar open and lifting her head.

Stretched in an arc on her neck above the collarbone was a wide, angry scar—a red slit that looked somehow barely closed, as though it might open and allow blood to gush forth at any second.

"Good God!" Barnett exclaimed.

"Dear me," said Holmes. "What an unusual mark. I have made something of a study of scarring, and I have never seen another like it." He stood up and took a magnifying glass from his pocket. "May I?"

"If you like," she said. "Why not?"

Holmes gently pushed apart the collar even more and peered closely at the wound. "A sharp blade," he commented, "but that, by itself, would not cause this. The wound is fairly old, quite well healed I would say, and yet the scar itself looks almost fresh. What accounts for this?"

"The chief of surgery at the Pitié-Salpêtrière Hospital is, I'm afraid, responsible for the appearance of the scar," Louisa said. "He put some salve on it while it was healing, and it had a bad reaction. The scar formed a sort of scab and, after a while, turned this color. It had been healing well before that. Still, as he almost certainly saved my life, I cannot speak ill of him. As for the scar itself, the man you seek is, I believe, responsible."

"Ah!" Holmes said. "Then—"

"Perhaps you should let her tell her story, Sherlock," the abbess suggested, "then ask such questions as you have."

"Of course," Holmes said, leaning back in his chair and sliding the magnifying glass back into his jacket pocket. "You must forgive me, mademoiselle. My eagerness sometimes causes me to get ahead of myself."

"And way ahead of those around you," the abbess commented wryly.

Mlle. Deschamps held the glass out to the abbess, who, after a moment, nodded and reached for the flask of cognac.

"It has been two years," she said. "I was a dancer at the Montagnes Russes. Not in the chorus, you understand, but a principal. I had admirers, but none above the others, if you see what I mean."

"Yes, of course," Holmes said. "Go on."

"There was this man—the one you describe—who would come almost every night. He sat all alone at a table in the front, drank a bottle of champagne, and stared at the girls. But of course there were many men who did that." She stopped talking and turned to look at the abbess, who, after a second, took up the story.

"At that time," said the abbess, "there was a man—a madman—loose in Paris. He was given the horrible sobriquet of 'the Belleville Slicer' by the press, since his first known victim, a sixteen-year-old schoolgirl, was found in an alley off the rue Ramponeau in Belleville. But he soon graduated to attacking women in their own homes at night."

"Strange," said Barnett, "I don't remember—"

"It received curiously little attention in the press," the abbess said. "Curious, that is, until you reflect that the Paris Exposition was about to start, and the authorities didn't want anything to discourage the thousands of tourists that were destined to come and gape at Mr. Eiffel's new tower and wander among the many pavilions and admire everything Parisian—everything French. One could not allow the occasional butchery of a young woman to distract from all that. After all, the monster was only attacking the *filles clandestines,* not respectable women or tourists."

"The *filles* . . . ?" Barnett began.

"The term used by the authorities to describe unregistered prostitutes, as opposed to the *filles soumises,* who have their identity cards from the gendarmes. Everything in France is regulated. The poor girls are not given any assistance, you understand, but they are regulated."

"You sound . . ." Holmes began.

"Yes, I do, don't I," agreed the abbess, smiling a tight little smile. "As you may have noticed in the past, I have little respect for those who feel they have the right to tell others how to behave."

"And you an abbess?" queried Holmes. "How do you reconcile—"

"It is, how shall I put it? A marriage of convenience between myself and the Church, but not necessarily of conviction—on either part. My superiors turn a blind eye to much of what I do, and I to much of what they do."

The abbess picked up three stem glasses with her right hand, holding them upright between her fingers, and filled each with about three-quarters of an inch of cognac. "Here," she said, handing one to Holmes and one to Barnett. "Let us fortify ourselves for the narrative." She held the decanter up with a questioning glance at Mlle. Deschamps, who shook her head.

"No more for now," she said.

"Well, then," the abbess said, resuming her story. "Louisa was the monster's last victim. He was, as you have certainly surmised, the gentleman who sat at the front table. It was her misfortune that he had turned away from the *filles éparses*—the streetwalkers, and she somehow caught his eye."

"He must have followed me home at some time," Louisa said, "for he knew where I lived. Indeed I have reason to believe that he had been in my flat several times in my absence. I had, on occasion, noticed things disturbed ever so slightly. I assumed it was the cleaning lady or the concierge, who took a healthy interest in the lives of her tenants. But . . ."

"Go on," said Holmes.

"On this occasion he was waiting for me in my bedroom, sitting on my bed. When I entered he leaped up and grabbed me by the"—she swallowed and went on—"by the throat and dragged me back over to the bed. I was too startled even to be afraid, it was so sudden. But also I was too startled to do anything to help myself. I dropped my candle when he grabbed me, and the room was dark, but I knew who it was almost instantly—he was giggling the whole time, and that same . . . noise . . . would escape from him from time to time while he was watching the girls dance at the club. A feeling of dreadful fear came over me. It was clear that he was a madman and I would be lucky to escape from this alive." She stopped speaking and closed her eyes.

"If you don't want to continue—" the abbess began.

Louisa shook her head, and she said, "However, I will, perhaps, take a little more of the cognac, if you don't mind."

"Of course," said the abbess, reaching for the decanter.

"I have not spoken of this but three times since it happened," Louisa said. "Once to the gendarmes, again to the *juge d'instruction,* and to madame the abbess, who consoled me and gave me the will to go on." She held her glass out to the abbess and then took a sip of the cognac. "He cut me," she continued. "First cutting through my blouse and my corset and, quite incidentally I'm sure, cutting through my skin. I still have that scar also."

"You are very brave even to talk about it now, years later," said Barnett.

"Thank you," she said. "I do not feel brave. I feel frightened that there is the possibility that he is once more on the streets. Very frightened."

"He is in London, not Paris, if it is indeed he," said Holmes.

"How did you escape this madman?" Barnett asked.

"I was unable to scream," she said, "but in thrashing about I, quite accidentally, overturned the night table by the bed. A large ewer fell to the floor and shattered. A few seconds later my brother, Jacques, came rushing into the bedroom. He grappled with the man, who wrenched himself free and fled down the stairs, leaving behind his hat and a large, very sharp knife."

"So the man got away?" Barnett asked.

"For the moment. Jacques thought it more important to tend to my wounds, and so I lived. Had he chased the man he might or might not have caught him, but I surely would have bled to death."

"Your brother lived with you?" asked Holmes.

"No. Jacques is a sailor. He was home on leave from the battleship *Marceau* and had been asleep on a couch in an alcove off the parlor. I didn't even know he was there. Obviously the Belleville Slicer didn't either."

"You were quite fortunate, mademoiselle," said Holmes. "What happened then?"

"My brother's yelling woke the concierge, who came upstairs to berate me for having a man in my rooms. Jacques sent her for an ambulance, and I was taken to the hospital."

"And your assailant?"

"I told the gendarme who interviewed me at the hospital when I was able to speak—well, I wasn't actually able to speak, but with a writing pad I was able to convey information. This was, I believe, three days later. I had been unconscious from loss of blood and shock. They were not sure I was going to live."

"My poor pigeon," said the abbess.

"I told him that I had recognized my assailant, that he was a regular at the cabaret, but I did not know his name. An agent of the Sûreté was sent to the Montagnes Russes to ask the manager if he perhaps knew the man's name."

Holmes leaned forward. "He identified him?"

"Better. The creature was sitting at his usual table when the agent arrived. He seemed surprised, I am told, that he could be wanted for any offence. As for the rest . . ." She held a hand out to the abbess.

"He went willingly," said the abbess, taking up the story, "and with many a giggle back to the police station. It was all a misunderstanding; he had done nothing wrong. His name, it transpired, was Georges Bonfils d'Eny, and he owned a draper's shop on the avenue Weil. A search warrant was obtained for the shop and his flat on rue des Eaux, and many horrors were found. It soon became clear that he was, indeed, the Belleville Slicer."

"Horrors?" asked Barnett. As the abbess prepared to speak, he held up his hand. "On second thought," he said, "perhaps we had best not hear them. There is no need—"

"*Au contraire,*" said Holmes. "Every morsel of information about this man, no matter how distressing, might be of use to us." He turned to Mlle. Deschamps. "If you'd like to be excused while Madame Irene speaks of this, we will certainly understand. There is presumably nothing you can add to the story of what was discovered when you were in the hospital or otherwise not present."

"I'll stay," Louisa said firmly.

"Very well," said Holmes. He turned to the abbess. "You know what was found?"

"I do," she said. "The *juge d'instruction* was a special friend of mine at the time. It was he who asked me to give what aid I could to Mademoiselle Louisa, who was, understandably, suffering from more than her physical wounds."

"So you had an insider's view of the case?" Holmes asked.

"You could say that. I did see an inventory of what was found in Monsieur d'Eny's flat. There were—" She paused and looked at Louisa, considering, but then went on. "There were body parts from perhaps a dozen unidentified women preserved in large jars in some sort of fluid. Also several, ah, appendages that had been removed from small boys. The rest of the bodies of these unidentified victims have, to my knowledge, never been found."

Barnett shook his head. "It must have been a horrendous trial," he said.

"There was no trial," the abbess said. "Georges Bonfils d'Eny was adjudged 'incompetent to stand trial by reason of insanity' by a special panel of the *cour d'assises* and whisked off to an asylum. As a journalist friend of mine discovered, it was not encouraged that anyone should write about this case or inquire too closely as to Monsieur Bonfils d'Eny's current condition or course of treatment. In some six months time it became known that Monsieur Bonfils d'Eny had died—of pneumonia, I believe."

"In what asylum did Monsieur Whosis de Whatsis reside?" Barnett asked.

"La Maison de Fous de Sainte-Anne la Belle, which is just outside the town of Brunoy, to the south of Paris."

"Run by a religious order?" Holmes asked.

"Perhaps at one time," said the abbess, "but in recent years it has been staffed by a group calling itself Le Sacristie de l'Agneau de Dieu."

"Sounds religious to me," Barnett observed.

"So you would think," Abbess Irene agreed. "Indeed, the order claims the imprimatur of the bishop of someplace-or-other, but it is not listed in any official Church documents that I am aware of."

"So," said Holmes, "it seems a reasonable inference that the Belleville Slicer is still alive and practicing his craft, albeit on the other side of the Channel. But why, and at whose behest? It is at the *maison de fous* of the beauteous St. Anne that I imagine the answers to the questions are to be found. We must take ourselves thither."

Barnett rose. "Thank you, Abbess, for your assistance, and you, Mademoiselle. Deschamps, I admire your courage, and we are most grateful for your help."

"Please," she said. "Determine whether this monster is alive or dead. And . . . and . . . and if he is alive—kill him."

CHAPTER TWENTY-ONE

THIS DAY'S MADNESS

Yesterday This *Day's Madness did prepare;*
To-morrow's Silence, Triumph, or Despair:
Drink! for you know not whence you came, nor why:
Drink! for you know not why you go, nor where.

—OMAR KAYYAM (TRANSLATED BY EDWARD FITZGERALD)

BUCKLE STREET SLUNK OFF of Commons Road at an oblique angle, twisted around to the left, swerved to the right, and ended at a brick wall. The street was inhabited by decaying warehouses and yards filled with the detritus of long-closed businesses, discarded furnishings, and cast-off lives. Beyond the wall was a narrow yard haphazardly filled with parts for trams from a defunct attempt to create a short-line steam railroad.

The house at the left edge of the yard was boarded over and fenced in, and it had been unoccupied for three decades before Colonel Auguste Lefavre had discovered it. When Lefavre had returned to London as "Macbeth," the house had filled the need for a secret gathering place, a supply depot, and a prison. For the past two months the madman Bonfils d'Eny, known as "Henry," had been kept in an upper room under guard, allowed out only in brief intervals to further the baleful needs of the Sacristy and his keeper, Macbeth.

For the past three weeks the Prince of Wales had been lodged in a comfortable but secure room on the ground floor, under the impression that he was being held for ransom. He was not pleased.

"He has complaints," said Prospero.

Macbeth looked up from his writing. "Which one?"

"The prince."

"Which one?"

"His Highness. The real prince. Although your bloody friend Henry ain't no walk in the park neither."

"What's his complaint?"

"The prince? Aside from the usual as how we can't do this to him and the like, he wants his morning *Times*, he wants to get some exercise, he wants to see us tried in the dock as common criminals, and he wants to know why his ransom hasn't been paid."

"Yes. And Henry?"

"He wants to know why he's being kept inside all day, and he wants his bit o' skirt." Prospero grinned. "And he wants to know why he can't meet the prince."

"Ah!" said Macbeth. "So he knows who our guest is, does he?"

"He may be crazy as a loon," Prospero offered, "but he ain't stupid."

"See that his needs are met," said Macbeth. "The day is almost upon us, and we need him eager, but not rabid. Tomorrow we move to the Russell Court house and clean him up for the big moment."

"We's got a trollop set for him now," Prospero said. "She ain't much, but she'll do."

"Ah!" said Macbeth. He pushed himself up and bounced around on the balls of his feet for a few seconds like a pugilist entering the ring. "Let us commence the evening's festivities."

Prospero moved ahead of him down the hall. "I don't like this part of it, I tell you," he said.

"Necessary to the day are the evils thereof," pronounced Macbeth.

Prospero turned to look at him for a moment, then shook his head. "I don't like it. Nohow."

The girl was waiting for them by the front door where the carriage driver had dropped her. She was young and frail-looking and reasonably clean, with dark eyes and a full mouth. She wore a high-necked gown of light gray taffeta that had once been elegant, but that was several decades and many owners ago. "Say, what sort of place is this?" she asked as Macbeth led her down the hall. "It sure ain't much to look at from the outside. From the inside neither if it comes to that," she added, looking around.

"It suffices for our needs," said Macbeth. "Come this way."

She held back. "I were promised a quid," she said, her voice showing how unbelievable she had found the offer.

"And a quid you shall have," Macbeth reassured her. "There's the door," he pointed. "Your gentleman awaits."

"Say, he don't want to do nothing kinky, do he? I ain't into that kinky stuff."

"I assure you," Macbeth said, "all he wants to do is satisfy his carnal desires."

She looked puzzled for a second, but then her face cleared up. "'At's all right then, innit?" she said, going to the door. She knocked cautiously and was rewarded with a giggled "Come in, my dear, come in."

She went in.

The screams didn't start for about ten minutes. They were eating supper in a small room down the hall, and the sounds were muted and distant through the walls. They affected not to hear. After the second scream Prospero pushed his chair back. "I have eaten enough," he said. "I think I'll go outside. Smoke a cigar. Take a walk."

Macbeth stood up, his jaw tight and the muscles in his neck twitching slightly as he struggled to remain impassive. "You think this is simple?" he demanded. "We are attempting to overthrow an entrenched monarchy, or at least create such discord that all of Britain's gaze will be internally fixed for the next two years, and we have but one tool. It is imprecise. It is distasteful. But it's what we have. A few lives are lost, mostly meaningless people the world will not miss. Think of the cost in lives if Britain goes to war with France. Weigh that against the life of this *cocotte*."

"I think I'll take a walk," Prospero said.

It was less than two minutes before the screaming stopped.

A few minutes later Henry's door was pulled open and he peered into the hall. He giggled. *"Je suis fini,"* he announced.

Macbeth stood up and felt in his waistcoat pocket for some coins. Counting out one pound's worth, he tied them into an oversized hand-kerchief and went to get a couple of men to help him do what had to be done.

[CHAPTER TWENTY-TWO]

WHO THINKS EVIL

*It is a fact that cannot
be denied: The wickedness of others
becomes our own wickedness because
it kindles something evil in our
own hearts.*

—CARL JUNG

MYSTERIOUS DISTURBANCE AT COVENT GARDEN OPERA HOUSE
ROYALTY PRESENT

SPECIAL TO THE EVENING CALL
TUESDAY, 30 SEPT., 1890

The Call has just received information regarding a disquieting event that occurred four evenings ago at the famed Covent Garden Opera House. While the evening's opera was in progress an unknown assailant made his way into the backstage dressing rooms and attacked Mlle. Mathilde van Tromphe, the opera's prima donna, with a large knife, causing a grievous wound on her neck. The timely arrival of Sergeant Albert Cottswell of the Metropolitan Police caused the aggressor to break off his attack and prevented this appalling incident from becoming an even greater tragedy. Sir Vincent Poberty, a local surgeon, came up from the audience to assist, and Mlle. van Tromphe was taken to St. George's Hospital, Hyde Park, and released to recuperate in her flat. She is expected to make a complete recovery, although it is not yet known whether she will be able to sing again. The singer stated that she did not know her attacker and can think of no reason for his actions.

According to our informant, His Royal Highness Prince Albert Victor was present at the performance, and was actually backstage at the time of the attack, but he sustained no injuries and was apparently unaware that the outrage was taking place. It is not entirely clear just what His Royal Highness was doing at Covent Garden that evening, as his visit was not on the published Palace schedule, and was not announced beforehand.

When asked to comment on the affair, a Palace spokesman said that the Palace had no knowledge of the incident. He further stated that the prince declined to give an interview.

The opera being performed was 'Mefistofele,' a retelling of the Faust legend by the Italian composer Arrigo Boito, which has not been seen on the London stage for over twenty years. Mlle. van Tromphe was singing the role of Margaret. The assault took place after the third act in the singer's dressing room, where she was resting and awaiting the final curtain to take her curtain calls. The call from the stage for assistance caused some comment, coming as it did in the middle of the act, but no one in the audience was aware of just what had occurred, although there was some remarking about the fact that Mlle. van Tromphe did not come out to take her final bows, a fact almost unprecedented in the annals of the theatre.

Interviewed at his station house the next morning, Sergeant Cottswell stated that he was only doing his duty and he was pleased that Mlle. van Tromphe would recover. He declined to answer any further questions, averring that it was for others to say what had happened.

There is some talk about earlier outrages of a similar nature that are alleged, by a source who wishes to remain anonymous, to have taken place at various locations about London in the past month.

BODY FOUND IN THAMES

The mutilated body of a young woman was pulled out of the Thames at the foot of Narrow Street, Limehouse, early this morning. The police surgeon estimates that it had been in the water no more than a day. This is the latest in a series of such finds over the past month. None of the women has been identified, the action of the tides and the river creatures having added to the original disfiguring sufficiently to make the bodies unrecognizable, although it is believed that they were all women of the streets.

REMINISCENT OF THE WHITECHAPEL MURDERS

Could these indignities signal a return of the infamous Jack the Ripper, whose outrages in the Whitechapel district two years ago (continued on p. 7)

"Help yourself to the kippers," His Grace Albert John Wythender Ardbaum Ramson, sixteenth Duke of Shorham, told Clarence Anton Montgrief, fifth Earl of Scully and hereditary holder of the baronetcies of Reith and Glendower, with a gesture toward the serving tray on the sideboard. "They're tasty, very tasty." He then waved a hand at the butler. "Horrock, fix His Lordship a plate."

"I can't eat," said His Lordship, clasping his two hands firmly over the third button of his waistcoat and shaking his head. "I seem to have a delicate tummy these days. Anything I put in it goes around twice and then comes up again."

"Rum go," said His Grace. "What you need is some good strong curry. I'll have my man fix you up a bowl of *Bharleli wang*. It'll do wonders for the touchy tum."

Lord Montgrief's face turned an interesting shade of pink at the thought. "I don't think so," he said. "Thanks anyway." He got up, clutching the chair firmly, as Professor Moriarty entered the room a few steps ahead of Mycroft Holmes and Sir Anthony Darryl. "Ah, there you are," he said. "I presume you have something to tell us."

They were in the breakfast room of the duke's new London domicile, erected a scant twenty years before, shortly after Chimbraughtenly (pronounced "Chimley") House, the duke's four-hundred-year-old ancestral residence in the city—where Queen Elizabeth had dined, where, legend had it, Charles I went to hide from the Long Parliament in an attempt to flee to the Continent—was razed to make way for several hundred very profitable rental homes.

"Perhaps you'd better leave us now, Horrock," said His Grace, with another wave of his hand, "and shut the door behind you. We are not to be disturbed until I ring."

"Yes, Your Grace," murmured Horrock, backing out of the room and closing the door.

Moriarty paused in the doorway to adjust his pince-nez and then continued into the room. Mycroft strode over to a soft chair by the sideboard and settled down, and Sir Anthony found a straight-back chair in a corner of the room and proceeded to be unobtrusive.

"Things are pulling together," Moriarty said. "I have word from Mr. Barnett, the journalist who has gone to Paris on our behalf, that a man answering the description of our unknown assailant was active in Paris about two years ago. He was known locally as 'the Belleville Slicer.'"

"And we heard nothing of him over here?" asked the earl.

"We were preoccupied with our own slicer at the time," Moriarty reminded him. "Besides, we don't pay much attention to news from France unless it concerns an Englishman or a war. And they, I should note, return the favor. We regard the French as being slightly foolish, and they regard us as being awfully stuffy."

The earl plumped back into his chair and sniffed. "Stuffy?" he said. "Well, really!"

"Tell us," said the Duke of Shoreham, "about this slicer fellow."

Moriarty nodded. "The Belleville Slicer, who turned out to be a gentleman named George Bonfils d'Eny, was apprehended a bit over two years ago, after killing several young women and, apparently, young boys. Mr. Holmes's brother, Sherlock, has returned from whatever distant bourn he had been investigating and has been of some assistance to us in Paris. It was through a connection of his that this information was garnered."

Mycroft, who had been carefully pouring a bottle of stout into a suitable glass, looked up and added, "My brother and Moriarty's journalist friend Mr. Barnett have uncovered what may well be the genesis of this plot," he said. "It has the sort of convoluted logic of a bevy of madmen, but is nonetheless dangerous for that."

"And the Thingummy Slicer?" asked the duke.

Mycroft waved the glass at Moriarty, who took up the story. "Monsieur Bonfils d'Eny was found to be insane and was confined to the asylum of St. Anne outside Paris, where, some six months ago, he is said to have died. Sherlock Holmes and my associate Mummer Tolliver went to St. Anne to ask about d'Eny and were shown where he was buried in the small cemetery just outside the rear gates. There is a discreet tombstone marking the spot."

"But if he died—" began the duke.

Moriarty held up his hand. "I am of the opinion that the reports of his death are greatly exaggerated, as Mr. Twain once said, and probably specious."

"You mean he didn't die?" asked the Duke. "But if there's a gravestone . . ."

"Ah!" said Moriarty. "That's the thing, that tombstone. I direct your attention to that tombstone. St. Anne has been caring for the criminally bewildered for some two hundred years, and many of its residents have died there—with, according to Holmes and Tolliver, nary a stone to mark the spot. If some relation did not care to claim the deceased for private burial, then he was removed to an unmarked pauper's grave in Montparnasse Cemetery under an ancient grant from the city."

The duke put a finger to his nose and rubbed it thoughtfully. After a few moments he asked, "So?"

"So when something quite unusual happens, there may well be a quite unusual reason for it," said Moriarty. "A stone has been erected for Monsieur d'Eny in a cemetery currently reserved for the deceased members of the Order of Le Sacristie de l'Agneau de Dieu, which has run the place for the last score of years. Among some much older graves, there are a dozen or so holding defunct members of the order, and the one for Monsieur d'Eny. It would seem that someone wants to be able to point to the stone and say, 'See, he's deceased. There he lies.' Which might make a curious mind consider the fact that he might not, after all, be as deceased as all that."

"You're saying he might be our madman?" asked the earl.

"He fits the description," said Mycroft. "Not only his physical appearance but in the manner of his assaults. I would say there's little doubt that d'Eny is very much alive, and is our substitute prince."

"So now we know who," said His Grace the Duke of Shorham, who was pacing furiously back and forth along one side of the great table that took up the center of the room. "All that remains to be discovered is what, where, when, and for the love of God *why*! What have the French, or at least the Order of Le Sacristie de l'Agneau de Dieu, against us that they should devise such a heinous plot?"

The earl stared briefly at His Grace the duke and then turned to Moriarty. "Just who, or what, is the Order of the Sacristy of the Lamb of God?" he asked.

"I can give you some information on that," Mycroft interjected. "The Most Secret Service has been keeping an eye on them for the past few years."

"We have a Most Secret Service?" asked the duke. "I didn't know."

"Hence the name," said Mycroft. "The existence of the service is known to only a few highly placed officials in the Foreign Office and Scotland Yard and the prime minister."

"And yourself," said the duke.

"Of course," Mycroft acknowledged. "It was at my instigation that it came into being some years ago. Several ministers considered it unsporting, but when I showed them what other governments were doing here in Britain, they came around. As a matter of fact that young man"—he waved a large hand in the direction of Sir Anthony—"is one of our best agents. Completed a delicate task for us in Tangiers two or three months ago." He gave a slight laugh. "And as a reward he's been dragged into this mess."

"Wherever I'm needed, Mr. Holmes," Sir Anthony said from the corner.

The duke settled back into his chair and took a deep breath, and then another. "Tell us about the Sacristy, Mr. Holmes," he said.

"As far as we have been able to determine," said Mycroft, "although the Sacristy has the trappings and accouterments of an ancient order, it dates back no more than forty or fifty years. It began as a religious order of flagellants who spent their time mortifying the flesh and planting turnips and kale. About twenty years ago it would appear to have been taken over by a small group of army officers who resigned their commissions after the Franco-Prussian War. How they managed the takeover is unknown. It would seem, however, that the parting from the army was less than it appeared. The Sacristy's continuing deep connections with the upper echelon of the army, and especially the general staff, have been noted by our people. Some high-ranking staff officers have been known to take leaves of absence to spend time in contemplative cogitation with the Sacristy and then return to active duty. The Sacristy's stated aim, according to our informant, is to 'regain the honor of France.' "

"Along, I suppose, with those parts of Alsace and Lorraine that were ceded to the Prussians in the peace treaty," observed the duke. "Honor is flexible, land is eternal."

"I, also, would suppose that," agreed Mycroft. "It would seem that, under the guise of being a religious order, the Sacristy has become a cabal dedicated to starting another war with Prussia, and presumably winning it this time. Although whether they can succeed with this mission is doubtful. French military doctrine still stresses that 'elan' will carry any battle."

"If their object is to start a new war with Germany, then what on earth are they doing *here?*" demanded the duke.

"Yes," agreed the earl. "Why are they doing this, and how can we stop them?"

"As to motive, I am baffled," admitted Mycroft. "It makes no sense to me that anyone could consider these killings as working toward his benefit, or the fulfillment of any end that isn't totally insane. Although killing in the name of God is an ancient sport, evil purely for the sake of evil is usually the province of the more sensational of the penny dreadfuls." He turned toward Moriarty. "What say you, Professor?"

Moriarty removed his pince-nez, polished the lenses thoughtfully with a square of flannel from his waistcoat pocket, and replaced it on his nose. "I'm afraid, Mr. Holmes, that you may be too far into the trees to see the shape of the woods," he said. "You have the most perceptive and consistently logical mind of anyone I know—"

"There is my brother," suggested Mycroft.

Moriarty sighed. "Yes, there is Sherlock," he agreed. "To continue; as you've suggested, the revelation of these monstrous acts, with the presumption on the part of the public that HRH is the perpetrator, might well have the effect of destabilizing the government and perhaps even bringing down the monarchy, or at least its present, ah, occupiers."

"We've been discussing that," said the duke, "at the highest levels. We believe that we could weather the resulting storm, but it would be a damnable nuisance. Damnable."

"Perhaps," Moriarty suggested, "that *is* the object."

The Earl of Scully, who had been slumped over in his chair, sat straight up in his chair. "What?" asked the earl. "What?"

"It might be prudent," Moriarty suggested, "to consider the probable result as the intended result. Perhaps the Sacristy wishes— intends—to destabilize the British government, threaten the monarchy, and throw the country into chaos. Perhaps it's not an incidental consequence, but the only purpose of this ghastly charade."

"Again," said the earl, "I ask you; whatever for?"

"I have one possibility to suggest," said Moriarty. "It is a hypothesis, nothing more, but—"

"Let's hear it, man!" urged the duke.

"Hypothesize away," agreed the earl.

"Let me present the facts—the broader facts, if you will—as we know them," Moriarty began. "The Sacristy, as Mr. Holmes has said, is basically a cabal of army officers intent on restoring the honor of France, as they would have it."

"Just so," said Mycroft.

"Which we can interpret to mean avenging the Franco-Prussian War, or as the French call it, the War of 1870. Rectifying the results; reclaiming what was lost."

"The Prussians gave them a smacking that time," said the duke. "No question of that."

"Let us assume that Mr. Holmes is right, and that the Sacristy is preparing to return the favor—and sometime soon."

"How would they manage that?" asked the duke. "The French people are not in the mood for another war. They're not quite over the horrors of the last one—and its aftermath—yet. The siege of Paris, the communes. Horrors quite as bad as anything in the French Revolution itself."

Mycroft harrumphed. "People have short memories for the horror of war and long memories for the insult of defeat, " he said, puffing out his cheeks and then letting the air out through pursed lips. "A pretext can be arranged. It wouldn't be the first time that a cross-border 'outrage' of some sort provoked a war. As a matter of fact . . ." His voice trailed off. "The general staff of the French army is looking for something to take the people's minds off last year's Boulanger affair," he went on after a few meditative breaths, "and there's nothing like a good war to rally the rabble."

"It would be incredibly stupid," the Duke of Shorham said thoughtfully, "but it wouldn't be the first time for that either. Or the last, I'm sure. Most wars are incredibly stupid. But"—he turned to Moriarty—"what has that to do with us?"

"I think the Sacristy wants to make sure that you—that Britain— will stay out of the war once it begins."

"Why on earth," asked the duke, "would we get into such a mess?"

"I doubt that we would," Moriarty agreed, "but the French don't know that."

The duke turned to Mycroft. "What do you think, Mr. Holmes? It seems a bit thin to me."

Mycroft stared thoughtfully into space for a long moment before replying. "I think I'll have a kipper," he said, pushing himself to his feet and turning to the sideboard. After some consideration he filled his plate with a kipper, several rashers of bacon, two sausages, some buttered parsnips, and a muffin. Then he returned to his chair and raised his fork. "The professor may well be right," he said, stabbing the air in Moriarty's general direction with the utensil before returning it to its intended use. "Less than a hundred years ago we were at war with France, and since then there have been a number of misunderstandings."

"Crimea," muttered the earl darkly. "What was the saying that went around then? 'If you have the French for an ally, you don't need any enemies'?"

"Just so," said Mycroft. "Then there is the fact that Kaiser Wilhelm is Victoria's grandson."

"The government certainly wouldn't allow that to influence British foreign policy," said the duke.

"Yes, but can the French general staff be sure of that?" asked Moriarty. "Wouldn't it be more prudent, from their point of view, to get the British government, and the crown, so embroiled in some domestic matter that they are unable to take the time to stare across the Channel?"

The duke stared at Moriarty for a long minute and then screwed his monocle into his right eye and stared for another minute. "By gad!" he said finally. "So this madman is running amuck in London, slaughtering innocent women and children while impersonating His Royal

Highness—and someone presumably is shielding him and guiding him, and I suppose providing him with shelter in between his deadly forays. And all this is to make it easier for France to attack Prussia? Is that your notion?"

"Yes, Your Grace," said Moriarty. "That's about it."

"By gad!" said the duke.

"Do you suppose, honestly suppose," said the earl, "that Prince Albert is still alive?"

"Oh, yes," said Moriarty. "I'm sure of it. The necessary culmination of this murderous scheme is to have His Royal Highness caught in the act, or at least shortly after the actual act."

"I think that is a reasonable assumption," Mycroft agreed. "Although our knowing the true story won't help unless we manage to capture the real culprit—this d'Eny fellow. Without him, or at least his body, to back up what we say, who would believe such a tale? I doubt whether *I* would."

"When do you suppose the final act of this melodrama will commence?" asked the earl.

"Any day—any moment now," Moriarty told him. "This last . . . outrage, had it gone as planned, would have been impossible to contain. A whole theater full of people. So whatever was scheduled to come next was probably the chef d'oeuvre. As my friends in the confidence rackets might call it, the 'convincer.' After the bit of scrum at the theatre they'll need a little time to refine their plan, but not very long, I should think. Notice that news of this latest outrage has reached the daily papers. It may be that one of the people involved talked to a reporter, but I think it likely that those behind this plan are preparing the public for what is to come."

"So we just wait?" asked the duke.

"Oh, no," said Moriarty. "We seek, we probe, we prepare."

"Prepare how?"

"Ah!"

Moriarty strode over to the door to the room and pulled it open, almost upsetting Horrock, the butler, who had been not-quite-leaning against it on the other side. "Hampf, erp, mumph," mumbled Horrock by way of explanation, pulling himself up into a more butlerlike posture. The Duke of Shorham glared at his offending servant but said nothing. One does not reprimand the staff in front of guests.

"Horrock," Moriarty said, "where did you put the lady who arrived with me?"

"The front sitting room, sir," said Horrock, "and her servant."

"Escort them here, would you?"

"Very good, sir." Horrock turned and headed with a rapid but stately stride toward the front of the house.

Moriarty turned to the others. "The coming outrage has certain . . . shall I call them goals?—that our antagonists will try to achieve, and that, therefore, we can look for. They will need some location that is public, but contained. A place that has a fair number of people to witness the attack, but where our pseudo-prince can flee before he can be caught. Then, in the search for the attacker, the real prince must be discovered, probably with a suitable amount of blood and gore on his clothing."

"And the pseudo-prince must be able to escape or disappear safely," added Mycroft. "If he were to be found, the whole scheme would be exposed."

"Once his usefulness to the cabal has ended," Moriarty said, "d'Eny will probably be killed and his body disposed of or rendered unrecognizable."

Horrock appeared at the door, murmuring, "This way, madam, if you please," and bowing deeply enough to satisfy a duchess, then he scurried away before the Duke could catch his eye.

Cecily Barnett, in what the fashion writers would call a fetching light blue bonnet and royal-blue high-waisted tailored dress with puff sleeves, paused momentarily in the doorway and then entered the room, extending her hand to Moriarty. Her maid came in behind her, holding her parasol and a slightly larger purse than was quite the fashion.

"Good day, Professor," Cecily said.

"Good day, madam," Moriarty said, taking her hand and bowing ever so slightly over it. He turned to the others. "May I present Mrs. Cecily Barnett, Your Grace. Mrs. Barnett, this is His Grace the Duke of Shorham, His Lordship the Earl of Scully, Sir Anthony Darryl, and Mr. Mycroft Holmes."

"Mr. Holmes and I have already met," Cecily said, dropping a deep, formal curtsey in the general direction of the others, "and it is my pleasure to meet Your Grace, Your Lordship, Sir Anthony."

The men murmured appropriate responses and looked inquiringly at Moriarty.

"Those preparations I mentioned," Moriarty said, "Mrs. Barnett has enabled, perhaps I should say refined, one of the more important of them for us."

"Really?" The duke peered at Cecily with interest. "How so?"

Cecily turned and gestured. "Pamela, my day book, please."

Her maid came forward and handed her the book. "Here, mum," she said before retreating back to her spot a respectful distance behind.

Cecily stood, book in hand, while two peers of the realm stared at her thoughtfully. Slowly their visages clouded into puzzled frowns.

Mycroft chuckled. "Very clever," he said.

"I'm afraid I don't follow . . ." said His Grace.

Mycroft chuckled again. "Regard!" he said. "She's the invisible woman. You see her, but you don't see her."

"How is that?" asked the duke. "I see her quite clearly, and what has the book to do with . . . with whatever?"

"Not Mrs. Barnett," Mycroft explained, "her maid!"

"Her maid?"

"Quite right," Moriarty said. "Let me introduce Miss Pamela Dilwaddy, the only person who we know has stared at the face of our killer's keeper and can recognize him again."

"A maid?" The Duke of Shoreham looked puzzled. "But I thought the gel who, ah—"

"Mrs. Barnett kindly offered to instruct Miss Dilwaddy in the ways of an upper-class lady's maid."

"Not a lady, eh?" asked the earl.

"A lady's maid can go anywhere," Moriarty said. "To any gathering or social occasion. All she needs is a lady to attend, but a lady needs an invitation."

"Come forward, my girl," Mycroft said, beckoning to Pamela. "Let's see what you look like under the light."

Pamela curtseyed and walked carefully forward to a spot next to Cecily, where she stood and stared demurely at the carpet somewhere in front of her.

The duke eyed both women suspiciously, as though someone were trying to accomplish something that he couldn't quite follow. It had never occurred to him to wonder how ladies' maids got to be ladies' maids. Or, for that matter, just how ladies got to be ladies beyond the matter of birth to the right parents. "Tell me, Mrs. Barnett," he said, "what sort of expertise does it take to train a person in the domestic arts?"

Cecily considered the question. "Aside from the carrying and fetching, an upper-class lady's maid must speak properly. My father teaches English to American heiresses and others who have the misfortune of believing that they already know how to speak it properly. I learned the pedagogy from him. Teaching proper speech to someone who realizes that it must be learned, like Miss Dilwaddy, is comparatively simple, although equally time-consuming. Many hours of practice are necessary, and the manners—the way of walking, of holding one's hands, of giving deference to those who believe they are entitled to it—that also is a matter of practice and constant drilling."

"Um," said the duke.

"What about that other gel?" the earl asked Moriarty. "The coat-check gel at the Château de Watchamacallit. Didn't she see the two men, ah, in question?"

"She only saw them masked," Moriarty told him. "She's useless for this purpose."

"Just what is this purpose?" asked the duke.

"I propose that Miss Dilwaddy be seconded as maid to various ladies who are invited to dinners, fetes, or charity events that might attract our evil friend."

The duke pursed his lips as though he were trying to pull a thought into focus. "What do you suppose this 'friend' might be doing at such events?" he asked after a moment.

Moriarty shrugged. "Advance preparation. Checking out the lie of the land. Noting the security arrangements, ascertaining which rooms are likely to be unused during such a gathering, plotting ingress and egress and places of concealment. It isn't merely a question of committing a murder, remember; it involves arranging for one person to commit the crime and then be spirited away so that another, who must then be produced, may be blamed for it."

Mycroft, who had been staring at his now empty plate, raised his head. "Large house," he said. "Not a hall or theatre or establishment of any sort, I fancy. Not for the final act. They'll want a residence where people of quality are mingling. Enough rooms so that the switch can be handled. Enough people so the thing can't be hushed up."

"A ball?" the earl suggested.

"A ball, a reception for someone high up in the social or political world, a society wedding perhaps."

"So this young lady is to wander about looking for one face among the dozens—perhaps hundreds—of men at such an event. What is she going to say if she is stopped—questioned?" The duke turned to her. "Well, what about it young lady, what would you say?"

Pamela dropped a slight curtsey. "Please, sir," she said, "her lady-ship misplaced her reticule. She sent me to find it. It's dark blue with"—she described small circles with her hand—"a sort of rose pattern on it. You haven't seen such a thing, have you?"

"Really, girl?" the duke said, fixing his eyes on her, his voice rising with feigned doubt and displeasure. "Just which ladyship would that be, now?"

Pamela shot a brief glance at Cecily and then met the duke's stare. "Which ones have you got?" she asked.

"Which . . . which—" the duke sputtered. Then he broke out laughing. "I think you'll do, gel," he said, slapping his knee. "By God, I think you'll do!"

The earl harumphed and turned to Moriarty. "What should we—what can we—do if this young lady happens to recognize our antagonist?"

"We should have a couple of men inside if that can be arranged, or loitering about outside if necessary," Moriarty said. "What I would suggest is that they break in and shoot the blighter right then and there, but I don't suppose that's feasible."

"Afraid not," the duke admitted. "Country of laws and all that."

"They'll have to keep a close watch on him while he is—wherever he is," Mycroft said, "in case this is the actual mission rather than a mere reconnaissance. If he leaves without causing an incident for which he can be arrested, he'll have to be followed. And God help the man who loses him!" He turned to Sir Anthony. "I believe I'll put you in charge of that."

"Many thanks, Mr. Holmes," Sir Anthony replied.

CHAPTER TWENTY-THREE

WESTERLEIGH HOUSE

They have much wisdom yet they are not wise,
They have much goodness yet they do not well,
(The fools we know have their own paradise,
The wicked also have their proper Hell).

—JAMES THOMSON, "THE CITY OF DREADFUL NIGHT"

HE FELT STRANGELY CALM. Westerleigh House was not a castle, it was only sixty or seventy years old, it was on Totting Square right in the heart of London, and he really preferred the countryside. His castle in the countryside if it came to that. Still . . .

The die was cast, the Rubicon was crossed, the . . . the . . . he searched his mind for another simile. The Ides of March were—no, perhaps not the Ides of March. Forget about the bloody Ides of March. The bloody Ides . . . He was practicing using "bloody" in a sentence. British gentlemen, he believed, said "bloody." Not around ladies, of course. Bloody.

The hall was ready, the invitations were sent. The Dowager Countess of Neath had agreed to be hostess—no unmarried young lady would attend an event without an official hostess, so Macbeth had assured him. Even then her mother or a maiden aunt would come along as chaperone. Assisting as hostess was a service that the dowager countess performed regularly, and her price was reasonable. Now the acceptances were coming in. Many of the best people—the *very* best people—were curious about this Earl of Mersy and his claim to be the last Plantagenet and direct heir to the throne. If only four hundred years of history could be reversed.

As indeed they could—so Macbeth told him, and surely Macbeth should know. Those Germans on the throne didn't realize how shaky was their . . . their seat. How slender was the thread by which they stayed in Windsor Castle and Buckingham Palace and all those other places that his ancestors—*his* ancestors—had probably once owned. Just which castles had the Plantagenets owned? He'd have to ask someone.

Albreth Decanare, son of a butcher—a very rich butcher, to be sure, but still a butcher—and now claimant to the title Earl of Mersy and aspirant to the highest position in the British realm, was, with the aid of that fierce and frightening man he called Macbeth, going to turn those aspirations into reality. He was going to replace that doddering old lady in her widow's weeds and take his place as the rightful king of England—and, of course, Scotland and Wales, and the overseas dominions—and emperor of India. He didn't know anything about India. He'd have to look it up after he took the throne.

Albreth's musings were interrupted by the sound of heavy footsteps in the hall outside his study (in the *gallery* outside his *drawing room,* he corrected himself—precision in language was the mark of the true aristocrat), and Colonel Auguste Lefavre, henceforth known as Macbeth, opened the door and flung himself into the room. Exuberant in every motion and positive in every action, that was Macbeth. Even when standing still he gave the impression that it was merely a brief pause before he'd be dashing off.

"I'm surprised," Albreth said petulantly, "that you don't break furniture more often, the way you slam about."

Macbeth glanced at him with an amused smile. "If you stay still too long," he said, "it may catch up."

"What may?" Albreth asked.

"Précisément," said Macbeth. "One never knows. That is the problem."

Albreth looked blankly at Macbeth for a moment and then changed the subject. "So," he said, "where are we? In our plans, I mean," he added as he saw Macbeth glancing around the room.

"It is good," said Macbeth. "It marches. At the reception on Saturday I will have the pleasure of introducing you to the Princess Andrea Marie Sylvia Petrova d'Abore, a lovely young lady who is, I believe, sixth in line for the throne of the Duchy of Courlandt, which is somewhere around Estonia. She is unmarried, and would be a suitable match for you."

"Ah!" said Albreth. "So she is coming to meet me? Is she attractive?"

"She is said to be quite handsome. She is coming," Macbeth added, "because she will go to any fete or ball that is suitably upper-class and where they serve food. Although her pedigree is impeccable, her family is penniless. Were it not for that, she would certainly wait for the sanctioning—if that is the word—council of the House of Lords to approve your patent of nobility before attending any *rassemblement* that you sponsored."

Albreth hung his head like a dog that has been chastised by its master. Then he brightened up. "The patent cannot be long in coming, and then she and a dozen like her will be dancing at my balls and hoping to catch my eye, and vying for the royal favor."

"I think you've left out a step or two," Macbeth said dryly.

"Yes, but my day will come!" Albreth spun around with little dancing steps, holding his frock coat away from his body so that it billowed like a sail. Then with a sudden lurch he stopped spinning and turned to Macbeth. "The Outrage," he said, "will it be long in coming?"

Macbeth looked at him silently for a moment, thinking . . . whatever he was thinking. "It will come," he said. "In due course. At the proper moment."

"Yes, but when?"

"You don't really want to know," Macbeth told him.

"I don't?"

"Please, trust me on this as you have on so much else."

Albreth considered this. "I'd really rather not know," he agreed. "I'd rather not know any of . . . this. I know it's weak, but when I think about that man, Henry, and what he does——"

"Don't," Macbeth advised. "He is a necessary tool, that's all. And those he, ah, eliminates are nobodies, worthless lives that do not matter. If a dozen people stand between you and the throne, then we do what must be done."

"I know," Albreth sighed. "The omelet and the eggs and all that, but still——" He paused and squinted in Macbeth's general direction. "A dozen?"

"More or less."

"But I thought . . ."

"Have to keep him happy between times, you see. The ones that we didn't want to be, ah, public, were disposed of. If they're found after the Outrage, it will just add to Prince Albert's score."

Albreth shook his head. "I'm sorry," he said. "It may sound weak, but I don't like it. I'm just not comfortable——"

Macbeth grabbed him by the shoulders and stared into his eyes. "If you want to be a king," he said with considerable force, "you must think like a king, act like a king. How many people do you think your royal ancestors eliminated to get or hold the throne? Have you thought of that?"

"I try not to," Albreth said.

CHAPTER TWENTY-FOUR

FRENCHIES

Glory be to God, who determined,
for reasons we know not,
that wickedness and stupidity should rule the world.

—ARTHUR DE GOBINEAU

"YOU WANTED FRENCHIES," said the master of the Mendicants Guild, "and Frenchies is what I 'as got for you."

They were in the professor's study, Moriarty settled in the great swivel chair behind his desk and Twist pacing the floor with an occasional lurch or hop, which the professor affected not to notice.

"What sort of Frenchies?" Moriarty asked cautiously.

"The usual sort," replied Twist with the sideways leer that passed with him as a smile. "Ones what speak French and wear bespoke suits that are just a wee bit too tight all over."

"Ah!" said the professor. "And where have you found these sartorial paragons?"

Twist looked at him suspiciously for a moment and then nodded. "It's this'ere way," he started. "I put me chaps about where you suggested they ought to 'ang out—"

"Chaps that speak, or at least understand, French?" Moriarty interrupted.

"What does yer take me for?" asked Twist in an aggrieved voice.

"Go on."

"A lot of the brothers, when they found out they was to get a shilling a day in addition to what they could make off the maund, suddenly found, deep within their livers, an intimate, as they says, knowledge of the French language," Twist explained, "but I weeded out the genuine parlay-vooers from the scrum by the simple expedient of having a chap who was a genuine Froggie—staying with us a bit whilst avoiding some officious rozzers back in Paree—gab a bit with the lot. Them as didn't take the snuff was excused except for a carefully selected group of stalkers and a few who was kept as runners, if they could run, or as watchers if they was particularly immobile—as with having no legs to speak of. Beggars make useful watchers, as you yourself have noted. Begging don't draw no attention past the act itself and the momentary decision whether to part with a ha'penny or a swift kick, and they is soon forgotten. Some particularly nimble lads was kept as carriage followers."

Moriarty nodded. "The process you employed sounds eminently satisfactory," he allowed, "and the results of your eleemosynary efforts? What interesting information have your minions gleaned?"

"You got me there, Professor; I admits my iggoranced."

"How's that?" asked Moriarty.

"Eel-monsy who, when he's at home?"

Moriarty thought back for a second and then said, "Hah! 'Eleemosynary' is the word." He spelled it. "It means pertaining to charity or good works."

Twist leered again. "I could just listen and listen as the words plop from your mouth."

Moriarty leaned back in his chair. "Amusing you is my singular goal in life," he said.

"Very funny," said Twist, dropping into the overstuffed leather armchair on his side of the desk. "And don't forget to give me the dollop with what to pay the lads afore I leaves. Eight quid I makes it, give or take a tuppence or two."

"First the information," said Moriarty. "Then we'll see about the dollop."

" 'At's right," Twist admitted. "You ain't got to pay for the ride till we gets where we're going—and that's the whole of the law." He pulled a long, rolled-up paper tied with a bit of red twine from an inner pocket of his ragged jacket and set it on the desk. "What I got for you is a bunch o' spots and a possible."

"Let's hear."

"The lads done as you suggested, and put their begging bowls or other accouterments of the profession, as it were, hard onto the Frenchies' embassy by Hyde Park and the consultulate at Finsbury Circle and tagged those who came out talking French or sounding like they should be talking French, if yer see what I means."

"With French accents?" Moriarty suggested.

"Like that." Twist agreed. "They was a lot of the blighters, too. It seemed like half of the blokes what came through them doors were Froggies."

"Quelle surprise," said Moriarty.

"All of that," Twist agreed, "but as luck would 'ave it, there is a lot of us." He pulled the twine on the rolled-up paper and spread it open on the desk, revealing a sketchy but carefully drawn map of London. "I 'as the spots marked out for you. We give a number to each of the Froggie gents, and scribble on this'ere chart where 'e—or in a couple of cases she—was picked up and where 'e went. Them as walked, our runners scrabbled after; them as took carriages, our lads 'opped on the backs when they could. They is pretty good at 'opping, our lads."

"So what have we found?" Moriarty asked, fastening his pince-nez firmly on the bridge of his nose and peering down at the map.

"Well." Twist paused dramatically and then stabbed a finger onto the map. " 'Ere," he said, "right 'ere, we might 'ave got a glimpse of the cove yer looking for."

Moriarty leaned back in his chair. "Really?" he asked, drawing out the syllables until that brief word sounded like a sentence.

"Could be, could be," Twist said.

"Right at"—Moriarty peered down at the map—"Randall Court?"

"'Ouse number 7, to be prezact. My man Shivers, who followed another bloke to the 'ouse, seen the bloke you want come out of the door and get into a grandiloquent carriage like for dukes and earls and suchlike, and ride off."

"Were there markings—a crest or insignia of any sort—on the carriage?"

"Nary a blob."

"Interesting," allowed Moriarty. "What made him think it was the right man?"

"'E fitted the description what you gave. Tall posh bloke, skinny, and what to clench it, 'e giggled a bit as 'e were escorted to the carriage."

"Escorted?"

"Right enough. By two other blokes. One sort of short and solid-looking, and the other dressed like a footman, but Shivers sez 'e weren't no footman, 'e were a toff dossed out in footman togs as you might say."

"How could he tell?"

"Shivers, 'e sez, 'Well, 'e didn't walk like a footman, did 'e? And 'e was giving orders to the other two like what no footman ought to do,' 'e sez."

"What sort of orders?"

"Just what I asked 'im. And Shivers, 'e sez, 'Well, I couldn't tell you that, now, could I? 'Cause they was palavering in French, most likely. Anyway, it were French to me,' sez Shivers."

"And—"

Twist held up his hand as though to stop the onrushing question. "I knows what yer going to ask," he said. "No, 'e didn't follow the carriage. 'E couldn't nohow 'cause the footman bloke stayed out there watching as it trotted away."

Moriarty nodded and stood up. "Here," he said, reaching into his desk drawer and removing a small cloth bag. "Here's twenty pounds in silver. Distribute it amongst your crew with my thanks."

"That's a bit of all right," said Twist, taking the coins and stuffing them into his clothing. "More than what I expected, but right enough all the same. You want us to stop, then?"

"No," said the professor. "Keep on as you were, but leave number 7 Randall Court to me now. If your lads find anything else of interest, report it back to this house with due haste. Mr. Maws will know where to find me if need be."

"Always a pleasure doing business with you," the master of the Mendicants Guild opined.

CHAPTER TWENTY-FIVE

COME FOLLOW, FOLLOW, FOLLOW . . .

Oh evil ones,
Ye are a seed of the evil mind,
Ye are a seed of arrogance and perversity,
And so are those that honor you!

—ZOROASTER

THE EARL OF SCULLY TURNED from the great globe in the corner of Moriarty's office, which he had been spinning, idly noting, with some satisfaction, how much of the earth was British. "So finally we have some tangible information," he said. "The question is, what are we to do with it?"

"We could raid the building and arrest everyone inside," suggested Duke Albert, leaning back in the overstuffed chair in the other corner and staring intently across the desk at the professor. "I could have Scotland Yard surround the building with an hour's notice, and in two hours we'd have the lot."

"Indeed," Moriarty agreed, "but quite probably the wrong lot. And no telling what might happen to His Highness if he isn't in the building—or even if he is."

"Harumph!" said the duke.

"Then what do you suggest we do?" asked Sir Anthony.

"That we follow—discreetly—anyone of interest who leaves the

243

building. With a modicum of luck that will lead us to someone, or something, that will shed the required light on their intentions."

"Very good," said the duke. "I can get a dozen men from the Yard—"

Moriarty shook his head. "Excuse me, Your Grace, but I fear Scotland Yard men are not temperamentally suited for this job. Their inclination is to be gruff, forward, and positive. If they are tasked with keeping a place under surveillance, they don't so much hide as lurk. We cannot allow these people to become aware that we're watching. We need men who are shy and retiring to the point of invisibility."

"Where do we find these invisible men?" asked the duke.

"Among the class of men who have come to me for advice in the past," Moriarty told him. "The more discreet sort of burglars or the subtler sort of thieves would be best."

"Humph!" said the duke. "What makes you think that sort of chap would be willing to assist us in this endeavor?"

"Money will be one incentive," Moriarty said, "and, interestingly enough, for reasons I cannot fathom, most villains are mawkishly patriotic."

"Interesting, indeed," said the earl. "So we are to set a thief to catch a fiend. Of course, we'll have to have some Yard men lurking somewhere about in case—in the hopeful case—an arrest must be made."

"We still need to keep the circle of people in the know as small as possible," said the duke. "Your average constable is just as unable to keep something like this a secret as would be a shopgirl."

"I think that's a bit unfair," protested the earl. "There are many reliable men on the force."

"And many taciturn shopgirls," added Moriarty.

"Someone will have to know what they're doing and why," the duke pointed out.

"Perhaps," suggested Sir Anthony Darryl, "the two officers who were involved in the Covent Garden affair. They already have some idea of what's happening, and they seem to have kept their mouths shut about it."

"Excellent idea," agreed the earl. He turned his gaze to Moriarty. "How are we to use our, ah, forces?"

"I thought perhaps that if you have access to a hansom cab or a growler or two," Moriarty said, "and men who can be trusted to follow instructions with a modicum of intelligence to drive them, we could watch the house whilst remaining unobserved and contrive to follow anyone of interest who emerged."

So the forces of order and the children of disorder gathered the next morning, Friday the third of October it was, in the streets a few blocks away from number 7 Randall Court. Three carriages were provided, with a driver and a passenger for each. A growler with a small rat-faced jarvey above and Police Sergeant Albert Cottswell seated below, uncomfortably rigged out in evening garb, down to a top hat and gold-handled ebon cane, waited in Upper Berkley Mews a block to the East of Randall Court. A hansom with a bow-legged ex-jockey atop and a pert-faced young lady with a golden pimpernel-bedecked bonnet seated in the cab loitered in Spottsworth Crescent to the south. A block over on Bixly Street a second hansom lurked, pulled by a burly-looking brown carriage horse with a large white star on its forehead, with Mr. Maws, Moriarty's butler, as cabman in the driver's seat and PC Bertrand Higgins, dressed in his closest approximation of a young man-about-town, as its passenger.

Four people whom Moriarty neglected to identify to the constabulary set about to, each in his own way, keep a close and careful watch on the house at number 7. Shortly before dawn Jimmy "the Squeek" Tomms had shimmied up the side of the four-story sandstone building at number 12, across the way, and settled in on the roof with a bag of pastries, a jug of sweet cider, and a collapsing telescope. His partner in various enterprises—a young man known as "the Beak"—had squirmed to the top of the residence on the next block, where he could watch for signals from Tomms and relay them to the growler driver waiting below. In case someone decided to venture forth through the mews that ran behind number 7, Red Sally had worked her magic with locks on the door of a conveniently vacant stable a way down the mews and was settled inside at the window, with just enough of the grime wiped off so she could see every which way through it. A string had been run to the back of the stable and through the wall, and a small red weight tied to the end outside. With a series of twitches on the string Sally could convey whatever needed to be told to Alphonse, her eight-year-old son, who had been schooled in the secret code of string twitches and was waiting outside, prepared to signal Mr. Maws a block away.

All was ready—but for hours their quarry, whoever that might turn out to be, stubbornly refused to emerge from the building. PC Higgins was beginning to take it personally. Here he was on special duty, and no telling what might come of that, engaged in an adventure that he could tell his grandchildren about—if he was ever to be allowed to speak of it.

"The lad is waving at us," Maws said, interrupting Higgins's thoughts.

Higgins stood up in the cab and shielded his eyes. The lad, Alphonse, was indeed waving a large once-white rag at them. *One-two-three-four from side to side,* a four-wheeler; *one-two up and down,* two passengers; *one-two-three from side to side,* headed east as it left the mews.

"We're off, then," said Maws. "Better sit yourself down."

"Right, right," Higgins agreed, quickly sitting and closing the little folding doors as Maws clucked the horse into motion.

Not too fast, didn't want to appear to be following. Not too slow, didn't want to lose the blighters. Mr. Maws, with his grimy topper and his wide mustache—assumed for the occasion—looked like the compleat cabman. Higgins contrived to look like the perfect upper-class silly ass that he felt himself to be in his sand-colored morning suit with the light red kerchief peeking out of the breast pocket and the brown bowler that was ever so slightly too small for his head. Nobody would give them a second look or for a second assume that they might be following anyone.

The carriage they were following, a maroon brougham with black wheels and a glossy finish, and with somebody-or-other's coat of arms on the door—Higgins could only get glimpses of it as they rounded corners, and couldn't have identified it anyway—proceeded east at an unhurried pace along Watney High Street for perhaps half a mile, then pulled over by a tobacconist's, and one of the two passengers hopped out and darted into the store.

Mr. Maws drove the hansom past the brougham without stopping, and Higgins got a brief view of a sharp nose and the brim of a top hat through the brougham's window. Maws made a right turn at the next corner—Pomfrey Street—and went halfway down the block before pulling to a stop and jumping down to lead the horse around in a tight U-turn. "We'll just await the blighter here," he said. "You might want to stick that mac over your suit to sort of change your appearance, in case they was looking behind them." He pulled a rag from his coat pocket and, producing a small flask from another pocket, dampened the rag and proceeded to wipe the horse's forehead with it, whereupon the white star miraculously disappeared.

Higgins pulled the stiff black coat up from the floor of the cab and drew it over his shoulders. "It smells," he complained.

"So it do," Maws agreed, climbing back up to the driver's seat.

It was perhaps ten minutes later when Higgins saw the brougham passing the street corner ahead of them. Mr. Maws clicked his horse into motion, turned right at the corner, and once again began the slow-speed chase. After another twenty minutes or so it brought them finally to Totting Square, a small park with a fenced area in the center dominated by a larger-than-life-sized bronze statue of a stern-looking man in a doublet and jerkin, puffy pantaloons, and an onion-dome hat with a wide, flat brim. Mr. Maws slowed his horse down to a walk to allow the brougham to keep well ahead of them.

Higgins reached over his head and tapped on the driver's panel, and Maws slid it open. "Do you suppose that's Mr. Totting?" Higgins asked, indicating the statue.

"Or Sir Totting," said Mr. Maws, leaning over to speak to the top of Higgins's head, "or Lord, or General; but I'd say he's some Totting or other."

The brougham went three-quarters of the way around the square and pulled into a gated courtyard just big enough for a carriage to turn around. Which it promptly did, after depositing its two passengers at the door of the Georgian mansion that took up most of that side of the square.

"You jump out and watch them blokes," Mr. Maws murmured down to Higgins. "Carefully now, without them twigging to you. I'll be back directly as soon as I see where yon brougham finishes up."

Higgins decabbed hurriedly, and Maws urged his horse into motion as the brougham pulled out of the courtyard and headed out of the square. A light drizzle had begun, and Higgins turned up the collar of his jacket and regretted having left the mac, smelly as it was, behind in the cab. The two men he was watching scurried into the house as soon as the door was opened, leaving Higgins to lurk in the doorway of the house across the square, where a steady trickle of water fell on his head as the drizzle turned into a shower.

Lights came at one of the first-floor windows, and Higgins could see someone moving about inside. He pulled out his pocket watch and peered down at it. It was seven after three in the afternoon, but the heavy overcast was doing a good job of obscuring the sun and most of its light. Higgins watched the figure in the window until it moved out of sight, and nothing further happened to hold his interest. He crossed over to the park and walked along the narrow brick path to the fence around the statue. Slowly he followed the fence, trying to find a plaque, or a sign, or some words chiseled into the side of the six-foot-high marble base.

"You are looking," a voice from somewhere behind him said softly, "at the bronze statue of Captain Robert Percival Totting of Her Majesty's Seventh Foot Regiment. The 'Her Majesty' in this case being, of course, Queen Elizabeth."

Higgins spun around to see a slender, angular man in a brown check suit emerging from a low bush behind him, one where he would swear no man had been but moments before.

"What the—" Higgins began.

"My apologies," the man said. "Didn't mean to startle you, but I thought I'd better speak up, as you were certain to see me when you turned around."

"Where . . . ?"

"I was sitting quietly next to—well, actually pretty much in—that yew bush. You would have seen me if you looked over as you passed."

"Yes, but what on earth—"

"Am I doing hiding in these bushes? The same as you, I'd say," the man said. "Watching that house, seeing who comes and who goes." He brushed himself off with a quick gesture. "I'm Sherlock Holmes, by the way," he said. "And you are?"

"Higgins," said Higgins. "PC Higgins."

"A pleasure."

"I've met your brother," Higgins volunteered. "How did you know—"

"I recognized your driver, Maws. Works for Professor Moriarty. Used to be a pugilist. It was an obvious deduction. How is Mycroft? Has he any new information on the workings of this plot?"

"What sort of information?" asked Higgins.

"Well, whatever, for example, brought you here?"

"We were following that brougham," explained Higgins.

"Yes, I could see that," said Holmes, "but why? How did it attract your attention?"

Higgins related what he knew, which was not much. "They don't burden me with details," he said. "They tell me, 'Dress like a toff and sit in that there hansom, and Mr. Maws will tell you what to do.'"

"The life of a constable," Holmes agreed. "Yours is not to reason why . . ."

The hansom cab with Maws atop rounded the corner and pulled back into the square. Holmes and Higgins walked over to meet it. Maws touched his whip to the brim of his topper. "Afternoon, Mr. Holmes," he said.

"Good afternoon to you, Mr. Maws," Holmes said. "You don't seem surprised to see me."

"Never surprised to see you, Mr. Holmes. You do turn up in the oddest places."

Holmes gave a sharp laugh. "I think," he said, "that I'd better speak with my brother and, I suppose, Professor Moriarty. You wouldn't happen to be headed in their direction, would you?"

"Climb aboard, Mr. Holmes," Maws offered. Then, leaning down to Higgins, he said, "There's a mews around the block that holds a carriage house for that there establishment. But as we can't cover both doors, and the hansom would be a mite conspicuous loitering about, I think you'd best stay and keep a watch on yon front door. Here, take my inverness, it'll keep you a bit dryer; that old mac is not fit to wear. I'll have someone come around to relieve you in a bit, and perhaps an extra pair of eyes for the mews."

"They'll find me by the gate under them stairs," Higgins said, indicating the entrance to a nearby building, "if the owner doesn't chase me away. There's enough of an overhang to keep me a bit less wet. I fancy I can see right enough over the railing."

"Hop to it, then," said Maws, and Higgins trotted off while Maws, with a snap of the reins, headed the cab back down the street.

"I've always admired your study, Professor," Holmes said, taking off his greatcoat and looking around the room before lowering himself into a chair. "It looks so erudite that it artfully conceals . . . what we both know you to be."

Moriarty sighed. "Ah, Holmes," he said. "You don't know how I've missed you and your puerile accusations."

Mycroft, who was settled in an oversized chair in a corner of the room, harumphed loudly. "Enough! Sherlock, Professor," he said sharply. "We have no time for ancient animosities." He turned to Sir Anthony Darryl, who was standing by the door. "Are the others coming?"

"I have sent messengers," Sir Anthony told him.

"We will just have to fill them in when they arrive," Mycroft said. "Well, Sherlock, what have you to tell us?"

"You, I presume, received my last cable?" Holmes asked.

"This morning," Mycroft said, "if this was the last one." He pulled a neatly folded form from his jacket, unfolded it, and read aloud:

RETURNING SOONEST STOP GAMES AFOOT STOP SH

"That's it," Holmes agreed.

"Elucidate," said Mycroft.

Holmes took a silver cigarette case adorned with the arms of a member of the Austrian royal family from his waistcoat pocket. "There is an asylum called La Maison de Fous de Sainte-Anne la

Belle," he said, removing a cigarette from the case and tamping it down on the engraved wild-boar head on the crest, "located in the forest outside of Brunoy, a small town south of Paris."

Mycroft nodded. "We know about that," he said, "and the supposedly deceased Monsieur Bonfils d'Eny. I'm just trying to save time," he added when his brother turned to stare at him.

"Of course," Sherlock agreed. "To continue, Professor Moriarty's assistant, Mummer Tolliver, and I visited *la maison* yesterday to inquire after Monsieur d'Eny, and were told of his death and shown the stone marking his grave. We appeared satisfied and went off. The mummer returned to Paris, I believe—"

"And thence to London," Moriarty interrupted. "He arrived here less than an hour ago."

"Ah!" said Holmes. "After the little man left, I remained in concealment on the road leading away from the *maison*. About twenty minutes later a man, one of the brothers, by his dress, left the *maison* and headed to Brunoy in a dogcart of the sort the French call *dos-á-dos*. I followed him."

"Were you seen?" Mycroft interrupted.

Sherlock glared at him briefly.

"My apologies," said Mycroft. "Of course not."

There was a clattering at the front door, and the Duke of Shorham and the Earl of Scully stomped into the hall, divested themselves of their raincoats, and were shown into Moriarty's study. In a few terse sentences Mycroft brought them up to date, then gestured to his brother to take up the tale.

Holmes paused to take a light for his cigarette from the lamp on Moriarty's desk and then turned back to face the others. "The man I was following entered the telegraph office and sent a cable. I was able to obtain the telegraph form under the one on which he had composed his message, and thus recover the writing with the aid of a soft lead pencil."

"What was the message?" asked Sir Anthony.

"It was addressed to Macbeth, at Westerleigh House, Totting Square, London," Holmes said, taking out a slip of paper and passing it to him.

ANGLAIS ICI POSER DES QUESTIONS SUR HENRY VU LA TOMBE
PARTI

"English here asking about Henry saw grave went away," Sir Anthony translated.

"Henry?" The duke looked around the room. "Does this help? Who the bloody hell is Henry?"

"I would say that Henry is Bonfils d'Eny, who achieved a sort of local renown as the Belleville Slicer," Moriarty said dryly.

"That is who we were asking questions about," Holmes agreed.

"Ah!" said the duke.

"Of more immediate interest," Moriarty suggested, "is who Macbeth is."

"I," said Mycroft, "concur."

"I went from boat to train to cab and arrived at Westerleigh house in eighteen hours," Holmes went on. "I stationed myself outside the house. The relevance of this address to our problem was confirmed when I saw PC Higgins and Mr. Maws arrive, as they must have had additional information from another source drawing them there."

"Umm. Westerleigh House, Westerleigh House," mused the duke. "Now where have I—" He snapped his fingers. "Of course!"

The others looked at him. "Of course?" asked the earl.

"That damned invitation! My wife wants to go, don't you know, but I've told her that it's impossible, just impossible. Parvenu scallywag!"

"To which particular parvenu, ah, scallywag are you referring, Your Grace?" asked Sir Anthony.

"That chap who's calling himself the Earl of Messy, or some such. Trying to claim the title. Says his great-great-grandfather was the last earl. On top of which the blighter claims to be the, as he puts it, 'last of the Plantagenets.'" The duke shook his head. "What is it all coming to, these days? Anybody thinks they can do anything, claim to be anyone. Americans come over and expect to be accepted into society."

"Only very rich Americans," Sir Anthony said.

"That's little excuse. Rich Americans bring their daughters over here and marry them to some impoverished peer, trading money for a title. Then the gals expect to be called duchess or countess or baroness or whatever."

"I would say they've earned the title," said the earl.

"And the nobleman has often earned the money," Sir Anthony added.

"Bah!" said the duke.

"What about this Westerleigh House, Your Grace?" Mycroft asked. "What invitation?"

"That house—it's where the supposed Earl of Messy . . . Mersy?—has moved himself and his entourage."

"You said something about an invitation," Mycroft reminded the duke.

"How's that?" The duke looked puzzled for a moment; then his face cleared. "Oh, yes. The bally upstart is throwing a bally ball, and he had the bally nerve to invite my wife and me. Won't go, of course. The duchess wants to go—get a look at him and that sort of thing. Something to gossip about, I imagine. But how would it look? I mean, really?"

"I heard about that chap," said the earl. "Got an invitation myself. He's invited half of London. Almost everyone of quality—any sort of quality whatever, it seems."

"When is the ball?"

"Saturday night."

"We'll have to go, of course," said Moriarty.

"So," Holmes said, rubbing his chin thoughtfully. "You think that's it then?"

"It would seem to all come together nicely if we assume that Saturday night is the witching hour," Moriarty said.

"Indeed," Mycroft agreed. "In front of dozens—hundreds—of people. No way it could be hushed up."

"We'd better have our people there," suggested Sir Anthony.

"Without a fuss," added the earl. "How will we manage?"

"The caterers," said Moriarty. "Leave it to me."

CHAPTER TWENTY-SIX

DO I HEAR A WALTZ?

¿Qué es la vida? Un frenesí. ¿Qué es la vida? Un ilusión,
una sombra, una ficción, y el mayor bien es pequeño;
que toda la vida es sueño, y los sueños, sueños son.
[What is life? A madhouse. What is life? An illusion,
a shadow, a fable, and the greatest good is slight,
as life is but a dream, and dreams are dreams.]

—PEDRO CALDERÓN DE LA BARCA

THE RENTED CHINA AND SILVER PLATE arrived Friday evening
in three carriages: twelve large wooden chests, which were lugged in
through the service entrance and stacked in the downstairs pantry
and adjoining hallway. The caterers arrived Saturday noon: in the
service entrance, down the hall past the downstairs pantry and the
cold pantry, through the bucket room, through the bottle room, up
the stairs into the upper kitchen and butler's pantry, and then to work
unpacking and distributing the kitchenware and cutlery which they
had brought with them, and commencing the cutting, peeling, boil-
ing, baking, pounding, ripping, and swearing that the jars of duck
confit must be somewhere amongst the comestible supplies that had
been sent ahead earlier, packed carefully in ice chests. It was not to be
a formal dinner but a floating buffet, which was certain to strain their
resources and their patience. Maisgot, the seneschal, had used that
dreaded phrase "His Lordship leaves the decisions to your good judgment." Which in practice meant His Lordship reserved the right to

carp about the food choices until the very last moment, when it would be impossible to alter any of the major decisions.

The extra staff, supplied by Cogswell's Superior Servant Exchange, began arriving shortly after and set to unpacking and sorting the china and plate and polishing and buffing the odd piece that wasn't up to Cogswell standards, and trying to find out from Maisgot where to put it all. He referred them to the caterers, which resulted in several muttered comments that he affected not to hear.

The orchestra arrived at four, except for the flautist, who was half an hour late and showed up in a state of nervous excitement over a contretemps with his landlady, and had to be calmed with a cup of hot tea and lemon and a biscuit before he could join in the rehearsal. In the tradesmen's entrance they went, up to the ballroom, pausing for an admonition from Maisgot that food and beverages would be supplied as requested, but they were not to mingle with the guests, and then up to the players' balcony, which overlooked both the entrance hall and the ballroom, with high railings and bars like a seraglio to prevent the cellist from leaping down and mingling with said guests.

On the far side of the ballroom was a second balcony, similar to the first but smaller, opening only onto the ballroom, with heavy red velvet drapes covering the three walls. Two ornate red-velvet-covered chairs, on which over the past two hundred years various monarchs and other royals were said to have stationed themselves when they merely wished to make an appearance but didn't wish to mingle with the mere nobility or commoners, faced the room down below.

At five the man who no longer thought of himself as Albreth Decanare, except in the wee hours of the morning when he awakened from a troubled sleep and, for a few frightening moments, couldn't remember where he was or why, looked around the ballroom from the privileged balcony. "It seems so large," he said.

"There will be," Macbeth told him, "over two hundred guests as of the latest tally. The room will not seem large. You have hired twenty-two extra staff, not counting the caterers."

"I have?"

"And all will be utilized. You'll see."

"I shall be recognized!" exulted the prospective Earl of Mersy.

"After tonight, if all goes according to plan, your name will be on the lips of everyone in the English-speaking world."

"Plan?"

Macbeth made a sweeping gesture with his arm, encompassing the ballroom and all it would contain, the past and the future, Albreth's hopes and his fears. Macbeth was good at these sweeping gestures. "You must be regal," he said, "and yet humble. Be firm, and yet flexible. This is the beginning!"

"Gracious!" Albreth said. "The Princess Andrea, she is still coming, is she not? I am anxious to meet her."

"She will definitely be here," said Macbeth. "We are sending a carriage for her."

"We are?"

"We want to assure her presence, do we not?" asked Macbeth.

"We do? I mean, of course we do. I just assumed she had her own carriage."

"Her mother, the grand duchess, didn't want her to come," said Macbeth. "I arranged for *un petit pot* for the mother and a carriage for the daughter."

The almost earl turned to look at his mentor. "You paid her to come?" he asked, a querulous whine in his voice. "You actually *paid* her?"

"I gave a small consideration to the grand duchess, and then Her Grace graciously permitted her daughter to come," said Macbeth. "Not quite the same thing. I have reasons for wanting the princess here."

"Yes, yes," Albreth agreed. "To see if she is suitable."

Macbeth, who was thinking of something else, looked surprised for a second. "Suitable?"

"As my bride," Albreth explained.

"Oh, yes. That. Of course."

"What else?"

Macbeth took a deep breath, put his arm around Albreth's shoulder, and said, "We have much to do, milord. We can discuss this later."

Milord. It had a certain pleasant ring, Albreth thought. *Milord.* He nodded and then gasped. "The silver!"

"The what?"

"The silver, the plate, the china—has it arrived? I don't see it."

"It is here. Maisgot assures me that everything is in order. The silver service is in the kitchen awaiting food. The plates will be brought out as soon as the plate warmers are placed and lighted. Most of the service will be done in the dining room." Macbeth pointed toward the two pair of double doors leading to the dining room. "Small tables, each seating four, will be scattered about for people to sit and eat. At nine or nine thirty the tables and chairs will be cleared away, and the dancing may commence. That is the schedule."

"Ah!" said Milord.

It was just after five when a black brougham swung through Totting Square, rounded the corner, and pulled up by the carriage house in Totting Mews. A tall man who looked a lot like the Prince of Wales emerged, giggling at something only he could see, and was escorted by his short, stocky companion through a concealed side door to Westerleigh House. About ten minutes later a second carriage arrived at the carriage house, and a tall, slender man enveloped in a dark cloak was helped out by two companions. He appeared to be drunk, or drugged, or otherwise incapable of walking on his own, and his companions carefully guided him through the side door, and the carriage pulled away.

CHAPTER TWENTY-SEVEN

THE PRINCE AND
THE GIGGLER

Come, thick night,
And pall thee in the dunnest smoke of hell,
That my keen knife see not the wound it makes,
Nor heaven peep through the blanket of the dark,
To cry, "Hold, hold!"

—WILLIAM SHAKESPEARE

THE SMUG, THE EPT, THE UNCURIOUS, the socially insecure thought it best to avoid the fete at Westerleigh House. The adventurous, the bored, the curious, the hungry, the uncertain thought it might be quite interesting to attend and meet the parvenu earl. Some unfortunates were hobbled by husbands or wives who felt that they couldn't—they simply *couldn't*—be seen at such an event, but the lure of good food, entertainment, dancing, mingling with the nobility, and meeting the most talked-about man in London that week was an intriguing idea. So they came.

The guests began to arrive a few hairs before seven. They shed their outer garments in the cloakroom and were announced as they entered the ballroom by a grandiloquently attired majordomo with a great gold-tipped ebony staff that he thumped on the hardwood floor before and after each name.

Thump. "The Honorable and Mrs. Jacob ValVoort." *Thump.*
Thump. "Baron and Baroness Strubell." *Thump.*
Thump. "The Honorable Professor James Moriarty." *Thump.*

Invitations are easy to forge, if you know someone who makes his living drawing pound notes freehand.

The star of the show, the possible Earl of Mersy, was not in evidence as the guests arrived. He had wanted to be—had pictured himself—standing just inside the ballroom door, smiling and nodding and graciously accepting all the bows and curtseys of his guests as they came through, but Macbeth had convinced him that it would not be wise. There were those, Macbeth suggested, who would choose not to bow or curtsey to a man who, after all, was still a commoner, no matter how close he was to gaining the privilege of being hanged by a silken cord, if convicted of a capital crime.

Now Macbeth had unaccountably disappeared, leaving Albreth standing by the door to his bedroom and trying to decide on his own just when the proper moment would be for his descent down the great staircase.

"How many?" he asked, intercepting a maid who was scurrying down the hall and clutching her arm as though he thought she would run off if he let go.

"'Scuse me, Your Lordship?" (He *would* be called "Your Lordship" in his own house.)

"How many guests have arrived? How many people are downstairs?"

She considered for a second and then curtseyed. "I don't rightly know, Your Lordship. I'll go down and find out for you."

"Yes, yes," he said. "Do that."

"If you'd let go of my arm . . ."

"Oh. Sorry." He released her, and she scurried off.

Two minutes later she scurried back and stopped a respectful distance from His Lordship. "Mr. Maisgot says as how an hundred and twenty-seven persons have passed in through the front door so far," she volunteered. "Not counting a few servants and the like."

"Ah!" said Albreth. "Go back and tell him to inform me when the number reaches two hundred. At that time will I reveal myself."

"Yessir, Your Lordship," said the girl, and she scurried off again.

"He's here!" Sir Anthony whispered, looking casually about as though he just happened to be standing next to Moriarty.

"No need to whisper, Sir Anthony," said the professor. "No reason why we shouldn't be talking to each other, and if anyone sees you talking out of the side of your mouth like that they may wonder about it."

"Ah," said Sir Anthony, turning to face Moriarty. "You're quite right, of course."

"Who's here?" Moriarty asked.

"The Belleville Slicer, and quite probably the prince. Sherlock Holmes is watching in the mews, and he got word to that woman—Red Sally—who's lurking by the statue, and she sent that very short person, Mummer, who told me as I was coming in. He saw a carriage pull up and a chap who looked to be the Slasher come through into the house. A few minutes later a second vehicle disgorged a cloaked man who seemed to be incapacitated and was helped inside. That would be the prince, or I'm an octopus. Holmes would have stopped them then and there, but there were three burly chaps, and he feared for the safety of the prince."

"Ah!" said Moriarty. "The wisest course, but it must have been difficult for him to restrain himself, given his impetuous nature."

"He didn't say," said Sir Anthony.

"Now it's up to us," Moriarty said, tapping his thumb thoughtfully on the beak of the silver owl head that was the handle of his walking stick.

"What should we do?"

"Who have we inside the house?"

"In addition to you and me? There's the earl and Mrs. Barnett, who has come in as his niece, and Miss Dilwaddy, her maid. And the duke and duchess, who is pleased that her husband is doing what she wanted to do for once. I don't think he has told her the reason for his change of mind about attending. And some of the waitstaff, I believe?"

"Two of the servers are my people," Moriarty confirmed. "Following my instructions, they should leave their putative jobs as soon as they can manage and begin searching the house. Of course, it's a big house."

"Won't they be stopped?"

"Quite possibly. However, the regular staff are all new and probably don't know each other very well yet, and my lads have glib tongues, so they have a good chance of talking their way out of any situation that may arise."

There came a riff from the orchestra that might have been a prelude to something, and then a few bars of "Boot and Saddle" from the trumpet, and then expectant silence. The assemblage looked up to the orchestra balcony. The orchestra leader pointed across the room. Their gaze shifted.

The possible Earl of Mersy was standing on the second balcony and leaning forward at a precarious angle toward the crowd.

"My friends."

Slowly the sounds from those in the ballroom ceased as all looked up and waited.

"It was good of you to come. I am your host. My name is Albreth Decanare. My great-great-great"—he stopped and counted on his fingers, then nodded to himself and went on—"great-grandfather was the Earl of Mersy, and his title has fallen into disuse. My family has been away from England too long. I wish to come back, as my great-great-, ah, ancestor would have wished, and assume my right-ful place in the affairs of this country, my country, which I have al-ways loved."

A smattering of applause broke out from the crowd, but it quickly petered out.

"I invited you all here," he continued, "to my new London home so we could get to know each other. As the evening continues I hope to meet each of you and thank you personally for coming. So—let us get on with it! Eat! Drink! And shortly we shall dance!" He twirled around once and then disappeared behind one of the heavy drapes that lined the walls of the small balcony.

"The perfect place!" Moriarty said.

"How's that?"

"That balcony, it's the perfect place. Visible yet unreachable."

"The perfect place for what?"

"Murder," said Moriarty. "You stay here. Find Mrs. Barnett and Pamela—Miss Dilwaddy—and stay close to them. If she sees anyone she recognizes, or if anything else of note happens, attract my atten-tion."

"How will I do that?" asked Sir Anthony.

Moriarty considered. "A loud noise," he suggested. "Drop a tray. If no tray is available, have a seizure. Here." He unpinned the green carnation from his lapel and fastened it onto Sir Anthony's jacket. "I told my people that if they have anything to report and they can't find me, go to the man with the green carnation."

"Very good," said Sir Anthony. "And then I drop a tray?"

"Do whatever seems appropriate," Moriarty said. He smiled for an instant and then walked away toward the great double doors leading to the hall.

"It is a pleasure, and an honor, to meet you," said Albreth, with a minuscule bow.

"Yes?" said Princess Andrea. "For me, also." She extended her gloved hand, which Albreth took and seemed loath to let go of.

They were standing in a private, or at least empty, alcove off the ballroom, where Macbeth had arranged for them to meet. Princess Andrea Marie Sylvia Petrova d'Abore was everything Albreth hoped, and secretly dreamed, she would be. She looked to be somewhere between seventeen and twenty-five—Albreth wasn't good with women's ages—and had long light brown hair that was done up in one of those fancy things that women do their hair up in, topped by a tiara that sparkled with hundreds of tiny diamonds centering around one large green stone that had an inner light of its own. She was tall for a girl, and slender, and dressed in a green gown that discreetly hinted of possible delights beneath.

"Tell me," Albreth continued, "how long are you going to be here?"

"My mamma wants me home by midnight," said the princess, "like *Aschenputtel,* you know. But I may stay longer. She's almost always asleep by midnight anyway."

"Aschenputtel?"

"Yes. You know—the girl with the cruel stepsisters who goes to the ball."

"Cinderella?"

"Oh yes? Cinderella? *Cinderella?*" She rolled the word around on her tongue. "So, unlike Cinderella I may stay until the new day has begun."

"Actually," Albreth said, "I meant how long are you staying here, in England? Before you return to Courlandt."

"Sadly," Princess Andrea said, shaking her head sadly, "we cannot return to our homeland at this time. We are guests of your queen, and thankful for her hospitality."

"Ah!" said Albreth.

Macbeth appeared from somewhere behind them. "You must

mingle," he told Albreth. "Wander about amongst your people. Go now. I will escort Princess Andrea."

"His people?" asked the princess.

"I will explain," Macbeth told her, leading her away. Albreth drooped sadly for a moment, but then straightened up, squared his shoulders, and marched back into the ballroom. A to-be-king has his responsibilities.

CHAPTER TWENTY-EIGHT

FEET, FEET

The trumpet shall be heard on high,
The dead shall live, the living die,
And Music shall untune the sky.

—JOHN DRYDEN

DINNER WAS DONE. The staff rushed politely about taking up the tables and chairs and clearing away the debris. The time for dancing, or standing around the side of the ballroom with a glass of wine and watching others dance, was approaching. Several servitors in classic Polichinelle costumes—long, baggy white jackets over even baggier white pantaloons and black domino masks—wandered among the guests distributing dance cards. The guests were, for the most part, using this time to inspect the other guests. Two dukes were in attendance, perhaps three, some said, along with a smattering of barons and honorables and sirs and ladies and a real-live princess; from a Balkan country nobody had ever heard of, but a princess nonetheless. Such a pretty young thing.

—No, that's not her, that's Lady Coreless. *That's* the princess, over there with that man with the funny mustache.

—Well, she's still a pretty young thing.

Pamela stepped up behind Cecily Barnett and clutched at her arm.

"Ouch!" said Cecily. "What is the matter?"

"It's 'im," Pamela gasped. " 'Im."

"Him? Him whom? Which one?" Cecily looked around the crowded ballroom.

"'Im with the 'feet, feet,' it's 'im!"

Pamela let go of Cecily's arm and, with one last "'im," her eyes rolled up toward the ceiling. Slowly she slid toward the floor. Cecily and Sir Anthony were just able to catch her before she collapsed.

"Over there," Cecily said, pointing with her chin. "There are some chairs by that wall."

They half led and half carried Pamela over to the chairs and propped her up on one. Her eyes opened and she began taking deep, slow breaths. After a few seconds she sat up. "It was 'im," she said. She reached up and pulled a long hatpin from her hair. "Where did 'e go?" she asked, waving the hatpin in front of her like a dagger.

"Careful with that thing," Cecily said.

"I ain't letting 'im near me. Where is 'e?"

"Which 'him' did you see?" asked Sir Anthony, searching around the room for someone who could be "'im."

"'E were standing over there with that princess," Pamela said, pointing to the other side of the room with the hatpin.

"The Slicer?"

"No, not the bloke what killed Rose, but the bloke what were with 'im. The 'feet, feet' bloke. But I don't see 'im now."

"Ah!" said Sir Anthony. "You two stay here and keep looking. I'll go after him."

"What should we do if we see him?" asked Cecily.

"Ah, drop a tray on the floor. Scream like you've seen a mouse. Something like that. The professor will be listening."

"I ain't afraid of mice," Pamela said.

"Of course you're not," Sir Anthony agreed. "What about spiders?"

Pamela nodded. "I could scream if I saw a spider," she agreed.

"Okay, then. A spider it is!" He headed off across the room.

"Or a bat," Pamela added, calling after him.

Macbeth opened the narrow door in the right-hand corner of the small balcony. "It's time," he said in French, peering into the small room. "How do you feel? Do you remember what you have to do?"

Henry was sitting motionless on a short stool in the corner, his face impassive, as though he had somehow been turned off. Macbeth's words served to turn him back on, and he slowly looked up, thought for a second, and then giggled. "I know," he said. "I always know what I have to do."

A look of mixed irritation and disgust crossed Macbeth's narrow face. "Not that," he said. "The rest of it. How to act, where to go . . . Why is it so dark in here? Turn up the light."

"The dark is my friend," Henry said, but he turned the screw on the wall sconce by his stool and brightened the flame. "I can accomplish much in the dark."

"Yes," Macbeth agreed. "It seems you can."

Henry sucked in his cheeks and then released them with a popping sound. "I know what you think of me," he said. "You think I am a tool, that I can be discarded when you are done with me." He sucked in his cheeks again and stared at Macbeth for a long moment. *Pop.* "Perhaps you are the tool. Perhaps your very reason for existence is to help me in the Great Design. Have you not seen that I increase daily? That I get larger with every thread?"

Design? Macbeth thought. *Thread?* "I was unaware of that," he said.

"You'll see," said Henry. "You'll see . . . Are we ready?"

Macbeth nodded. "We are."

"I feel the greatness growing inside of me. Leave me now to prepare."

Macbeth backed out of the room and closed the door behind him. For a few seconds he stared at the wooden panels; then he turned and went downstairs to join the crowd and await the working of the Plan.

His plan, not, he sincerely trusted, Henry's Great Design. But suppose . . . No. He shook his head. Besides, after Henry had served his purpose this evening, it was arranged that he would be no more.

Ten minutes passed.

Henry pranced through the doorway and onto the small balcony and danced forward to the railing as though he were on springs. At first no one noticed him as he bounced gently from foot to foot and surveyed the crowd below. Then an elderly colonel of the Horse Guard saw him and poked his neighbor, and a plump woman saw him and *ahemmed* to her husband, and the sighting spread and the room grew quiet except for the low buzzing of muted voices identifying what, or who, they were seeing. A tall, slender man in the elaborate dress uniform of the 10th Hussars, bespangled with medals and ribbons across the chest, he looked, remarked one young lady who was almost overcome by being so near, just like his picture in *Vanity Fair*.

"It's His Royal Highness, that's who it is, right up there. Trust me."

"Prince Albert Victor, that's who it is. I was in the royal box at Ascot with him last year, no farther away from him than I am from you right now. You have my word, and that's him."

"I didn't think any of the royals would be coming to this event," said a knowledgeable young man. "I actually spoke to the Honorable Hortense, invited her to come along with me, don't you know, and she said none of them were coming on instructions from the palace."

"I suppose His Highness can go where he wishes without permission from Grandmama," opined his companion.

Pamela Dilwaddy, her eyes fixed on the man on the balcony, mouthed, "It's the other 'im," and rose from her chair. Cecily put her hand on the girl's arm and said something to her, but she heard not a word and slid out of the grasp as though it weren't there and started walking slowly across the room.

For a minute the putative HRH stood on his perch in a regal pose and stared down at the people below and smiled a secret smile. A few who were close thought they heard a giggle, but perhaps it was a random noise from the great room. Then, all at once, Princess Andrea of Courlandt came through the door and appeared beside him. Had she been pushed into the space? It seemed that it took her a moment to regain her balance. She looked around her as though she were not sure just what she was doing there.

Just as those below were thinking, because one could hardly keep from thinking, *Tall, handsome prince, petite elegant princess, perhaps . . .* they saw the prince take her hand.

Well . . .

With a sudden gesture the princess pulled her hand free as one would recoil from a deadly adder and took a step back, a look of horror on her face.

What?

The prince turned toward her and giggled—that was clearly a giggle—and grabbed at her shirtfront, pushing her up against the curtain. There was a long silver object in his hand. A knife?

Why would he . . . ?

The princess gasped and tried to break free of his grasp, but he held fast. He raised the knife. She screamed.

Those below were curiously silent, as though they were watching a play and didn't know how they were meant to react to this scene. Some sort of joke, of course, but in very bad taste.

"My God!" It was Albreth, their host, yelling at the top of his voice and running across the room toward the balcony "Not here, not now, not *her!*"

Henry turned and leered at the crowd below, then turned back and slashed—

—at where the girl's throat had been a moment before. But the princess's blouse had ripped, loosening his grip, and she dropped to her knees, her hands up to avert the blow. His blade missed its target, cutting her arm and slashing the side of her head. He looked annoyed and grabbed for the princess, who had fallen, screaming, to the floor beneath him.

The door at the rear of the balcony suddenly swung open and Moriarty pushed in, thrusting and slashing the air ahead of him with his walking stick. With one sharp blow he knocked the knife from Henry's hand, and then the two were grappling and swaying at the edge of the balcony, a furious Henry clutching madly at an implacable Moriarty. They twisted this way and that so that first one and then the other was pushed against the railing. Then, with a sickening cracking sound, the railing gave way, sending the two of them in a roiling mass to the floor below.

Henry landed on top, and within seconds he had risen and launched himself into the crowd. Moriarty, stunned, lay where he had fallen for a few seconds longer before pushing himself to his feet and stumbling after.

From somewhere about his cummerbund Henry produced a second knife, a long, thin, wicked blade, and he lunged forward, the guests parting before him like the Red Sea before Moses. In this open lane stood only Pamela, mute and eerily composed, directly in his path.

Henry grabbed Pamela and lifted her, and she went limp in his arms. He continued forward, using her body as a shield as he ran toward the door.

Pamela twisted slightly in his grasp and seemed to punch him in the chest, and a look of surprise came to his face, but he kept moving. Then she thrust at him again and again, in the chest, in the neck, in the face, and he staggered. Blood was coming from wounds in his neck and face. He stumbled.

Pamela was on top of him now. With a heave of his body he threw her off and tried to rise, but she was back in an instant, sobbing and thrusting again and again with the long hatpin between the fingers of her closed fist. A peculiar gasping noise came from his mouth, and his body shuddered and was still.

Cecily ran over to them, and in a moment of inspiration quelled the muttering from the people behind by calling out in her clear soprano voice, "My God—it's not His Highness at all—it's an impostor!" Then she knelt beside Pamela, who continued to stab the body, and tried to stay her arm. "You can stop now," she said. "He is dead."

"Not dead enough," Pamela cried and stabbed him once, twice, three more times before crumbling in a faint beside the body.

Sir Anthony was in a long hallway now, trying to work his way toward the small balcony, which was somewhere to his right and above. He tried the doors as he passed them—small room, small room, toilet—aha! Here was a flight of stairs leading up. It was unlit, but the door above was open, spilling light onto the steps. He started climbing.

Suddenly a tall man appeared on the landing below him, silhouetted by the light behind. He was brandishing a long blade, which gleamed in the reflected light. Before Sir Anthony had a chance to react, the man stopped and peered up at him and then lowered his weapon. "It's you," he said. "What luck!"

"Moriarty!" Sir Anthony exclaimed, feeling his heart pounding in his chest. "By God, man, you gave me quite a start! What's happening?"

"Come and help me," Moriarty said, sheathing the sword back inside the protective body of his owl-headed walking stick. "The slasher is, I think, dead, but his master is still at large. But first—it will take the two of us, and we must be quick!"

"Help you do what?"

"His Royal Highness is in a small room behind the balcony, and he's under the influence of some powerful narcotic. We have to get him out of here."

Moriarty joined Sir Anthony, and they hurried up the stairs and pulled open a door next to the one leading to the balcony. A man who was undoubtedly HRH was leaning against the wall, looking with wide-eyed wonder around him. The prince's uniform jacket was spattered with blood, and his tunic was torn. "My God!" said Sir Anthony, touching the blood smears, which felt dry and cold under his fingers. "What on earth . . ."

"They were setting the stage for His Highness to be found after the princess was stabbed," Moriarty said. "It is, I imagine, cow's blood or pig's blood, but it would have done the trick. Help me get him downstairs. We'll take him out the back way."

Sir Anthony took one arm and Moriarty the other, and between them they eased His Highness out of the room and along the corridor. A very short man in servitor's costume poked his head out from a door farther down. "This way, Professor," he called in a stage whisper that reverberated down the hall. "I has found the egress."

"Very good, Mummer," said the professor. "You lead the way."

Along the corridor, into a narrow hallway, down another flight of stairs, and into a room with a large brick oven, perhaps once used as a bakery.

"Hello," said a man in a leather apron, coming in from a doorway in the far wall. "You some of the daily help, are you? Waiters, I fancy, by your garb."

"You've got it, mate," the mummer agreed.

"What's all the fuss and commotion I'm hearing upstairs?" the man asked, pointing with his finger in the general direction of upstairs.

"Some sort of accident," Moriarty told him. "Perhaps you should go help. This chap has fainted, and we're taking him outside."

The man nodded, seeing the wisdom in this. "Too much alki-bloody-hall," he opined. "Shouldn't partake whilst you're at work, I says. Through that door there will get you out the back."

They nodded their thanks and continued out the door with their burden.

The beam from a bull's-eye lantern turned to shine on them as they came out into the mews. "Ah!" said a familiar voice, "you've made it—and with His Highness. Good, good."

"Is it you, Holmes?" Moriarty asked. "The Belleville Slicer is dead, but his companion—his keeper—is still at large in the house. Unless he managed to leave during the ongoing festivities."

"He tried to," Holmes said. "I have him here." He turned the lantern so the beam shined on a man sitting on the sparse sidewalk and glaring up into the light. "I imagine this is the man you want. He was one of the gentlemen who brought His Highness in, and he seemed to be in charge. So when he emerged in something of a hurry a few minutes ago, I scuppered him up. He was not happy about it, and there was something of a scuffle, but I prevailed. I found this in his pocket." Holmes waved a crumpled scrap of paper at them. "It's the 'Macbeth' cable from France."

"Ah!" said Moriarty. He turned to the man. "Then you must be the fabled Macbeth. A pleasure, I must say, to finally make your acquaintance."

The man struggled to his feet. His evening jacket was in disarray, his heavily starched collar was pulled out in front, and his extravagant mustache was pointing up one one side and down on the other, giving his face a look of bewildered indecision. "You will release me at once!" he demanded, waving his manacled hands in front of him. "This is an outrage! You cannot do this to me!"

"Really?" Moriarty asked, sounding sincerely interested. "Why not?"

The man came to a position of attention, or as close as he could manage with his hands tied. "I am Colonel Auguste Pierre Marie Lefavre of the French general staff, currently serving as military attaché to the French ambassador. I have the diplomatic immunity. Whatever you may think I have done, it is of no consequence. You must release me immediately!"

Silence descended on the group as they considered this.

"You could just shoot 'im, Professor," the mummer suggested.

"I couldn't watch such a thing," said Holmes. "I'd have to turn my back."

"What?" Lefavre took a step back. "No—you couldn't . . ."

"Why not?" Moriarty asked. "You seem to have little hesitation about taking a life—or two—when it serves your purpose."

"That was different."

"How?"

"Those people were . . ." Lefavre paused.

"Expendable? Sacrificed for the greater good?"

Lefavre said nothing.

"We shall not shoot him," said a quiet voice, and a dark figure stepped out of the shadows by the doorway.

"Your Grace," said Holmes.

Moriarty turned and recognized the Duke of Shorham, who walked slowly forward until he was standing in front of the man who had been Macbeth.

"I didn't think—" Lefavre began.

The duke raised his hand, and Lefavre was silent. "You will be taken from here directly to the Tower of London," pronounced the duke. "You will not communicate with anyone between here and there. Once there, you will be held at Her Majesty's pleasure. I would say that Her Majesty's pleasure might well include taking you out into the courtyard early one morning and putting a noose around your neck, but that's not up to me."

"Pity," said Holmes, turning to Moriarty. "I've never actually seen you shoot a man, Professor. It would have been an enlightening experience."

Lefavre said, "You can't—"

"I can," said the duke. "In the name of Her Majesty and by the power intrusted to me by the Special Committee of the Privy Council, I will." He turned and whistled, and a carriage started toward them from down the street. After a brief and curiously silent struggle Lefavre was thrust into the carriage, the duke went in behind him, and the carriage began its unhurried journey to the west.

Sir Anthony murmured something.

"What's that?" asked Moriarty.

" 'We 'ave 'eard o' the Widow at Windsor,' " Sir Anthony recited,

" 'It's safest to let 'er alone: / For 'er sentries we stand by the sea an' the land / Wherever the bugles are blown.' "

"A bit of Kipling," said Holmes, "never hurts."

CHAPTER TWENTY-NINE

A MIDNIGHT DREARY

He, who through vast immensity can pierce,
See worlds on worlds compose one universe,
Observe how system into system runs,
What other planets circle other suns,
What varied Being peoples every star,
May tell why Heaven has made us as we are.

—ALEXANDER POPE

IT WAS NINE THIRTY TUESDAY MORNING; the sky was overcast, and the air was moist. Benjamin and Cecily Barnett left their hansom cab at the Brook Street corner of Hanover Square, unfurled a large black umbrella, and walked the short distance to the Roman pillars marking the portico of the otherwise stolid brick facade of the Earl of Scully's London residence. They were admitted by a butler, stoic of face and precise of dress, who led them to an oak-paneled room at the back of the house with large bay windows overlooking the garden.

The earl, the Duke of Shorham, Sir Anthony, Moriarty, and the Holmes brothers were sitting around an oval mahogany table strewn with cups of coffee, the remnants of an extensive breakfast, and two copies of every London morning and evening newspaper.

"Good day, good day," said the earl. "Welcome. Coffee? A spot of breakfast? Cruther, bring them what they want."

"We're fine, thank you milord," said Cecily.

"Very good, then. Ah. Sit down, sit down. I was just going over the newspapers. The story of Saturday night's, ah, events is on the front page of every paper except *The Times*. Still today, three days later." He lifted a couple of papers from the pile in front of him with the air of a man examining a dead hedgehog and allowed them to drop back down. "They're all coming up with more details, more facts, more theories, and each of them has it quite wrong and turned about."

"The presence of HRH is still not mentioned, or even hinted at, in any of them," observed the duke. "They're not even all agreed that it was His Highness that the madman was trying to imitate. So we may ride clear of this yet."

"And Miss Dilwaddy comes off as quite the heroine," said Sir Anthony. He turned to Cecily, who was sitting quietly by the door. "How is she doing, if I might ask?"

"Outwardly she's quite recovered," Cecily told him, "but I'm afraid the events of that night will be with her for some time."

"Ah, yes," said Duke Albert. "Whatever are we to do with Miss Dilwaddy? We can't send her back to, um, her former, um . . ."

"I am taking her into my household," the Earl of Scully said. "I have spoken to my wife," he added hastily, a spot of color appearing in his cheeks, "and she quite agrees."

"Good, good," said the duke.

There was a silence, which was finally broken by Sherlock Holmes. "I sent a cable to Paris," he said.

They looked at him. "Saying what?" asked Sir Anthony.

"Here." Holmes pulled a form from his pocket and passed it to Moriarty. It was addressed to Princess Irene, Abbess of the Paris chapter of the Holy Order of the Sisters of Mary Magdala, and it read:

TELL MLLE DESCHAMPS HE IS DEAD SHERLOCK

Moriarty read it and passed it on.

"Good thought," said Barnett. "Very good."

"That little princess is going to be all right," offered Sir Anthony after a pause. "The scar on her forehead should be barely visible in a few months, although the one on her arm is going to be more troublesome. Or so says the surgeon."

"Good, good," said the duke. "Horrible experience, what? Have to see what we can do for her. I'll make a note." He turned to Mycroft. "What are we to do about that chap, whatchamabobby—the chappie who claims he's the Earl of Mersy?"

"I don't think," said Mycroft, "that the Crown Office is going to find any merit in his claim. He can have his castle, somewhere just this side of Scotland, I believe, but not his title."

"But was he involved in this scheme?" asked the duke.

"Almost certainly," Mycroft said, "but we could never prove it."

"Ah, well," said the duke. "Living somewhere just this side of Scotland may be punishment enough."

"This affair would seem to be over," said the earl, "and the truth of it may never come out."

"*Can* never come out," said Sir Anthony.

"Just so," agreed the duke.

"This is odd," said Holmes some minutes later, tapping a story he had been reading in the *Morning Standard*. "You wouldn't know anything about this, would you, Professor?" The tone of his voice and his arched eyebrow indicated that he rather thought that Moriarty might indeed know something about whatever it was.

"About what?" asked Moriarty.

Holmes adjusted the paper and read, " 'Strange Discovery in Nottinghamshire. Secret Room Revealed.' " He paused to glare at Moriarty and then began again:

STRANGE DISCOVERY IN NOTTINGHAMSHIRE.
SECRET ROOM REVEALED

Sometime Monday afternoon workmen installing indoor plumbing at Widdersign-on-Ribble, the country estate of his lordship Baron Thornton-Hoxbary, accidentally broke into a hitherto-secret room adjoining the baron's ground-floor library and discovered a trove of valuable jewelry and works of art, including objects that are believed to have been stolen from nearby estates over the past three years. The discovery came during the annual Ribble Wetten's Day celebration when most of the town's inhabitants are gathered on the baron's copious back lawn to wish each other good fortune and to pick the fairest maiden in the town and throw her into the Ribble.

Widdersign-on-Ribble, which is just outside of Wedsbridge in Nottinghamshire, has been the principal residence of the Barons Thornton-Hoxbary for the past two hundred years and was recently the scene of a robbery with violence, which resulted in the death of two men and became known locally as the Widdersign Outrage.

"Hmm," said the duke. "A secret room, eh? There's a secret passage in Wythender Hall, don't you know, but I wouldn't care to put any valuables in it. Cold and damp, and not all that secret anymore if it comes to that. My grandson and his chums play Robin Hood or what-you-like in it, as did my son twenty years ago. As, come to think of it, did I."

"Isn't that the house you were accused of robbing some months ago, Professor?" asked Holmes pointedly.

"Read on," said Moriarty.

> Among the objects discovered in the room, which was fit-
> ted out in the manner of a gentleman's sitting room, were a
> small statuette of John the Baptist attributed to Michelan-
> gelo, and an etching of a windmill believed to be by Rem-
> brandt, both of which went missing from the estate of Lord
> Whigstow last year, and the "Bain of Thorncroft," a twenty-
> carat imperial topaz, believed to be the world's largest,
> owned by the Marchioness of Cleves, which was taken dur-
> ing a robbery at Cramden Pimms, the Nottinghamshire es-
> tate of Lord Chaut.
> How these items got into the room is not known. Attempts
> to question the baron on the matter have failed, as the baron
> disappeared from the estate before the police arrived.

"I sense your presence in this, Moriarty," Holmes said, shaking the newspaper in the professor's direction before putting it down.

The start of a smile flitted across Moriarty's face and then disappeared. "I confess I may be indirectly responsible for the baron's troubles," he said. "I spoke of my conclusions regarding Baron Thornton-Hoxbary to some of my friends, who may have mentioned it to some of their friends, and, well . . . I fear that some of the smaller items that were in the room when it was discovered may not make it into the official inventory."

"What sort of conclusions?" asked Sir Anthony.

"While I was incarcerated I asked my friend and colleague Mr. Barnett to visit the village of Wedsbridge and see what he could discover about the baron," Moriarty said. "I knew that I was not responsible for robbing him, and it would be in my interest to discover who was. It seemed to me quite possible that the baron was robbing his own houseguests. What Mr. Barnett found out verified this opinion and led me to think that he was also responsible for the cluster of robberies in the various great homes in his neighborhood, and that there was quite probably a hidden room in or near the library."

"What I told you?" asked Barnett.

"Oh, yes."

"That's quite a stretch, thinking that the baron might be robbing himself," said the earl.

"Not himself, just his guests," said Moriarty. "He might arrange for something of his to be taken for an air of verisimilitude, but it would go right into the secret room."

"What did Mr. Barnett tell you that made you think there was a secret room?" asked the duke.

"The fact that yon innkeeper was reciting poetry."

"I don't follow," said Barnett.

"He was reciting poetry because he had been put in charge of stacks of books gathered on the floor while the baron had new bookcases put in."

"That's right," Barnett agreed. "He had old oak bookcases pulled out to replace them with new ones made from the, ah, something-or-other—Widdersign Ash, which had recently come down."

"Of course he did," said Moriarty, "and he brought in artisans from Italy to do the job because there aren't any British carpenters who need the work. The Italians only spoke Italian and went home when the job was done."

"When you put it that way," Barnett said.

"So the baron—" began Mycroft.

"Spent his nights stealing from his neighbors, and on occasion from his guests," said Moriarty. "Every once in a while, one would assume, he would sneak off to his secret room and smoke a cigar—"

"A cheap cigar," interjected Barnett.

"Surrounded by his stolen treasures."

"Where do you suppose he has gone off to?" asked the duke. "Now that his, ah, secret vice is known, where can he hide?"

"He has a boat," said Moriarty. "A small yacht berthed in Grimsby. My agent has alerted the authorities."

"I thought you didn't have agents," said Sir Anthony.

"I couldn't be there myself, as we had this other matter to attend to," Moriarty explained. "So I deputized a trusted friend."

"Hmmph!" said Sherlock Holmes.

"Oh yes, oh yes," said the Duke of Shorham, "speaking of the 'other matter,' I almost forgot." He turned to Cecily Barnett, who was sitting quietly on the far side of the table. "You are to be recognized, my dear."

Cecily raised her head. "By whom, and for what, Your Grace?"

"Teaching Miss Dilwaddy so effectively and standing by her at the, um, critical moment. And the ringing cry of 'impostor!' you sounded at just the right moment. At the queen's special command you are to be appointed a Dame Commander of the Order of the Bath."

"Well!" said Cecily.

"Congratulations, my love," said Barnett, giving her a hug.

"Yes, but, Pamela—Miss Dilwaddy—certainly did more . . ."

"I'm afraid that Her Majesty is not ready to give an order of chivalry to a woman in Miss Dilwaddy's former profession," said the duke.

"At least not to one who was quite so openly known to have been in that profession," corrected Mycroft.

"Just so," agreed the duke.

"Mr. Benjamin and Dame Cecily Barnett," said Benjamin. "It has a good sound."

CHAPTER THIRTY

ON THE MOOR

Mediocrity knows nothing higher than itself;
but talent instantly recognizes genius.

—ARTHUR CONAN DOYLE

"AH, WILCOX," SAID THE PROFESSOR, "there you are. Is that blink spectrometer aligned yet? I'd like to try to get a series of shots of Venus this evening."

"The mount is a bit wobbly as she sits," his chubby assistant said, rubbing the bald spot on the back of his head, "but we could likely clamp 'er in place on the scope."

"Fair enough," said Moriarty, "Let's give it a try."

"Glad to see you back, Professor," said Wilcox with a rare burst of feeling. "I was a mite worried there."

"As was I, I confess," admitted Moriarty, "but truth won out, as she occasionally does, and here I am."

"And done a spot o' service for 'er Majesty, so says Tolliver."

"Surely the mummer should know," said Moriarty with a smile.

Wilcox nodded. "His ways are deep beyond his size, that's for sure. By the by, that skulking gent is back, hiding out behind a hillock off to the east a few hundred yards."

"Really?" Moriarty adjusted his pince-nez thoughtfully. "How did you happen to notice him?"

"I caught the glint of a telescope lens about an hour ago, so I sent one of the lads to creep around and take a glom, and there he was."

"Ah!" said Moriarty. "Send someone around to Mr. Holmes with a flask of cocoa and a biscuit in a little while. It promises to be a cold night."

"Don't he never give up?" asked Wilcox.

"Perhaps," said Moriarty, "in a world where there is a Professor Moriarty, it is a good thing that there is a Sherlock Holmes. Perhaps each of us needs the other." He sighed. "Or perhaps not. Who can say?"